"Who hired you to follow me?"

Her smoky voice could melt a snowman. And Gabriel O'Shaunessy was no snowman. "I can't tell you that, sweetheart. You know the rules."

"Rules. I even used to play by them."

"Okay. Dave Townsend from Oval studios."

Her look said by taking this case, Gabe had put her in danger. "They sure bought you easy, didn't they?" she accused softly.

"If you were a man, I'd call you on that." But she wasn't, so Gabe covered her mouth with his. She kissed him back, too—even if, a moment later, she left without a backward glance.

And then Gabe heard the report of a car backfiring, followed immediately by another. Except they weren't backfires. Through the window, he saw her fall, and he raced for the street.

But her body was gone! Mysteriously vanished. On the pavement lay only her fox stole, with one lonely glove beside it.

And an ever-widening pool of blood.

ABOUT THE AUTHOR

Harper Allen lives in the country in the middle of a hundred acres of maple trees with her husband, Wayne, six cats, four dogs—and a very nervous cockatiel at the bottom of the food chain. For excitement she and Wayne drive to the nearest village and buy jumbo bags of pet food. She believes in love at first sight because it happened to her. This is her first novel.

The Man That Got Away
Harper Allen

Harlequin Books

TORONTO • NEW YORK • LONDON
AMSTERDAM • PARIS • SYDNEY • HAMBURG
STOCKHOLM • ATHENS • TOKYO • MILAN
MADRID • WARSAW • BUDAPEST • AUCKLAND

To my sister Renata, with love.

AUTHOR NOTE

"It Happened One Night" swept the Oscars in 1934, not 1935, as mentioned in this book. The author applied a little poetic license, in order to have Clark Gable appear at the 1935 Oscars ceremony.

ISBN 0-373-22468-0

THE MAN THAT GOT AWAY

Copyright © 1998 by Sandra Hill

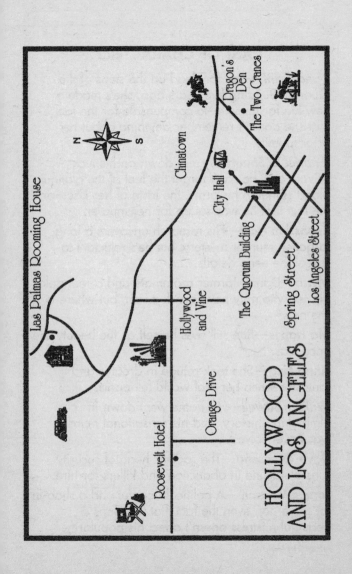

HOLLYWOOD
AND LOS ANGELES

Roosevelt Hotel

Orange Drive

Hollywood
and Vine

Las Palmas Rooming House

N

S

Chinatown

City Hall

Dragon's
Den

The Two Cranes

The Quorum Building

Spring Street

Los Angeles Street

CAST OF CHARACTERS

Dana Smith—Left for dead on the steps of the Quorum Building five years ago, she's made a new life for herself—to compensate for the fact that she doesn't remember *anything* about her prior identity.

Gabriel O'Shaunessy—A down-on-his-luck private eye, he can't forget the feel of the platinum blond starlet in his arms, the taste of her kiss—and the fact that he was set up for her murder.

Sebastian Hart—His research uncovers a long-forgotten murder mystery, but he's reluctant to reveal the eerie details....

Myna—Dana's former roommate and a real gold-digger who may have struck it rich, but where is she now?

Ma Harris—She still sees herself as the beauty she once was.

Anna Ling—She took refuge in dreams and fantasies when her real world fell apart.

William Atwell—His name went down in filmmaking history, and his sensational murder was never solved.

Dave Townsend—The sadistic head of security runs a sideline in abduction and killers-for-hire.

James Mattson—A political hopeful and a shoo-in for governor, even the fact that he keeps a beautiful mistress doesn't affect his popularity.

Prologue

Los Angeles, 1930

Gabriel O'Shaunessy, private detective, had been tailing the blonde for the better part of a week, so when she walked into his office he knew she was trouble. He took a second look just to make sure. Also because she was the kind of woman who deserved a second look, he thought appraisingly—about twenty-three, with legs that went on forever and a glistening mouth that was made for kisses. Or lies. He'd seen her type before, just not in such a gorgeous package. She had a silver fox stole slung around her shoulders, and a cute little hat tipped forward over the platinum curls.

He'd just pulled open the drawer with the bottle in it, thinking one more wouldn't hurt, but then he looked at those big green eyes and decided against it. This was definitely a time to have all his wits about him. The dame wasn't here on a social call.

"Mr. O'Shaunessy?" Her voice did things to a man. Those smoky, husky tones, combined with that hundred-watt gaze, could melt a snowman.

A snowman he definitely wasn't.

"You're looking at him, doll. But office hours are over.

Make an appointment with my secretary tomorrow." He stood up. Turning away from her, he reached behind him for his hat.

"Keep your hands away from your body, Mr. O'Shaunessy, and turn back around very slowly."

Maybe he was a snowman—that would explain the cold trickle he felt at the back of his neck. Or maybe it was the fact that she was pointing a tiny pearl-handled gun at him. That kind of thing tended to give Gabe O'Shaunessy a chill. He turned around slowly, like the lady had said.

"Listen, lady—"

"No, you listen, gumshoe. I want to know why you've been following me. Who hired you?" Her voice was still low, but there was a quiver of nervousness in it. The little gun wavered.

Like a sap, he'd taken his .45 out of the shoulder holster earlier, and put it in the desk drawer along with the bottle of Canadian bootleg. He flicked a glance at the drawer, wondering whether he could make a jump for it.

"And don't try anything. I've never used one of these, but before they took my daddy's farm away from him, I was pretty good at keeping the vermin down with a shotgun. This can't be too different."

He knew when he was beaten. He abandoned plan A, which was escape, and shrugged.

"What makes you think I've been following you?"

"I'm not stupid, Mr. O'Shaunessy, and I don't have much time. You're good at your job, but I've been looking over my shoulder lately. Most times I see you, or that beat-up coupe you drive around in. So tonight I turned the tables and followed you here. One more time—who's paying you?"

Professional ethics and a nickel will get you a cup of java, O'Shaunessy thought wearily. He'd never said he was a hero, and part of him was ready to spill the beans right then and there. But a long time ago, the name O'Shaunessy used to stand for something in this town. He hesitated.

"I can't tell you that, sweetheart. You know the rules."

For a moment she kept the gun pointed at him, and then something in her seemed to crack. She put it back in her purse.

"I know the rules. I even used to play by them." She sounded defeated. "Look, mister, if you're working for the guy I think you're working for, then it's no use appealing to your better nature." She hitched the stole higher and tossed one end over her shoulder, her chin nestling deeper into the fur. "But if you tell him where I went today, it'll be all over for me. If you can sleep with that on your conscience, then sweet dreams." She turned to leave, but not before the detective saw a shimmer in her eyes.

Hell, he was as much of a sucker as the next man when it came to green-eyed blondes. Even in Hollywood, where they were a dime a dozen, and where crying on demand was something you wrote on your resumé. But still…he could swear those tears were real.

"All right, sister. It'll probably cost me my retainer, but that's peanuts anyway. Dave Townsend down at the studio asked me to keep an eye on you—see where you went, who you met. It's my guess they've got some big plans for you, but with this new Hays Code, they want to make sure of what they're getting. Don't worry, I'll keep it out of my report that you went to the *Times* office today." He pulled a battered pack of Luckys out of his vest pocket and looked for a match. Striking it on the top of his desk, he peered through the smoke at her.

"You were trying to sell some studio gossip, right? Forget it. More than a few of those reporters are in Townsend's pocket, and if it gets back to him you can kiss your movie career goodbye."

She stood at the door, her back to him. "Is that what they told you? That the studio's checking me out?"

"Sure."

But something about her question tied in with a doubt he'd had himself. Why him? Townsend had half a dozen legmen to run errands like this. Financially, O'Shaunessy was in no shape to look a gift horse in the mouth, but when Townsend had approached him for this job he'd wondered why he was picking an outsider for it. The studios had the reputation of taking care of their own dirty laundry.

"They bought you easy, didn't they?" She turned and studied him, pulling on a pair of soft leather gloves, her head tilted to one side. "A big, black-haired Irishman, a tough guy. But you let them persuade you this was a clean little job for Oval Studios, maybe could lead to something permanent if you played your cards right. Deep inside, you know it's not." Opening the door to the outer office, she drew the tip of one gloved finger across the glass, where it said Gabriel O'Shaunessy, Investigations and looked with disgust at it.

"You should clean house once in a while, O'Shaunessy. Dirt sticks."

The contempt in her eyes was familiar. He'd seen it in the mirror all too often these last few years, but he'd learned to live with his own opinion of himself. What he couldn't take was the fact that she seemed to share it.

He'd let himself dream about her a little, dammit! Watching her this last week, he'd begun to anticipate her every move. He knew the way she walked, long-legged and confident. The way she leaned forward to allow her escort to light her cigarette, steadying his hand in a way that turned the casual courtesy into an intimate moment. The way her smile sometimes didn't reach her eyes.

It was crazy, but right from the start she hadn't been

just a job to him. She'd taken hold of his senses, possessed his thoughts in a way that no woman ever had. He'd even thought that maybe once this assignment was over, he might find some way to really get to know her. Take her dancing, maybe; have that secret little smile directed at Gabe O'Shaunessy this time, not some other man... And now she was looking at him as if she couldn't stand to be in the same room.

O'Shaunessy didn't stop to think. Before she could turn away, he reached out and pulled her close. The soft fur she was wearing crushed between them, releasing a scent of exotic flowers.

"If you were a man I'd call you on that remark," he told her. "But you're not, so this'll have to do."

He brought his mouth down on hers, hard. He was way out of line and he knew it, but he'd be damned if he let her go like that. She didn't move, maybe thinking that if she put on an ice-maiden act he'd give up. But he wanted to wipe that cold look of dismissal off her face, see it replaced with some kind of acknowledgment of him as a man.

He got more than he bargained for.

Just as he was about to let her go, cursing himself for acting like a heel, her lips parted under his and one gloved hand crept around the back of his neck. Her mouth tasted like vanilla and cream, and all of a sudden he felt like he'd stepped into an empty elevator shaft. *Going down, O'Shaunessy?* Hell, yes, he thought incoherently. And loving it. Her hair was silk under his hand, and when the tips of her lashes brushed against his face, his heart did a slow roll like a hotshot pilot at an air show, and then failed to pull out of its spin. He went down in flames.

She must have been riding the rocket too, because when they finally, slowly, pulled apart, he saw that her eyes were misty and unfocused and her mouth was soft, like bruised cherries. His leg was between hers, the thin material of her dress pulled up, and he felt the shudder that ran down her like a current of electricity. They looked at each other for a long moment.

"I thought love at first sight only happened in the movies." She gave a shaky laugh, but the green eyes were wide and serious.

"A week ago I would have agreed with you." He hadn't meant to say it, but as soon as the words were spoken O'Shaunessy realized that they were true. Holding her in his arms, he felt as if time itself had stopped for them, as if they existed in a private world of their own.

Suddenly the old regulator clock on the wall whirred and struck the hour, and the spell between them was broken. Abruptly she drew away from him, smoothing the wrinkles from her dress. When she looked up again, there was an odd expression of loss and regret on her face.

"Wrong time, wrong place, shamus," she whispered. She took his handkerchief from his pocket, wiped a smudge of lipstick from his mouth, and tucked it back into the jacket. Then she was gone, without a backward glance.

O'Shaunessy felt as if he'd been sucker punched. Obviously the last few minutes hadn't affected her the way they had him. He'd let himself forget that the lady was an actress.

He heard her heels clicking down the hallway and then the stairs, and he went to the window to catch a glimpse of her as she came out of the building. Why, he didn't know. Maybe to get a last look at her, to reassure himself that she was nothing more than he'd first figured—a cute little Hollywood starlet making the most of her assets. Better looking than most, sure, but playing the angles like everyone else in this town. What right did she have to judge him? Times were tough. A guy like him took what jobs he could get, and counted himself damned lucky to make the rent.

It didn't sound convincing, even to himself.

He heard the car before he saw it, and then it came swinging around the corner, headlights cutting through the blue city dusk just as she stepped out onto the sidewalk. She looked up in surprise, her face illuminated in the sulfurous yellow of the beams, and suddenly all of the doubts he'd had about the job became a certainty. He tore away from the window and out the office, taking the stairs three at a time, but even as he got to the ground floor he heard the sharp report of a car backfiring, followed immediately by another.

Except he knew they hadn't been backfires.

As he wrenched open the door to the street, a black sedan peeled off down a side street. The light was bad, but O'Shaunessy tried to catch the license plate. No dice, he thought in frustration. Then he looked down to see what he could do for her.

She was gone!

It was impossible.

In the gutter lay the fox stole, one lonely glove beside it. As he picked up the glove, he looked down the street and then the other way, as if he didn't know the terrain like the back of his hand. There were no alleyways nearby, no shop entrances where she could have hidden. And besides, there hadn't been time for her to run. Where the hell was she?

He squatted down beside the stole and lifted a corner of it. A ghost of her fragrance drifted towards him. There was something sticky and wet on the fur, and a sharp coppery smell overpowered the perfume. Suddenly the whiskey rose in his throat. He dropped the fur and wiped his hands on his vest.

IN THE POLICE REPORT that was written up that night, it said that Gabriel O'Shaunessy had blood all over him when the black-and-white came screaming up a couple of seconds later.

He was being held for questioning, the report added, in the disappearance of Dana Torrence.

Chapter One

Los Angeles, 1998

"But Julia's motivation is completely lost if we cut that! Get rid of the scene in the restaurant if you want to tighten things up." Dana Smith stopped pacing and raked her fingers through her hair distractedly. "And what's with this air conditioner anyway?"

It had been a long hot day on location, and the last thing they needed was to come back here to the office and melt, she thought. This morning she'd left her condo in a crisply ironed man's-style shirt and pants. Now she looked as if she'd gone swimming in her clothes.

"It's been on the fritz ever since you plugged the power adaptor into the wrong outlet yesterday." Sebastian Hart glared at his assistant. Normally an elegant man, even he was looking a little wilted. "And don't come at me with all guns blazing and then add on a bimbo-esque *non sequitur* to divert me—I pay you to play the devil's advocate, not Scarlett O'Hara. If you feel that strongly about the scene, we'll talk about it. Later."

He tossed a pencil onto the desk in front of him. "Right now, I'd like to go somewhere cool and eat cool food. Thoughts of a dewy glass of Chablis and an icy shrimp salad have been drifting through my mind for the last half hour. Maybe that little place down the street with the patio. Sound good?''

"Sounds great, but why me? Did you mislay your little black book?" Dana rummaged around in the bulky tapestry tote bag at her feet and pulled out her cosmetic case. Uncapping a bottle of skin freshener, she tipped some onto a cotton pad. "Just give me a minute here."

Sebastian lifted an eyebrow. "Going all out for our date, I see," he commented. "And no, the little black book has been retired. Temporarily, at least."

Dana looked at the cotton ball and grimaced. "This city is ruining my skin." She tossed it into a wastebasket and picked up the tote. "Edwina?"

"We've come to a kind of…well, an exclusivity agreement. For the time being," he added hastily. He opened the door for her and turned to lock it behind him.

She studied him with amusement. So, the Playboy of the Western World had come crashing to his knees! And over an English, classically trained actress two years older than himself.

"I always hoped you two would go the traditional route, you know." She clattered down the stairs ahead of him. The Quorum Building was designated as a historical structure, and when Sebastian had bought it for the production company's offices, he'd restored it as it had been fifty years ago, oak stairs and all. "Sebastian and Edwina," she mused. "And when you have kids, you can name them Marmaduke, or Cornelius, or Hortensia." She stepped out onto the street and flicked a wicked glance at him.

"Why I put up with this insubordination I don't know," he said. "All I have to do is make a few phone calls. You'd never work in this town again."

Dana smiled. Sebastian was a sweetheart, and she knew how lucky she was to have been taken on as his assistant.

He was only in his thirties, but he'd already won an Oscar. The film they were working on now, a remake of an old Hollywood classic, was shaping up to be a strong contender for next year, in her opinion. She put her hand on his arm.

"I sometimes wonder why you did hire me. Did you feel responsible for my life, in some way?"

"Because of how we met, you mean?" Sebastian asked. It wasn't a topic they often discussed, and the fact that she had brought it up now surprised him.

"Because you saved my life. Like the old Chinese saying—if you save someone's life, you're responsible for them forever."

They'd reached the restaurant and the owner hurried forward to greet them. A few patrons looked up as they weaved their way through the tables to the patio section at the back, but Sebastian hardly noticed them. He let his glance dwell on Dana walking ahead of him, her hair tightly bound in a French braid as if to obscure its rich autumn-leaf glow. Her straight back added inches to her petite height and her shoulders were set with determination. Responsible for her? he thought wryly. She'd never allow anyone to get past her defenses enough for that. He'd learned to be content with friendship.

"The past has been on your mind lately, hasn't it?"

She took the seat he held out for her. She toyed with the menu, and then looked up at him, her green eyes troubled. "I've been having dreams these past few nights."

"Dreams?" He looked up as the waiter came to their table with a carafe of wine, and waited for the man to leave. "You mean your memory's returning?" He lowered his voice as he spoke. This was another first, he thought. Dana never mentioned the incident that had left her without any memory of her life before he'd met her.

"After five years of psychoanalysis and hypnotherapy?

No, I've given up expecting that'll happen. And Dr. Gottfried says that trying to remember can bury the past even deeper, so I don't think about it very often.'' Lifting her glass in an ironic salute, she took a sip of wine. ''My dreams may have something to do with the project we're working on. They take place in the same time period.'' She laughed, trying to dispel the suddenly somber look on his face. ''You're probably working me too hard. All those nights of poring over photos of this town in the thirties, looking for period details and trying to get the sets just perfect.''

Sebastian looked at her intently. ''These dreams take place in the 1930s?''

Dana hesitated. ''Just since we've started this film. Which is as good an explanation as any, I suppose, except that everything in them seems so real. And everything is happening to a particular woman. I see everything through her eyes, as if it *was* a memory, and yet it can't be.''

''Because of the time discrepancy?''

''Right. People even talk like they did back then. You know, saying *heater* for gun, *dame* for woman, things like that.'' She attempted a laugh, but he didn't join in.

''This *dame*. Do you know what she looks like?''

''A Jean Harlow type. She looked into the mirror once and I saw my—her reflection.''

''Platinum blond, penciled eyebrows, dark red bee-stung lips?'' There was an edge of suppressed tension in his voice.

''Exactly!'' Dana leaned forward and lowered her voice. ''Maybe my subconscious is trying to compensate for the amnesia. Maybe it's trying to manufacture a past life for me, grabbing bits and pieces from my work, the photos we've been using, even old movies I've seen!''

Before he could answer her, the waiter came up to their table. As Sebastian ordered shrimp salad for both of them,

Dana leaned back in her chair and tried to relax. A small fountain, covered with blue clematis, splashed soothingly a few feet away, and in the restaurant an Ottmar Liebert tape was playing, the soft guitar music drifting out to the patio. It was that hazy half hour between the end of the day and the beginning of dusk, and the candles on the tables had been lit. They glowed in their glass bowls, like miniature beacons.

The serenity of her surroundings should have calmed her, but Dana was more perturbed by the dreams than she'd admitted. She hadn't told Sebastian about the feelings of dread and impending danger that came with them. She hadn't mentioned that she woke up from them drenched in sweat, shaking.

And somehow she couldn't tell him about the man she saw in them, night after night.

She couldn't see his face in the dream, but she could feel his hands moving over her and his mouth on hers, teasing her. At first she would try to resist, to tell herself that no man could make her feel like this, but each time it was the same. A slow feather of desire would uncurl somewhere deep inside her and stroke its way down her body, and she would feel his hand slide down her spine, finally cupping the fullness of her hips against his. He wore a jacket of some rough material that chafed her through the thin bodice of her dress, but even that only served to focus the nerve endings in her skin to fever pitch. He tasted like dark wine, and every night she melted into his arms, welcoming the intoxication.

And every night she lost him and walked into a nightmare that brought her to a violent awakening.

"Dana?" Sebastian's voice broke into her thoughts and with an effort she brought herself back to reality. "We've got to talk. I know Dr. Gottfried thought it might affect the natural return of your memory, but I think it's time you knew what happened the night I met you.''

She caught her breath. He'd never volunteered this information before. Was she about to get some answers to the questions she'd never dared ask?

"I've always wanted to know what happened that night, but for the first few weeks I was in the hospital, so sedated that I hardly knew where I was. I'd been shot, hadn't I?'' Of its own volition, her hand moved to her ribcage. Through the thin cotton of her shirt she could feel the scar, faint, but still there.

"Yes.'' Sebastian paused, choosing his words carefully. "If this upsets you, interrupt me. I'd been working late at the Quorum Building—the 'Nam film had finally been wrapped, and I was wondering if it would be possible to do a remake of a classic. I was running some old films through the projector.'' He looked over at the fountain vaguely, as if he was replaying the evening in his mind. "There was a girl in one of them...just a bit part, but somehow her face fascinated me; I kept rerunning her one close-up, staring at her.''

His voice trailed off and he poured himself another glass of wine, still not looking at Dana. "Then I heard a gunshot. Two, actually.''

As he spoke, Dana's hand tightened on the delicate stem of the wineglass. That was one of the features of her dream that she hadn't mentioned. She heard the shots in her mind, as she had heard them in her sleep the last few nights. One shot, then a squealing noise like tires on pavement. And a second shot immediately after. "Did you see what happened?''

"That was the strange part. There was nothing there. There's a streetlight just in front, but the street was empty.''

He fell silent as the waiter came with their salads, and

then went on. "You can imagine what the police thought of that little flight of fancy when they questioned me later on. In the end, I'm sure they pegged me as another Hollywood flake with pharmaceutical ideas of recreation. Anyway, there I was, scared out of my mind. Then I heard a moan."

She felt as if she was listening to a script being pitched by an overimaginative writer. It all sounded so far-fetched, so violent.

"As you know, I call in a SWAT team when there's a spider in the bathtub," Sebastian said wryly, "so how I found the courage to make my way down those stairs I'll never know. If I recall rightly, I had an umbrella in my hand."

Despite herself, she smiled.

"But when I opened the door, I saw you lying on the sidewalk. As soon as I realized you were still alive, I went back in and phoned for an ambulance and stayed with you until it arrived." He drew a shaky breath and reached across the table for her hand. "I never want to spend another ten minutes like that again. I'd wadded up a towel and tried to stem the flow of blood from the wound, but I was sure you were dying."

Dana couldn't speak. The world that had just been described to her, a world of mysterious gunshots and nearfatal wounds, wasn't her world. It couldn't be!

Why not? a tiny, unwelcome voice within her asked. *After all, you've got a huge blank where your memory's supposed to be. Maybe what you've forgotten is too terrible to remember.*

"I've upset you, haven't I?"

She picked up her fork. Pushing a piece of arugula to the edge of her plate, she said tensely, "What else can you tell me?"

He looked uncertainly at her. "Nothing. Your picture

was run in papers across the state, but no one ever came forward to identify you. You know that much.''

"What about my clothes, what I was wearing? Did I have a purse? Anything that could be traced?"

Sebastian looked away, his expression troubled. "This is where we run into Shirley MacLaine territory," he muttered. He took a deep breath. "You had on a Lilly Daché hat, a Schiaparelli dress that any costume museum would give its eyeteeth for, except that it was covered in blood, and your stockings were seamed and fastened with garters. Your dress had pulled up when you fell," he added, apologetically. "Your personal effects were shown to me later by the police. They included a platinum cigarette case, not engraved, and about ten dollars. None of the money, bills included, was newer than the late 1920s.''

He forestalled her attempt to interrupt with an upraised hand. "Your purse was made in France. Your gun was made in the good old U.S. of A. A pretty thing, as guns go, but unfortunately the company that made it went out of business in the depression. The Great Depression.'' He lifted his glass and drank his wine as if it was water. "Now tell me I'm crazy for what I'm thinking.''

"You should have told me before!''

They were back in the office. After Sebastian's revelations it had been useless to even pretend to eat. When the flower-filled patio had started to fill up with late diners, they'd left to continue their bizarre conversation with no chance of being overheard.

"Gottfried felt—''

"How dare he play God with my life! I feel like a puppet, totally controlled and manipulated!'' Dana's voice rose, and she jumped up from the leather couch, almost upsetting a vase of roses on the low table beside it.

Sebastian touched her shoulder placatingly. "His theory

was that confronting you with these details would do more harm than good. Don't forget, he counted it a major triumph when you started talking again. You were practically catatonic for a couple of months.''

She shrugged, still angry. ''It's all so—so Twilight Zone!'' He was silent, and she went on, calmer now. ''The whole setup, the clothes, the gun—it just doesn't make sense.'' His expression stopped her. ''Something tells me I'm not going to like what you're thinking.''

'' 'There are more things in heaven and earth, Horatio,' '' he quoted.

''What do you mean?''

Sebastian didn't meet her eyes. ''I think you may have been temporarily taken over by the ghost or spirit—whatever terminology you want to use, of a woman who died in 1930.''

Dana stared at him incredulously.

''I did consider the possibility that you'd been transported through time, but since the woman's dead, that's impossible. She was shot on the front steps of the Quorum Building and her body was dumped in a ditch on the outskirts of Orange County. It was all country around that area then. She wasn't found for a few months, but she had her Screen Actors' Guild card on her. Her name was Dana Torrence.''

The information hit her with the force of a hammer blow and her mind reeled. An image of stark horror had been conjured up by his words. A violent death, a body left in a ditch? That was terrible enough, but what she refused to accept was the possibility that, in some way, she was not completely in control of her own life. Possessed? The thought terrified her.

''What are you talking about? Just because I was wearing clothes from the thirties doesn't mean I was possessed! And my loss of memory—how do you explain that?'' She smoothed damp palms down the beige linen of her tailored slacks. "And why hasn't anyone ever come forward to identify me?"

"Take a look at this." Sebastian unlocked a drawer in the filing cabinet. He tossed a five-by-seven photo onto the desk.

Dana picked it up and felt an icy chill settle in the pit of her stomach. It had been taken with a flash, so the features of the face that stared back at her were washed out by the harsh light, but the heavy makeup compensated for that. It was recognizable. She was looking at the woman in her dream. The photo fell from her hand and fluttered to the floor.

"Damn!" Sebastian's arm was around her shoulders as he helped her to a chair. "Hang on, I'll get you some Evian."

"Where did you get that picture?" she whispered. She took the glass of water from him and tried to drink, but her teeth were chattering against the rim.

"Enough of this experiment," he said firmly. "I should never have ignored your doctor's advice."

"No! I want to know everything that you've learned about this woman who was killed. I can handle it, Sebastian—what I can't handle is being treated like an unstable child." She reached down and picked up the photo. "Where did you get this?"

Sebastian looked confused. "But I thought you knew! That's the photo of you that was run in the papers. It was taken at the hospital when they couldn't find any ID on you. Now do you understand why no one would recognize it?"

She'd told him she could handle it, but as Dana brought the photo closer and forced herself to look past the dated makeup, some part of her wanted to tear it up, as if by doing so she could deny the evidence of her own eyes.

The eyebrows, plucked, penciled and arched, were unlike her own thick straight ones, and it was hard to tell the true shape of the woman's mouth under the exaggerated Cupid's bow of the top lip. She knew that her own mouth was a little wider, but the heavier base makeup of the 1930s could hide that. Yes, she thought slowly, despite the superficial differences she could see that it was her own face, now that Seb had told her. Her expression was haunted and strained as she turned to him.

"But this is the woman in my dreams!"

He let out the breath he'd been holding. "I suspected as much." Taking the photo from her, he laid it face down on the desk. "Let me run my theory by you. Don't forget, I've had five years to investigate this little mystery, and I've come up with a few facts." He ticked them off on his fingers. "One—I've searched the records and found that a woman was killed outside this building back in 1930. Her name was Dana Torrence. Two—her murder was never solved. Three—she looked a lot like you, from what I can tell."

At her look of inquiry, he added grimly, "Oh, yes, I've seen her. I was running her close-up when I heard the shots that night."

For a moment she was too shocked to speak. When she did, it was in a tremulous whisper. "When they asked me at the hospital what my name was, I couldn't tell them— it was months later that I chose the name Dana Smith. Did I get it from you?"

Sebastian shook his head. "You chose it yourself, before I'd gotten that far in my investigation."

"Then maybe..." It was hard for her to say it, to acknowledge that the terror of her dreams could have any relevance in her waking life. "Maybe...I *am* Dana Torrence. Not possessed by her—reincarnated. But that sounds so crazy!"

Dana's voice rose on the last word and Sebastian shot her a worried look. Her face was pale, her eyes glittering with unshed tears. She was close to breaking down. He tried to defuse the situation.

"Do you realize what we're doing?" he asked. He attempted a laugh. "We're actually considering whether you've been possessed by a ghost or reincarnated! Can you believe it?" He dropped into the chair and rested his forearms on his knees. "Only in California."

For a moment Dana stared at him. Then the tense set of her body relaxed a little and she mustered up a weak smile. "Should I phone the *Enquirer?*"

"Hollywood Director and Assistant Really Gable and Lombard!" Sebastian improvised. His joke had the desired effect of chasing the shadows from her eyes.

She shot him a grateful look. "We'll knock poor Elvis off the front page," she predicted. "At least until the next time he's sighted in Boise."

The tension between them dissipated and they both burst into laughter. Sebastian sobered up first.

"My new theory is that we're both so exhausted we don't know what we're doing anymore. I think we should head home and get some sleep. Drop you off at your place?"

She considered his offer, then shook her head. "Thanks, Seb, but I'm so beat I think I'll just crash on the couch tonight. I've got a change of clothes and a toothbrush here."

She'd done it before, especially when she'd been working at the light table, straining her eyesight by peering at old photographs through a magnifier and trying to catch details that would add to the authenticity of *Scarlet Street.* Usually after a few hours of that she felt too tired to even call a cab. Tonight had been just as exhausting in a different way, Dana thought.

"Then I'll give you a ride to the set in the morning." Sebastian picked up his linen jacket and shrugged into it. He shoved his hands in the pockets and looked at her, apparently unwilling to leave. "We both went off the deep end tonight, but there *is* a mystery here, Dana. If you're starting to lose sleep over it, then we should bring it out into the open. Deal with it some way."

He hesitated. "This is between you and me and the couch over there, but there's a rumor around the studio that they're going to offer you your own picture next year. I want you to be ready for the responsibility. Nothing hanging over you."

"I'm getting my own movie?" A thrill surged through Dana at the news, although it wasn't totally unexpected. Long hours, missed vacations, extra courses at the film institute. Finally they had all paid off, and the future was within her reach. *This* was her life now, and she'd worked hard for this moment. The cloud that lay over her past was definitely not going to interfere with it, Dana thought determinedly. Even if she never discovered the truth about her previous life, she wasn't going to let this opportunity slip by.

"Seb, you darling! You had something to do with it, didn't you?"

"My opinion was asked. I gave it. End of story." He beamed, obviously pleased at her reaction.

"End of story, sure. You pulled strings, Mr. Hart."

"Call me Seb. You're the only one who's allowed to. I'd feel strange if you started giving me some respect at this late date." He laughed. "But seriously, don't sell yourself short. If you hadn't been as incredibly talented as you are, nothing I said would have helped. These are money people. They look at results."

"Well, I was taught by the master." Dana gazed at her friend, her eyes filling suddenly. "Oh, great, now I'm going to embarrass myself.'' She took the handkerchief he offered. ''But I'll miss working with you. We've been a team since I got out of the hospital and you gave me a job.''

''And one day you'll do the same. You'll give some bright kid a chance, promote her, work with her, and then wish her all the luck in the world when it's time for her to leave the nest.'' Seb's voice was a little husky, but he went on. ''I got that film scholarship myself when I was green; I'd never have been able to afford to go to university otherwise. Back then, I was holding down two jobs during the week and waiting tables on the weekend.'' He was silent for a moment, lost in his thoughts. ''I really don't know if I'd have made it if I hadn't gotten the Silver Shadows bursary.''

''You'd have made it.'' She paused. ''I know I've got an independent streak in me a mile wide, Seb. You were the only person I would have come to for help, because you never put strings on it. I'll pass the torch on when the time comes, but the debt I owe you can never be repaid.''

''Then consider it canceled.'' He ruffled her hair tenderly. ''We're getting too weepy here. We've still got *Scarlet Street* to finish, so I'm stuck with you for a few months yet. Pick you up around seven-thirty?''

Dana made a face. ''Seven-thirty. But don't you dare be cheerful at that hour.''

''I'll pick up a couple of cappuccinos and ignore you totally for the first half hour,'' he promised. ''Lock the door behind me. I'll set the main alarm downstairs.''

She did as he asked, and then went to the window, bending the slats of the venetian blinds so that she could watch him come out. His pale hair picked up the gleam from the streetlight as he walked down the block towards the twenty-four-hour garage where he parked his car. She stood there until he turned the corner.

Why had the spark between them never grown into a flame? Dana wondered. There was a rapport between them that she had never experienced with any other man, a comfortable camaraderie, but it had gone no further than that. Although, she thought with sudden insight, at times she'd had the feeling that Sebastian would have taken that next step if she had given him the slightest encouragement. The thought disturbed her and she pushed it away.

No, it was better this way. Relationships with other people had come and gone for both of them, although on her part they were never very intense. At this point in her career she was just too driven to spare much time for a social life. Of course she wanted a lasting relationship some day. But not yet.

And if you don't let yourself love someone, then it doesn't hurt so much when you lose them.

The stray thought flashed into her mind, and she frowned. That wasn't it at all! She wasn't afraid of falling in love. Why should she be? She just wanted to get her career on track first, Dana told herself impatiently. Once her professional life had taken off she'd have time for a personal one. That didn't indicate a deep-seated fear of loving someone, it was just good planning.

She turned her thoughts back to Sebastian. She was fortunate that their friendship had endured. Luckily, she got on well with Edwina. If Sebastian had finally found the woman he wanted to marry, then Dana knew that she would still be a welcome visitor to their home.

But it wouldn't be quite the same, she thought.

She walked around the small office, tidying up, flicking off the light in the kitchenette and closing the door to the rarely used darkroom. She picked up a rose petal that had fallen from the arrangement on the side table, and crumpled its silkiness in her hand. The faint scent touched the air and faded away.

For some reason the thought of making up the couch and getting ready for bed held no appeal. She'd gone past the point of tiredness, she decided. The evening had been an emotional roller coaster, from Seb's revelations about Dana Torrence to his final bombshell about her career.

Could she handle directing a movie on her own, with no one holding her hand? It was an exciting prospect, but with the excitement there was a pinprick of trepidation. What if she failed? Her emotions were rapidly becoming unraveled by these dreams. Her conversation with Sebastian tonight had only added to the questions in her mind, and neither of them had come up with any reasonable answers.

What connection could she possibly have with a woman who had died more than fifty years ago? If only she could remember something—anything—about her own past, maybe it would provide a clue to this psychic link she seemed to have with the long-dead Dana Torrence. Perhaps the actress had been related to her in some way. Somehow, it was easier to contemplate being haunted by someone in her family tree than to entertain Seb's notion of possession, Dana decided. She shivered suddenly.

It was time to halt that train of thought, she told herself. Her nerves, already frayed, were overriding her common sense. She'd make an appointment with Dr. Gottfried in the morning and he'd probably tell her that there was a simple psychological explanation for her haunted nights.

She hoped.

There was a scrap of paper on the desk. She didn't realize until she turned it over that it was the photo they'd been looking at earlier.

The dream woman. Herself.

She stared at the photo for a long moment and sighed. It was no use. In the back of her mind she'd prayed that the picture would jog something in her memory, that maybe even one piece of the puzzle would fall into place. In the past five years she'd learned to live with the void in her past, but always with the hope that one day her memory would return. Whenever Sebastian talked casually of his family back in Boston, or met with people he'd gone to school with, she'd felt a twinge of wistful envy. Surely there was someone out there who'd loved her, who missed her. Someone who was, even now, looking for her and wondering what had happened to her.

That hurt the most. Apparently she had disappeared out of a previous life and left no one behind who cared.

Even Dana Torrence had made more of an impression in her short life. The actress had obviously roused some emotion in the people she'd known. It eventually led to her death, but at least her disappearance had been investigated. As though her thoughts had subconsciously drawn her to it, Dana realized that she had walked over to the filing cabinet. The drawer that Sebastian had unlocked still stood open in front of her. She stood uncertainly for a moment, her curiosity battling with her conscience.

"It's my life." Her voice sounded unnaturally loud in the empty room. "I can't go on like this." In guilty haste she pulled the drawer out completely. There was little in it, and the only thing that interested her was the thin file marked D.T. Was there really a connection between her and Dana Torrence—as Sebastian had suggested? Dana dumped the contents onto the work table, ignoring her qualms.

Old newspaper clippings, police reports from decades ago and a few photographs slid across the polished wood. Setting the file drawer down on the chair beside her, she started sifting through the jumble. A typewritten description caught her eye.

The body was almost unidentifiable due to the length of time before it was found, but certain details lead me to believe that it is the missing actress Dana Torrence; the hair color matched, the height was not dissimilar to the known height of the victim, and a card case was found near the body with a Screen Actors' Guild identification card in the name of Dana Torrence. I hereby make positive identification. In my opinion, this is the body of Miss Dana Torrence. No known next of kin.

The statement was signed with an illegible scrawl, but the writer was noted under his signature as being the county coroner. A wave of pity washed over Dana. The poor woman! Left in a ditch. Obviously her life hadn't been one to envy. Even in the depths of her occasional self-pity, she had known that she had at least one good friend who cared about her, Dana thought. This woman had had nobody at all.

Suddenly ashamed of herself, she began to gather up the papers. If Sebastian wanted her to see them, she'd go over it all with him. But not this way. Not behind his back. A picture fell from the pile and she reached for it, intending to stuff it back in the folder with the others, but something about it stopped her. She adjusted the angle of the brighter desk light.

A man stared out of the photo at her, his dark gaze holding hers. His black hair was slightly longer than was customary for the period. A lock of it had fallen across his forehead and he had a shadow of stubble on his lean face. But it was his eyes that fascinated her. Their flat, accusatory stare gave him the tough, disillusioned look of a man who'd been pushed too far. He looked dangerous.

She had seen a timber wolf once in the San Diego Zoo. It had given off the same aura of caged violence and frustration, but it had possessed a kind of wild beauty. She'd had the insane impulse to tear down the barrier between them and place her hand on the animal. To caress it, whatever the consequences.

She had that same irrational impulse now. Who was he?

Dana pulled her gaze away from the photo and turned it over. There, on the back in Sebastian's familiar hand-writing, was a note. *Gabriel O'Shaunessy, held and questioned, but never charged in D.T.'s murder. Possibly last person to see her before murder. Could be murderer? Check further.*

The picture slipped from her fingers. A murderer! But why should that surprise her? Before she had even read Seb's note, she'd seen in his face that this O'Shaunessy had crossed a boundary line. A line between light and dark, the world of rules obeyed and of rules broken. Had moved into a world of no rules at all.

But what shocked Dana more than anything was her irrational desire to be in that world with him—a desire so overwhelming that she found herself trembling. It was as if she was poised on the edge of a precipice and had taken one step forward.

The regulator clock above the couch suddenly started striking midnight. Its hollow tones, usually comfortingly old-fashioned, were an intrusion, and Dana felt as if she had just been awakened from an uneasy sleep. Her hands shook as she put the photo back into the file. Seb was right; enough was enough. She'd end up back in the hospital if she didn't rein in her imagination.

A siren wailed and she realized that she'd left the window open. Another stupid move, she thought, especially in this city. Still clutching the folder, she snapped off the overhead lights and crossed to the window, closing it as the clock marked the last hour of the day. The sound of the siren ceased abruptly.

As soon as she turned back to face the room Dana knew that something was very, very wrong.

Chapter Two

The vibrations from the striking clock still hung in the air, as tangible as ripples in water, and Dana felt the hair lift on the back of her neck as she stared at the innocuous scene. The room was heavily pooled with shadows, the only light coming from a gooseneck lamp that cast a weak yellow glow on the scarred wooden surface of the desk. A primitive instinct warned her to remain motionless, although her mind had yet to identify the reason for her fear. Cautiously she slanted her eyes at the rest of the office.

The shape of the furniture in the corners of the room looked strange and bulky, unrecognizable as Sebastian's Italian-designed pieces. She wrinkled her nose slightly. The air suddenly seemed thick with tobacco smoke and the sharp smell of alcohol. Perhaps a bottle of developing liquid had spilled in the darkroom. Her mind, desperately trying to deny the alarm bells from her subconscious, seized on this explanation.

But a moment ago the strongest scent in the room had been the vase of white roses on the coffee table. What could possibly explain the smell of smoke? Of course! The air conditioner had finally come on again. It must be pulling in smog-laden air from the outside. She'd have to call the repairman tomorrow.

Still in a state of denial, she took a step forward and

then gasped in pain as she cracked her shin against a hard object. She glanced down. A chair! Who had been stupid enough to leave that right in her path? It hadn't been there when she'd crossed to the window, had it?

This chair hadn't even been in the room a minute ago!

At that, her defenses gave way and her conscious mind started receiving the information from her senses that it had been trying to block. Her grip tightened on the back of the chair. The whole room was different! The desk was closer to the wall than it had been. The bulb in the lamp didn't give off the clear tungsten light that it should have; in fact, it wasn't the same lamp at all. There was a coatrack behind the desk that she'd never seen, and a calendar hanging on the wall instead of the beautiful Dufy print that she'd given Seb last Christmas. Dana started edging along the perimeter of the room. Something was terribly, frighteningly wrong. She had to get out of here! How close was she to the door?

The door wasn't there.

She heard a whimpering sound and it took her a split second to realize that it was coming from her own throat. She cut the sound off abruptly. The door! Where was the door? In a panic, she backed up against the window and felt something at the side of her neck.

"No!" She whipped around to confront this new terror, grabbing at her neck and pulling the thin cord away from it.

There was a mighty clatter as the venetian blinds were released, shutting off the meager light from the street outside.

"What the—" The voice, slurred and sleep-roughened, came from the couch. "Hold it right there. I'm too drunk to wing you, but not too drunk to kill you."

Dana froze. "Please. My purse is over there by the coffee table. Or it was. Take it." She took a breath and tried to sound calm. *Don't provoke him, just let him have what he wants!* she told herself. "I don't have a lot of money. Look for yourself if you want."

Her earlier disorientation took second place to the immediate danger. Wherever she was, whatever had happened, she could deal with it later. Right now all she needed to know was that she was in a dimly lit room with an intruder. She tried to recall the sum total of the two classes of tae kwon do she had so far attended. Grab Tail of Tiger Coming down Mountain? No, that was a tai-chi relaxation technique.

"A dame." The voice was amused. "Deadlier than the male, as I know from experience, but I'll take my chances. Walk forward into the light." Out of the corner of her eye she saw him move behind her.

"Carrying heat, doll?"

"Heat?"

She gasped as she suddenly felt his hands move down her body. Without thinking, she spun around and raised her knee to where it would do the most damage. Tae kwon do be damned! she thought desperately as she heard his indrawn breath. The next moment she was facedown on the floor, her arms twisted behind her, and a weight pressing into the small of her back.

"Sweet move. Too bad your aim was off," her attacker ground out. "Not by much, though." She heard a clicking sound, and then the blinds falling to the floor. The room was immediately flooded with moonlight, and a cord was twisted around her wrists several times.

"That should hold you for a while. Now, let's have a look at you. And move slowly, I'm in a real bad mood and I was working on a hangover when you barged in."

"When *I* barged in?" Dana protested. Her voice cracked. Then she saw the face above her and her words died.

The cold light from the moon cut shadows under the lean cheekbones, and the dark eyes that met hers were narrowed in suspicion. The hair dropping carelessly across his brow was so black that it seemed to absorb and then quench the light that fell on it. Dana felt her own energy drain away as they stared at each other for a long moment.

All thoughts of escape seemed hopeless now. There was no fleeing from a ghost, was there? And that's what he was. Either that, or a photograph come to life.

"Welcome back, sweetheart. I've missed you." His voice was cold and flat and to Dana's fading senses it sounded as if it came from a great distance.

Then everything went dark and someone turned the sound off.

A ROUGH JACKET WAS covering her. It smelled slightly of tobacco and the harsh tweed tickled her chin where it had been tucked around her, but it felt warm and comforting. Especially after that weird dream she'd had, Dana thought hazily. Another cliff-hanger to tell Gottfried. Too bad she had to get ready to meet Sebastian; she could use a couple of hours more sleep after last night. Maybe just a few more minutes—

Last night!

She pushed the jacket away and looked wildly around her. She was lying on a faded red davenport, and the rest of the furniture in the room was just as unfamiliar. Even the door was in a different place. It hadn't been a dream.

Had her mind completely snapped? Maybe she was really in a hospital somewhere, fantasizing all this. She'd been under a lot of strain lately, and her mental health had probably been affected by it. It would all be connected to her amnesia somehow, and in a while she'd open her eyes and see the bearded face of Dr. Gottfried bending over her.

"You're awake." He had been sitting, motionless, behind the desk.

Apparently her fantasy was still continuing, because when she flicked her eyes over to the speaker, she saw that it wasn't Gottfried, but the man she knew as O'Shaunessy. He got up and started pulling the chair over to her. She studied him with interest.

She had to give herself credit, Dana thought approvingly. She was certainly hallucinating a devastatingly attractive man; even better-looking than the photo she'd seen of him. About six-two, with the shoulders of a linebacker, he was obviously what the Celts called black Irish, with soot-dark lashes half concealing eyes that were a true navy blue. Long legs and lean hips gave way to a solidly muscled torso just hinted at beneath his shirt.

His suit vest was unbuttoned, and as he moved the chair she saw he wore leather suspenders underneath. Tanned forearms contrasted sharply with the white of his rolled-up shirtsleeves, except for a pale scar that snaked its way from his wrist to his elbow.

It was the scar that did it for her.

It was obviously a few years old, and the skin had long since healed, but it still had an ugly connotation of whatever violence had caused it. It didn't belong in a delusion. Her mind would *never* have created a man with a scar.

This was really happening, Dana realized hollowly. No wonder she'd blacked out last night: something very weird and frightening was going on here. He was Gabriel O'Shaunessy, all right. Except that Gabriel O'Shaunessy had lived in the 1930s.... She sat very still, hardly daring to breathe, but behind her unnaturally calm facade a voice was screaming questions that she had no answers for.

Or at least, no answers that she could accept.

"It's time to talk." As he moved, he kept his eyes on her. He looked exhausted, as if he'd stayed awake all night, but there was a weary determination about him that told Dana she wouldn't be lucky enough to catch him off guard again.

She watched in silence as he reached into his pocket and pulled out a pack of cigarettes. Striking a wooden match against the leg of the chair, he lit a cigarette. Without thinking, she looked over at the desk where Seb's polite No Smoking, Please sign had always sat, but of course it wasn't there. In its place was a chipped glass ashtray, overflowing with butts.

No, this definitely wasn't Kansas anymore, Dana thought warily. Or the offices of Hart Incorporated, although it *was* the Quorum Building, as far as she could tell. Some details, like the position of the door, had changed, but most of the room's basic architecture was the same.

There was one way to find out if the insane suspicion that had taken hold of her was correct. As if in a trance, she swung her legs off the davenport and stood. Slowly she walked to the window, ignoring O'Shaunessy's sudden movement toward his gun.

Even before she saw the vintage cars in the street below her, she knew that she had somehow slipped into another time. The skyline of Los Angeles, the skyline that she had stared at so often from this very window, had totally changed. No building appeared to be over a few stories tall—ten or fifteen at the most. Gone were the office complexes that she was familiar with, the buildings that they'd had to be so careful about when they'd been shooting *Scarlet Street*. She recalled from her research for the film that there had been a height restriction on structures in L.A. until the 1950s.

Wait a minute! Dana's heart gave a little leap as she spotted the familiar outline of a church a few blocks away, but then her hopes fell. She felt as if she had run into an old friend in an unfamiliar country, only to be rebuffed. The church looked somehow cleaner. Newer. Like a building that had been recently built. In fact, looking closer she could see a construction scaffolding at the side of one wall.

She'd looked up the construction date of that same church for *Scarlet Street*. It had been built in 1935.

"You'd break your neck. There's no way out of here, lady." He'd come up behind her and Dana started.

"I wasn't going to jump." Her shoulders sagged and she leaned her forehead against the glass. "I've already fallen. Down the rabbit-hole, I think."

"Yeah, it's a crazy world." He took hold of her arm and gave her a little shake. "But then you're a pretty crazy dame, so that's just jake. You must be out of your mind, coming back here." He watched as she sat dejectedly back on the couch and let her head sink into her hands. "Right, sister, go ahead and cry now. I fell for your hard-luck story once. The biggest mistake in my life, and I've sure made some beauts. But not this time."

"What are you talking about? I've never met you before in my life." She lifted her head and stared at him. "I just want to go home."

He gave a short, unamused laugh. "Let's cut the acting. We're going downtown in a little while, and you can do some singing to a friend of mine, Lieutenant Oakes." He sounded bored, but there was an edge to his words. "But first of all you're going to go through it all for me. Call it a rehearsal."

He dropped his cigarette to the floor and ground it out with his heel, then leaned towards her. "I want the whole damn story; names, dates, everything. You can start with why you came back here. Are you in another jam? Did you think I was stupid enough to be your patsy twice?"

Dana wasn't ready for a confrontation. Her head felt as if it was filled with cotton wool, and her temples were throbbing. She tried to organize her thoughts quickly. As outlandish as it seemed, she had somehow traveled backward in time—how and why, she had no idea, but it was the only explanation for all this. The man who sat across from her obviously thought she was a criminal, although from what she knew about him, he had no right to judge her. He was a suspected murderer himself. She inhaled sharply as a thought struck her.

"Who do you think I am? No, please," she pleaded, as he started to reach for the phone. "Just humor me. Who am I?"

She hadn't realized that blue eyes could be so cold. "You're Dana Torrence, and you haven't changed enough to pretend you're someone else. Your hair's different, big deal. I've seen your lying face for the last five years in my dreams, laughing at me, and I'd recognize you anywhere. Just because you wipe off the makeup and tone down the platinum you think you can pass as an innocent little farm girl or something?" He lit another cigarette and looked at her in disgust.

She shook her head, bewildered. "But her body was found. She was killed."

"That was the official story. But I never believed it." A shadow passed over his face as he studied her. "Looks like I was right, doesn't it, sister? So who was she—the poor sucker who took your place?"

"I'm not the person you think I am! Look, I don't know how to explain this to you, but somehow I've been transported through—" She trailed off. How could she tell this antagonistic stranger the truth? *Transported through time.* First he'd laugh, and then he'd have her committed. A shudder passed through her. Psychiatric hospitals in this time had been primitive at best. She could be incarcerated for years.

"Transported here last night," she finished feebly.

"Yeah, I figured that, but who brought you? Why?"

Dana stayed stubbornly silent, and at first she thought that O'Shaunessy was going to lose his temper. The grim lines around his mouth whitened in anger.

She couldn't control herself. She started to shake with delayed reaction, and finally the tears she'd been holding back spilled over. She blinked them away. Should she go along with his assumption that she was Dana Torrence, or would that get her in more trouble than she was in already? And how did this time-travel phenomenon work? Should she try to stay in this office—was that the key? The Quorum Building was where she'd left her own time, and it was where she'd appeared in this time, so it seemed to be the one stable factor in all of this.

And the Quorum Building was where she'd first appeared to Sebastian.

"Look, whatever you're involved in, they'll go easier on you if you tell the truth now." O'Shaunessy sighed, and his severe expression softened as he watched the conflicting emotions chasing across her features. "Perhaps you're just a pawn, like I was, but you've got to talk to someone. Whoever you're protecting won't think twice before eliminating you, unless they know you've already spilled the beans." He reached for the heavy black telephone on the desk. "I've got no choice. If you won't talk to me, I'm taking you in."

Dana barely heard him speaking into the phone. If she accepted that she had moved backward in time, then what was to say that she hadn't once traveled forward in time too! She had been found on the steps of this very building five years ago, with no knowledge of who she was or where she was from. Dana Torrence had disappeared from here back in the thirties.

She and Seb had overlooked the one explanation that covered both of those facts, because they'd believed that the actress's body had been found and identified, but what if O'Shaunessy was right? What if Dana Torrence hadn't died? What if, in a moment of great pain and danger, and somehow aided by Sebastian's intense concentration on her film image that night, she had broken the rules of time and traveled forward? *And had become Dana Smith!*

"No, it can't be," she breathed. "There has to be some other explanation. There just has to be!"

"Come on, Oakes is waiting for us." O'Shaunessy was rolling his sleeves down in a businesslike manner.

He picked his jacket off the couch and Dana fleetingly realized that he had covered her with it during the night. So the man had a compassionate side to him, she thought. Could she persuade him to leave her alone here for a while? Somehow she had to get back to Hart Incorporated, to her life as Dana Smith, assistant director to Sebastian Hart. Back to the life she had built for herself in the future. If a doorway back to that other life existed, it had to be in this office.

"Tell the police I'll talk to them here. I'm not leaving this place." She drew herself up to her full height, all five and a half feet of it. Unfortunately she had to tip her head back to meet O'Shaunessy's eyes.

He grabbed his fedora off the hat stand and shot her an amused look. "Sure. I'll tell the lieutenant that, Duchess. And you can stand right beside me when I do, to pick him up when he falls down laughing." He snapped the brim over his eyes with a practiced motion. With the other hand he checked his gun in his shoulder holster. "All set?"

Dana sat back down on the sofa and folded her arms in response. "The only way you'll get me out of here is by throwing me over your shoulder and carrying me. Believe me, you don't want to try it, Mr. O'Shaunessy," she warned him.

Ten minutes later, she was being unceremoniously

dumped onto the front seat of a car. She tried to struggle to a sitting position, not easy since her hands were once again tied behind her. O'Shaunessy ran around and entered the driver's seat, pushing her upright as if he was handling a sack of potatoes.

"I hope you're satisfied. We could have done this the polite way," he muttered, breathing heavily.

Dana glared at him, and saw the broken skin on his cheekbone where she'd scratched him. "I'm satisfied. For now, anyway," she threatened. The scuffle in his office had been humiliatingly brief. As soon as she got back to the 1990s, she vowed, she was getting her black belt.

He looked over his shoulder as he reversed out of the parking lot. She felt herself flying forward, and only his arm in front of her stopped her from hitting her head on the dashboard. "Ralph Nader, where are you?" she gasped. "Don't tell me, seat belts don't exist, do they?"

"In a car? What for?"

"Just a frivolous luxury, I suppose," she snapped. "You win, O'Shaunessy. Untie me and I give you my word I'll stay put."

He stared suspiciously at her for a moment. "No tricks?"

"No tricks," Dana promised resignedly. "I just don't want to go diving through your windshield."

She leaned forward and felt his hands firm on her wrists as he warily untied the cord. Then, with O'Shaunessy still casting doubtful glances over at her, they pulled away from the Quorum Building with a squeal of tires. Dana rubbed her skin where the cord had chafed it, and felt as if she was walking away from the last lifeboat on the *Titanic*. As soon as this business with the police was over, she had to get back here. Somehow she had to get back to the future. But meanwhile she had to cope with the past, or the present. Whatever this was.

They stopped for a red light and she looked out the window. It was almost like a film set, she thought, intrigued in spite of herself. A small boy stood at the corner selling papers. He wore corduroy pants several sizes too big, held up around his skinny waist with a length of twine. A man paused, took a paper and tossed a coin in the air. Dana watched as the boy caught it and tugged at his cap while his customer sauntered on.

"Why isn't he in school?" She hadn't realized that she'd spoken aloud.

O'Shaunessy glanced at the newsboy and shrugged. He put the car into first gear as the light changed. "He's probably the only one in his family with a job. It's tough all over right now." He darted a curious look at her. "After five years of this damned depression, don't tell me you aren't used to it."

Somehow she'd forgotten that fact. The Great Depression. A man passed by on the sidewalk. His shoes were cracked and broken and he wore a sign fastened to his back that said *Will work for food.* As they overtook him, Dana craned her neck back for a better look. He seemed to be in his forties, and on his shabby jacket she saw a row of medals.

"Another hero of the Great War, reduced to begging on the street." O'Shaunessy shifted viciously into a higher gear. "Sometimes I'm glad my brother didn't make it back from the Argonne." He pulled around a truck, laying on the horn as he passed the slower vehicle.

The Argonne. It rang a faint bell in her mind. Had it been a battle of some sort? "Your brother was in World War I?" she attempted.

"What do you mean, World War I? The Great War, of course." His tone was bitter. "Unless there was another one that you know of."

Bad mistake. She pressed her lips together. Until World

War II started, the first war had been referred to simply as the Great War—people hadn't been able to conceive of another slaughter to equal it. She'd have to watch what she said. She focused on a woman in a tight skirt, with a small feathered hat perched on top of her head and short white gloves smoothed over her hands.

Dana looked down at her own sand-colored linen slacks and crumpled cotton shirt, the creases in them bearing witness to her night on the davenport. If she'd entered this time a couple of years earlier she'd have caused a scandal, but thank goodness she'd seen the occasional female in pants as they drove along. Still, she hardly looked like an upstanding citizen. A bag lady with illusions of grandeur was more like it. With all the miracle creaseproof fabrics she'd had to choose from, she'd gone time-traveling in linen and cotton.

As they swung into the police station parking lot, she gathered her thoughts, attempting to prepare herself for the ordeal ahead. If O'Shaunessy convinced the police that she was Dana Torrence and that she'd had something to do with the dead woman whose body had been found, they'd want to hold her for questioning. Or worse. They might even charge her with being an accessory to murder, and she couldn't allow that to happen. She had to get back to O'Shaunessy's office and try to reverse time again.

What was she going to tell them? She had no ID on her and even if she did, the dates would be all wrong. The truth wasn't an option. Could she simply refuse to talk?

That would really rouse their suspicions. Dana felt her stomach clench in apprehension. The first time she'd been questioned by the police, in the hospital five years ago, they'd been courteous and understanding when she hadn't been able to give them any information, but their sympathy had stemmed from the fact that they knew she'd lost her memory.

Back then it had been the truth, but would it work now that it was a lie? It was her only chance, she decided as they walked into the station, O'Shaunessy's hand clamped possessively around her arm. But she'd have to use every ounce of acting ability that she had if she was going to fake amnesia.

Of course, if she really had been an actress once, that shouldn't be such a problem.

"Hello, Jake. Harry's expecting me." O'Shaunessy obviously didn't have much faith in her promise of good behavior. He kept her close by him as he greeted the uniformed man behind the counter.

"Gabe! Long time no see." The desk officer looked with interest at Dana and noted O'Shaunessy's death grip on her. "So that's how you get a date. I always wondered."

"Officer, this man has assaulted and kidnapped me." Dana gave Gabe a freezing look, but for all the attention the two of them gave her, she might just as well have held her breath.

O'Shaunessy grinned at the other man. "It's the Irish charm, boyo. It drives the ladies crazy." He sobered and finally let go of her arm. "No, this little spitfire is here to clear my name."

"The Torrence killing? You know your friends never believed you had anything to do with that." Jake picked up the phone and dialed a number, his good-natured face troubled.

"Plenty of people did. It was enough to drive the paying customers away. Hell, city hall stonewalls me if I even try to track down a missing pooch by his dog license." He caught the other man's expression of disbelief. "Yeah, it's gotten that bad. Time was when I felt I was slumming, taking divorce cases. Now I track down canine runaways."

So that's why he'd been so hostile towards her. It was

the Dirty Thirties, with a soup kitchen on every second corner, and this man had had his livelihood ripped away from him—because of her, or so he thought. It was a wonder he hadn't marched her here at gunpoint. She almost felt sorry for him.

But she had her own problems, and one of them was the big Irishman on point duty beside her.

"The lieutenant can see you now, Gabe." Jake replaced the phone in its cradle and gave him a thumbs-up sign. "Good luck with the frail."

Frail! Dana fumed as she walked down the corridor a reluctant step ahead of O'Shaunessy. Another aspect of this unenlightened era that she found hard to swallow! Somehow, when she'd heard this kind of dialogue on the late show, she'd thought it was quaint, but having it directed at her was demeaning.

"Now, remember what I told you. Oakes isn't a bad guy, and if he thinks you've been straight with him, maybe he can pull some strings for you later on."

She shot O'Shaunessy a look of pure venom over her shoulder. "Thanks for the tip. Maybe he can help me get one of the cushy jobs in the prison laundry."

His face hardened. "Have it your own way, sister." He tapped perfunctorily at the door in front of them and opened it.

"Here she is, Harry, special delivery."

She felt a none too gentle nudge at her back and took an unwilling step into the office. It looked as if a bomb had hit it. Papers were strewn on every surface, photos hung crookedly on the dirty yellow walls, and a film of gray ash surrounded the overflowing ashtray on the desk like a UFO circle in a wheatfield. The only thing in the room that was free of dust was a silver-framed photograph beside the telephone. Oakes tilted his oak swivel chair back and looked at them.

"Nice parcel, Gabe. Too bad you couldn't wrap her up a little better, though." He cast a critical eye at her rumpled appearance. "So this is the dame you think is Torrence? From what I heard, she was always a sharp dresser."

This from a man with mustard on his tie, Dana thought, but she kept silent for the moment.

"Forget the clothes. She's obviously been on the lam for a while. Pull the photo out of her file and compare it with her." O'Shaunessy impatiently lit a cigarette while Oakes sifted through the mess of paper on his desk. "Jeez, Harry, don't you ever get a filing clerk in here?"

"Over my dead body," the other man answered absently. He placed a stained manila folder triumphantly in front of him, and started patting his pockets. "Now, where'd I put my glasses?"

Dana could see a pair of steel-rimmed spectacles poking out from under a folded newspaper. "Under there," she pointed, before she could stop herself.

"Thanks. I can't see a thing without them."

He carefully hooked them around his ears, while she cursed herself. Little Miss Helpful, she thought in exasperation. Why didn't she just offer to trot down the hall and have herself booked for murder one, to save them the trouble? From O'Shaunessy's amused glance she realized that he knew exactly what was going through her mind, and she looked quickly away. From now on, no more cooperation. Her freedom might be at stake.

Oakes had been looking at the photograph of Dana Torrence. It was a studio shot, from what she could see of it. For the second time in twenty-four hours she found herself looking at the platinum-blond hair and bee-stung lips of the woman who had been found by Seb on the steps of the Quorum Building. In this photo, the lighting was softer, the shadows around the eyes more mysterious, but it was the same face. Dana Torrence's face. Her face. Dana put out a hand to steady herself against the desk.

"I see the resemblance, Gabe. Hair, makeup—they've all been changed. But those are details." Oakes looked over the top of his glasses at her. "The basic facial structure and features match." He closed the folder with a snap. Taking off his glasses, he rubbed the bridge of his nose wearily, and then looked at her. In that instant his whole demeanor changed.

"Where've you been for the last five years, Miss Torrence? You realize that at the least, you've perpetrated a major hoax on a very busy police department. Why didn't you come forward sooner?"

He sounded as if he regretted her thoughtless behavior. Like a cat chastising a mouse for trying to escape, she thought. She forced herself to look away from the photograph, with its eerie and distorted image of her own face, and took a deep breath.

Underestimating this man, for all his previous low-key manner, could be fatal. He had the power of the law behind him and she had no protection at all. In the world she was used to, she would have a lawyer with her and the police would have to follow a strict procedure in questioning her, but she had the feeling that procedure was something that would be ignored in this decade, if it got in the way. She allowed her body to slump, and her eyelids fluttered weakly.

"Please, Lieutenant. This is all so confusing..." She looked around uncertainly. "Do you think I could sit down?" At his nod, she sank into the hard wooden chair facing him. "You keep calling me Miss Torrence, but that name isn't familiar to me. Could I see the photo of her?"

Oakes looked puzzled, but he complied. She took the picture and pretended to study it carefully. "It certainly does look a lot like me." She let an expression of hope cross her face. "This would explain so much!"

"Wait a minute—" O'Shaunessy pushed himself away from the wall that he'd been leaning against.

Oakes held up a commanding hand. "Let her finish." His eyes never left her face. "What are you saying? That you aren't Dana Torrence?"

Dana twisted her hands in her lap and shook her head. "I don't know. I just don't know!" She sounded on the verge of hysteria and wondered briefly if she was over-doing it. "I haven't known who I am for over five years now." She buried her face in her hands as if overcome by emotion. The words had come easily enough, because it was all true. From O'Shaunessy's tense attitude she knew he was ready to explode. But had she convinced Oakes?

He hadn't finished with her. "Amnesia. If it's true, it sure came at a convenient time." He pulled a cigarette out of a pack on the desk. "Got a light, Gabe?"

O'Shaunessy tossed him a battered lighter without tak-ing his narrowed eyes off Dana, and Oakes flicked it a few times before it caught.

"So what have you been doing all this time? Where've you been and why didn't you contact the authorities?" He slammed the lighter down sharply, making her jump. "Take it one at a time, lady. Where were you yesterday at this time?"

Her mind went blank. *Think,* she told herself. Her glance fell on the newspaper folded in front of her. The *Chronicle.* "San Francisco," she blurted. "I—I've been looking for work."

"She's lying, Harry. Look at her," O'Shaunessy de-manded. "She knows damn well who Dana Torrence is. She knew that the body had been identified as hers, she told me." Dana could feel the anger he was holding back. "Ask her who got killed in her place!"

The lieutenant's voice came out in a low rumble. "I'll ask the questions, shamus." He turned back to her. "Is that right? Did you know about the body?"

Before she could formulate another lie, the telephone rang. Oakes grabbed it with a muttered oath.

"I told you, no calls!" He listened for a moment.

Dana, watching him closely, saw him close his eyes briefly, as if he was in pain. With his free hand he grasped the little silver-framed photo and held it tightly. Was it her imagination, or did he suddenly look tired and old? She glanced over at O'Shaunessy, but he was staring out of the grimy window, his hands jammed in his pockets.

"I understand. No! That...that won't be necessary." The lieutenant gently replaced the receiver and rose from his desk. He laid the framed photo facedown. "Emergency. I'll be back in a couple of minutes, Gabe."

"What? We're in the middle of something here," O'Shaunessy protested.

Lieutenant Oakes kept his face averted from his friend, but as he walked out he met Dana's puzzled gaze. What she saw in his eyes shocked her. They burned with hate. Hate and something else. He reached for the doorknob with a trembling hand, and she realized that along with the hatred she had seen fear.

But why would he be afraid of her?

"Now that we're alone, suppose you tell me what the hell is going on?" O'Shaunessy sat on the edge of the desk and leaned toward her aggressively. "That amnesia story'll get blown out of the water with a few phone calls to 'Frisco, so why don't you drop it and start telling the truth?"

Since last night, Dana thought, she'd been manhandled, bullied and intimidated by this man. When she'd first seen his picture in Seb's file on Dana Torrence, she'd almost felt as if there were some bond between them. Face it, she told herself, you were attracted to him! But since then she'd been dragged into this police station against her will, and was possibly facing murder charges, all because this two-bit PI had a grudge against her. Any passing attraction she'd felt for him had obviously been a delusion.

"Listen, mister, if I told you the truth you wouldn't be able to handle it!" she flashed back at him. "The amnesia happens to be true, but that's the least of my problems right now. If you think I'm going to risk going to jail, forget it."

"Jail? You'll be lucky if they don't hang you, lady. And they will, if you don't start giving them some names." He shook his head. "I don't think you killed the woman who was identified as you. But I bet you know who she is. I think you're shielding someone."

For a long moment he held her eyes with his, his expression unreadable. Almost reluctantly, he reached out and pushed a strand of hair back from her face. "I never wanted you hurt, not even on the nights I woke up cursing the day you walked into my life."

His voice was barely above a whisper, and his touch was gentle, but Dana felt as if she had picked up a live electric wire. A white-hot current ran through her, and she caught her breath in a gasp. Denial was useless. There *was* something between them: the same something that she'd felt last night staring at his photo. And from his startled reaction now, he was feeling it, too.

She gave no conscious thought to what happened next. As if she had done this before with him, her hand slipped softly around the back of his neck, his hair brushing against her fingers. It all felt so right, she thought dazedly, as she felt him move towards her. So…certain. As if they were continuing something they'd started long, long ago.

The office door opened suddenly, shattering the moment.

"Gabe, the lieutenant says—" Jake walked into the room and stopped. He cleared his throat. "Sorry. But the lieutenant had to go out on an emergency call. He said to tell you that he'd be in touch, Gabe." He turned to Dana. "You're free to go."

O'Shaunessy shook his head like a man awakening from a dream. He straightened up, moving back from Dana.

"He said he'd be in touch?" Shoving himself off the desk, he stared at the other man in disbelief, his voice rising. "In touch? This is a murder investigation, not a tea party. He was questioning her, for God's sake!"

Jake shrugged, obviously uncomfortable. "All I know is that he said he had to leave. He signed a car out for the whole day," he added helpfully.

O'Shaunessy reached for his hat. "That's that, then," he said tonelessly. "Tell Harry thanks for seeing me, Jake. I knew I could depend on my friends." He started for the door and flicked a contemptuous glance around the office. Dana, following him, saw him check his stride for a second. He reached over and picked his lighter off the desk. Then he brushed by the other man and made his way purposefully down the hall.

She ran to catch up with him. Through some miracle, the police had lost interest in her, but there was no guarantee that they wouldn't have her picked up again. She had to return to the Quorum Building right away and she needed O'Shaunessy's help for that, but from the way he pointedly ignored her as he walked out of the building towards his car, helping her was the last thing on his mind. She put a restraining hand on his arm.

"O'Shaunessy, wait!"

He stopped so abruptly that she almost stumbled. "It was the phone call, right?"

Her hand slipped from his sleeve. It was as if the moment between them in Oakes's office had never happened.

The man who had touched her so tenderly simply didn't exist anymore. A cold-eyed stranger stood before her, looking at her as if she was an unpleasant form of life that he had never encountered before.

"How'd you do it? I've been with you all the time. You couldn't have gotten word to anyone." He sounded as if he was speaking to himself, but she answered him anyway.

"What are you accusing me of now?"

He turned away from her and headed for the car. "Forget it. I'm tired of your games. Just get out of my life, lady."

"Are you blaming me because your friend was called away? Is that it?"

He pulled his car keys out of his pants pocket, paying her as much attention as if she was invisible, and Dana felt something like panic rise in her throat. Damn the man! He couldn't just leave her stranded here! She had no money, no knowledge of this time and place. With a start, she realized that Gabriel O'Shaunessy was the closest thing she had to a friend in this alien world, and he seemed fully prepared to leave her standing in this parking lot.

"Just because he had more important things to do than listen to your accusations—"

"Harry didn't go anywhere. He's still in the station, waiting for me to leave." He reached around her and opened the door. "And if that's the way he wants it, then I'll oblige him."

"You're paranoid. What makes you think he didn't go out like they said?" Had the stress of the last few years affected Gabe? If he saw a conspiracy in a simple broken appointment—

"His glasses were still on his desk when we left. Harry wouldn't go out and leave them there and he certainly wouldn't try to drive without them." O'Shaunessy pulled out the choke and started the ignition. "So he was lying to me. The phone call must have been a message from your friends, telling him to lay off.'' He looked at her curiously. ''How much did they offer him? How much are you worth?'' His disillusioned expression told Dana that to him, at least, any price would be too high.

''I don't think he's on the take,'' she said slowly. She thought back to the scene in Oakes's office, and his face when he left. ''I think he was threatened.''

He'd already shifted the car into gear. At her quiet announcement, he put it back into neutral. He sat for a moment, and then reached over and unlocked the passenger door. ''Get in.''

The interior of the car was hot and dusty and the upholstery was ripped in several places, but she was grateful for the invitation. Her greatest fear had been that he would leave her with no way of getting back to the Quorum Building. Dana slid in beside him.

''I saw his face when that call came. He was frightened, I'm sure of it,'' she said.

O'Shaunessy tapped the steering wheel with his thumb. ''I don't buy it. Harry Oakes doesn't scare easy.''

''His hands were trembling. He was holding that little silver-framed picture and I could see it shaking,'' she insisted.

He stopped tapping the wheel. ''Janey's picture?''

''I couldn't see the picture in it. Why, who's Janey?''

''His granddaughter. The apple of his eye.'' His eyes closed briefly, and despite the tension of the moment, Dana noted the spiky sweep of his lashes against his cheekbones. She felt an odd pang of dismay that they hadn't met under more convenient circumstances. But, of course, she told herself, under normal circumstances they never would have met at all.

''So that's how they got to him. I should have known.''

He opened his eyes and looked at her. "Of course he'd back off, with Janey at stake."

"His granddaughter?" Dana was appalled. "But you must know that I didn't have anything to do with it. You said it yourself, I've been with you all the time, Gabe!" It was the first time she'd used his Christian name, and she saw that it disconcerted him. She hurried on, practically stumbling over the words in her desire to convince him. "You may not think much of me, but I'd never harm a child. Only a monster could go that far! And if I was involved with whoever threatened Harry, why would I tell you what I'd seen? You weren't watching when that call came. You'd never have known."

She leaned closer as she talked, forcing him to acknowledge her reasoning. Her face had a smudge of dirt on it and strands of hair had escaped the tight French braid that had originally confined them. But her eyes, green and intense, locked O'Shaunessy's doubtful gaze with hers. Finally he sighed, and nodded.

"I went to see a film of yours a couple of years ago, in a second-run theater in Santa Monica. *Follies on Broadway.* You had a bit part."

"One close-up," she murmured, remembering what Seb had told her.

"You were awful." The corner of his mouth lifted reluctantly. "Extremely decorative, but you couldn't act worth a damn. You're not acting now, are you?"

"Most of what I've told you really is the truth. I wish I could tell you everything, but it's all so unbelievable. And I don't have any way of proving it to you." Dana nibbled at her lower lip in concentration. "If only I'd brought something with—" She didn't finish her sentence.

She had a vision of herself last night, before this nightmare had begun, walking toward the window in Sebastian's office. She'd been carrying something. The file on

Dana Torrence! She was sure she'd had it in her hand when the time travel had occurred. But where had it gone?

"What is it?"

"I've just remembered something. When you cut the blinds down last night, was there anything underneath them on the floor?" She gripped his arm in her excitement.

Gabe shrugged. "I was occupied, if you'll recall. I didn't notice." A flush of color crept under his tan. "Besides, I'd been nursing a bottle of Scotch for a couple of hours. I was so far gone I didn't even notice you come into the office until you started knocking chairs over."

She made a gesture of impatience. "You wouldn't have anyway. Look, if you'll drive me back to your office I'll tell you everything. I've got a file full of newspaper clippings, photographs, even police reports. I don't know what else is in it, but it'll prove that I had nothing to do with whoever threatened Oakes and tried to pin a murder charge on you five years ago."

"Proof that you're not Torrence? Sorry. I'll give you the benefit of the doubt when it comes to everything else. I told you I figured you were being used. But you're the woman I met as Dana Torrence, and nothing can convince me you're not." He looked away. "Some things you just don't forget, sweetheart."

"I *was* Dana Torrence." A tiny crease appeared between Dana's brows. "At least, I think I was, a long time ago. But you have to look at this file. Please, Gabe. Trust me this once."

She held her breath, praying that he wouldn't turn her down. With Gabriel O'Shaunessy on her side, she could stay in his office for as long as it took to get back through the time barrier. She wouldn't allow herself to consider what she would do if the door, or whatever it was, had closed forever.

"Trust you once?" He flicked an ironic glance at her worried face, then sighed and started the car.

"O'Shaunessy, you never learn, do you?" he murmured resignedly.

Chapter Three

During the drive back through the city streets, Dana's mind was working furiously. What was she going to do once they returned to the Quorum Building office? Stand in the middle of the room and chant *Open Sesame?* She had no idea how she was going to reverse the process that had brought her here.

Just her luck, she thought, that she'd had to be the first person to test Einstein's theory of relativity.

Her immediate task was to convince O'Shaunessy that her crazy story was true. The file contained newspaper clippings that were dated later than this time, but would that be enough to make him believe her? He'd obviously been carrying a grudge against her for a long time, blaming her for the suspicion that had been directed at him, almost wiping out his business. She could understand that, but she couldn't fathom the edge of personal resentment she detected in his attitude, as if she had betrayed him in some way.

As a working theory, she had to accept that she had lived in this time before, under the name of Dana Torrence, and that somehow she'd known Gabriel O'Shaunessy in that life. It would help if she knew why he held her so responsible for his bad luck. How and when had their paths crossed?

Suddenly, an image came to her, unbidden and unexpected.

She was standing in front of him. His eyes burned with a dark blue fire; anger and something deeper. Before she'd known what he intended to do, he'd pulled her to his chest. She felt the heat of his mouth possessing hers, and for some reason, she didn't even think of resisting; it seemed useless, like denying fate. Her mouth opened under his...

Where had that come from? Dana sat bolt upright in the seat. Had that been a memory of something that had actually happened between them? The image had been so vivid that she touched her lips surreptitiously with her tongue, sure that she would find them swollen and tender. She'd felt the heat of his body against hers, had almost been able to taste him, and she still felt languid and softened, as if she had been dipped in warm honey and licked clean.

Hastily she rolled down the window, welcoming the cool breeze against her burning face. Had they been lovers once? Back in Oakes's office she'd felt a strange sense of déjà vu; had somehow known that whatever was about to take place was merely a continuation of an earlier intimacy. What if a fragment of her past had just fallen into place, like a pattern in a kaleidoscope?

She needed some answers from him.

"How did we meet? Did we know each other well—when I was Dana Torrence, I mean?" Her question sounded stupid, even to herself, but O'Shaunessy merely slanted a sardonic glance at her.

"Memory still playing tricks on you? Okay, I'll go along with you. I was hired by Oval Studios to follow you for a few days. As far as I knew, it was just a routine check before they offered you a contract. For the best part of a week I watched your every move; sitting in my car all night outside your rooming house, seeing where you went, who you met. Yeah, you could say I got to know you pretty well. Or I thought I did.''

He'd been tailing her? Dana felt unreasonably angry. She'd been nothing more than a job to him, someone whose privacy he'd been paid to violate! But that *couldn't* be all she'd been. For the first time since she had stumbled into this situation she had something besides O'Shaunessy's recollections to rely upon. The flashback she'd just experienced *had* to be a memory. It had been too intense to dismiss as a figment of her imagination. He wasn't telling her the whole truth.

"You watched me. That's all? We never met?''

"We met. Once.'' He shifted uncomfortably in his seat, his concentration seemingly focused on his driving. They came up to a yellow light, and he sped through it. "You saw someone at the newspaper that last day, and I figured at the time that you were just passing on a tip to one of the gossip columnists. You came to my office and asked me to withhold that information from the guy who hired me.'' He fell silent.

"And did you?''

O'Shaunessy accelerated as they approached another amber light, but as a police car cruised into view, he swore softly and braked. Impatiently he turned towards her. "I kept your secret, don't worry. That's what you wanted to know, wasn't it? How big a fool I was for you?'' He fumbled in his pockets, brought out a pack of cigarettes and lit one.

"No,'' he continued. "It wasn't me who sold you out. Even after I realized that you were involved in something a lot bigger and a lot dirtier than I'd thought. Big enough to scare you into trying to spill your story to the press, and dirty enough for someone to later buy off the reporter you talked to. Yeah, I was a conquest, darling.''

The self-mockery in his voice was all too evident. Dana

knew that she had opened a wound that hadn't yet begun to scar over, but after years of living in limbo, a fragment of her past had finally surfaced. That kiss had been the first memory powerful enough to rip aside the veil of her amnesia. She had to continue.

"What happened after I left your office?"

O'Shaunessy laughed shortly. "That's what I'd like to know. You were shot—bad enough so that I couldn't see how you'd gotten out of there—but somehow you did, leaving me to take the rap." His jaw tightened. "I was covered in your blood, dammit! The cops were grilling me, and all I could think of was that you might be dead!"

The raw emotion in his voice ripped through her.

"They asked me why you'd come to my office and I told them you'd asked me to follow a cheating boyfriend. I said I'd turned you down." He grimaced. "Then a wise-guy rookie noticed a smear of your lipstick on my handkerchief, and they took me in." The traffic moved forward again and he didn't see Dana's involuntary start. "I said you'd ended up crying on my shoulder in the office and one thing had led to another, but it was twelve hours before they let me go. Even then they kept pulling me in for questioning every couple of months."

O'Shaunessy turned down a side street. "After all, a dame had been shot as she walked out of my office. Hell, two minutes after she'd walked out of my arms. The police tend to take that kind of thing seriously, even in this town."

After she'd walked out of his arms? Then what she'd just experienced *had* been a memory! She could no longer deny the fact that she had lived in this time as Dana Torrence, and had almost been killed here. Hard as it was for her to accept, her life in the 1990s had been the false one.

No wonder no one had been able to identify her! No wonder she had been so traumatized that she had been unable to speak for months, and that when she could, her mind had blotted out all of her previous existence. In addition to battling for her life in the hospital, she had been fighting for her sanity. The only way she'd been able to cope with being seriously wounded and then traveling through time, had been by completely closing off part of herself.

She'd done a thorough job of it, Dana thought. Even knowing that she belonged in this time didn't alleviate her longing to return to the life that she had made for herself. She'd worked hard to get where she'd been in Hart Productions and it had finally started to pay off: she'd been taken seriously as a potential director and a creative talent. There was no way she could return to being Dana Torrence, a bit-part actress who'd ended up as a supposed murder victim. She'd progressed far beyond that.

Or had she? An eerie chill ran down her back, as if someone was walking over her grave. If she stayed in this time would she take up the life that had been interrupted so abruptly? Would she gradually take on the persona of Dana Torrence again, and fulfill the destiny she had temporarily escaped? She had been meant to die on the steps of the Quorum Building five years ago, but somehow she had managed to cheat death by traveling forward into the future. Perhaps her fate had merely been suspended, not evaded.

"Get down!" The urgency in Gabe's voice caught her attention. She shot a look of inquiry at him.

"Get out of sight! We've got visitors." He grabbed his hat from the seat beside them and pulled it low over his eyes. Hastily Dana slid down in the seat, making sure that she couldn't be seen from outside. She felt ridiculous.

"What's going on? What do you mean, we've got visitors?" She was in no mood to play cops and robbers.

He spoke out of the side of his mouth, his eyes fixed on

the road ahead. "We're just passing the Quorum, and there's a car waiting by the curb. I think I recognize it."

She could see the building as they drove by it, but from her worm's-eye view she couldn't see the car he was talking about. If there was one, Dana thought. She was about to sit up again, but then she remembered the fear she had seen on Lieutenant Oakes's face. Someone had threatened the granddaughter he loved. Maybe Gabe wasn't imagining things.

"What's happening?" she whispered, expecting at any moment to hear machine-gun fire raking their vehicle. She reined her imagination in firmly. This was what came of watching too many late-night shows on television. Her fantasies were running wild with scenes from gangster movies.

"All right, you can get up now." His voice had lost its edge, but his knuckles had whitened where they gripped the steering wheel. The scar on his forearm seemed more noticeable.

"Who were they? Were they waiting for you?" She pushed her hair off her face and was grateful that there wasn't a mirror around. She didn't want to know what she looked like.

"Three of Dave Townsend's thugs that usually work for him out at the casino he's invested in. Those boys aren't picked for their brains, though. They were standing right beside their car, smoking. They didn't spot me." Gabe sounded thoughtful. "If they're the ones who muzzled the cops, why bother staking out my office? Unless..." He glanced at her, obviously puzzled.

"Unless I'm telling the truth and I haven't had anything to do with these people," Dana stated. "Admit it. I've tried to tell you from the start, but you were determined to take me in to the police. Now they know I exist. This Townsend person might even be trying to kill me!"

"Townsend works for Oval Studios. He's the one that hired me to tail you in the first place. His goon squad crosses the line sometimes, but I saw him after the cops released me and he swore he'd had nothing to do with your shooting. Why would he want to kill you now?"

"I don't know!" Her frustration showed. "But it seems pretty suspicious. Within minutes of you parading me around in the police station, your friend receives a threatening phone call, and then when we get back to your office, there's a posse waiting for us. I may not remember much, but I still know how to add two and two together, and I don't like what's adding up here."

Even as she spoke, Dana wondered why she was so certain that she was the target of the men waiting outside of the Quorum Building. Her conviction went beyond mere logic. Again, she had the eerie feeling that she was reliving something that she had already gone through, but this time the prospect filled her with dread.

Was this how she had felt just before she had been shot five years ago? Was she experiencing the apprehension she had felt then? Her dream, with its overtones of impending disaster, was coming true, she thought wildly. A bubble of irrational terror rose in her throat.

"This is a setup, isn't it? You and your pals blew it last time, so now you're delivering me right to them!" She felt frantically for the door handle, but Gabe pulled her back.

"This isn't five years ago!" His hand reached out and covered hers as if he could read her fears. "Okay, it looks bad, but let down your guard a little, lady. I swear I didn't set you up with Townsend—now, or five years ago. We're in a tight spot here and we've got to start trusting each other."

"Trust? The only time you trusted me was when you had my hands tied behind my back!"

"If that's what's bothering you, I'll let you have your

turn with me some time in retaliation,'' Gabe shot back. ''I'll even let you tell me your side of the story from start to finish, no matter how crazy you say it is. Until then, we're partners. Agreed?'' His eyes held hers steadily.

She tried to pull away from his gaze and found she couldn't. It was insane, Dana thought. In the space of a few short hours, her life had been turned upside down. She'd traveled backward in time, and now, it seemed, she was on some gangster's things-to-do-today list. So why did she suddenly feel that the most immediate danger in this situation was staring right at her from a pair of impossibly blue eyes?

She looked down at her hand enclosed in his, resisting with difficulty the impulse to run her fingertips along the pale line of the scar on his forearm, resisting the desire to ask him how it had happened. She realized that he was still waiting for her response, and she wrenched her mind back to reality with an effort. She had no choice. They had to work together.

''Partners,'' she agreed briskly, withdrawing her hand in a businesslike fashion. Her attempt at a nineties-style power move was sabotaged by her voice, which came out in a rusty croak. ''But how do we get into your office? Is there another entrance?''

''Better than that. We'll leave the car here and come back for it later.'' If O'Shaunessy had noticed her mood swing he gave no sign. He turned into an alleyway lined with trash cans, touching the brake when a ginger-colored cat ran in front of the car. The cat jumped gracefully to the top of the wooden fence that separated the alley from the back of the buildings, and then paused to wash itself with feline indifference. Dana got out and looked around her. The traffic noises from the main street were muted, and except for the cat the alley seemed deserted.

''Follow me, but keep your voice down. This building

adjoins the Quorum, and Townsend might have someone watching the back entrances.'' He opened a gate in the fence and let the latch slip quietly down again. "Come on."

He made his way to a flight of steps leading down to a basement door. So quickly that she hardly realized what he was doing, he pulled a thin piece of metal out of his pocket and inserted it into the lock. The door opened soundlessly. "Good. Hildie still keeps this oiled. Old habits die hard, I guess." He noticed her look of inquiry. "Hildie runs a nightclub. Up until a few years ago it was a speakeasy, and this is where they used to deliver the booze at night."

They were in a passageway, lit only by a feeble bulb hanging from the concrete ceiling, but he seemed to know where he was going. He stopped abruptly before an iron door. Except for the buzzer beside it, it looked as if it led to a furnace room. He pressed the buzzer twice. He paused, and buzzed three times again. They waited.

Dana jumped as a panel in the door slid aside, revealing a shadowy face behind a grill.

"Who's there?" The question was hostile, the voice deep and husky.

"It's the cops, Hildie. We're charging you with watering down your liquor."

"The cops wouldn't know the difference, Irish." The door opened wide and Dana found herself the subject of a comprehensive scrutiny. She returned the favor, taking in the slim black woman barring the entrance. Hildie had pansy-velvet eyes, and a garnet-colored mouth set in skin so dark it seemed almost like black satin. Her hair was a gleaming waved cap cut short to her head. For a moment Dana wondered if she had passed inspection, as those wide eyes stared coolly at her, and then Hildie smiled, motioning them inside.

"You can come in, sister, but I don't know about the Irish bum you picked up." She held out her hand. "Hildie James."

The fine-boned hand she offered was weighted down with an enormous diamond-and-platinum dinner ring. She laughed at Dana's expression of awe. "Spoils of war, sugar."

"Some spoils," Dana commented.

"It was some war." Hildie grinned. She turned to Gabe. "You got lousy taste in clothes, shamus, but I can't fault your taste in women. Does this mean you're dumping me?"

Gabe lifted an eyebrow. "I never was enough man for you, darling. You told me that yourself."

Hildie walked ahead of him, her white dress a ghostly shadow in the low light. "I like to play in the minor leagues sometimes, Irish," she threw over her shoulder.

Dana followed them down the dank hallway, listening to their banter. The stunning black woman, with her jewels and her exotically made-up face, made Dana more conscious than ever of her own untidy appearance. Her hair was a flyaway halo around her head, and her cotton shirt had come untucked from the waistband of her pants. She trudged after them, her temper fraying. Where did this hallway lead to? And why weren't they trying to get to O'Shaunessy's office? This was hardly the time to pay a social call.

"Welcome to the Pelican Club." Hildie drew the bolt back on a steel door at the end of the hall and held it open.

As Dana stepped through, she felt as if she was entering another world, and she forgot her irritation. The room in front of her was decorated in shades of white, from the plush carpeting on the floor to the silk-hung walls. Bone-colored upholstery covered the seats of the Art Deco chairs, and the round, inlaid tables were set with sparkling crystal and translucent white china. In the center of the ceiling a glass chandelier glittered, reflecting off the curved and polished surface of the bar at the back of the room. Hildie stood in the middle of it all like a black opal surrounded by diamonds, obviously pleased at her reaction.

"Not bad for a little *chanteuse* from Fayetteville, is it?"

"It's stunning!" Dana breathed. Of course, she thought. This was the height of the Deco period, and all-white interiors were the rage. She knew collectors who would give their right arms for just one of the tables, with their mother-of-pearl inlay. Even in the Depression, the furnishings must have been prohibitively expensive.

She looked with renewed interest at Hildie, who was talking quietly with Gabe. It couldn't have been easy for a black woman in this time to have built up a successful business. She was obviously a fighter, not content with the currently accepted boundaries placed on someone of her sex and color.

"This big lug tells me you have to get into his office without being seen." Hildie draped an arm around Dana's shoulders. "Not a problem, but I'd say you could do with a place to clean up first, right? Men just don't think of these things."

"The big lug didn't even give me a chance to brush my hair this morning." Dana flicked a sardonic glance at O'Shaunessy, who had tossed his old felt hat on the gleaming bar.

"We had a crowded social calendar. Besides, you look fine the way you are, sweetheart," he replied absently, polishing a thick crystal tumbler on the sleeve of his disreputable tweed jacket.

The two women looked at him and then at each other in silent solidarity, and Dana shook her head in mock despair. Despite the formidable poise and beauty of the other woman, she was beginning to feel at ease with Hildie.

"You'll find everything you need in my dressing room. I used to live way across town, but my hours are different from most folks and it was more convenient to keep an apartment here." She stopped suddenly, arching kohl-accentuated eyebrows. "Was that your stomach, honey, or did someone let a bear loose in here?"

Dana laughed for the first time since she'd found herself in Gabe O'Shaunessy's office the night before. "I'm starving," she admitted frankly. "But we're on a schedule." She nodded in Gabe's direction.

"Come on, Gabe, the girl's about to pass out from hunger, and if she faints it'll hold you up even longer. Let me fix you two a couple of sandwiches at least." Hildie cast a disapproving look at the gumshoe lounging against the bar. "You can wash them down with that whiskey." She ignored his expression of hurt innocence and gave Dana a pat on the behind. "Last door on the left, marked Private."

Twenty minutes later, Dana felt reborn. The faint sandalwood scent of soap clung to her, her hair no longer trailed irritatingly around her face, and she'd wolfed down a chicken sandwich with a cup of scalding coffee. She was ready to face anything.

"We'd better push off, Hildie." Gabe retrieved his hat. "You'll be opening for business soon, and we've got to try and get in and out of my office without those goons spotting us."

"The less I know about that the better," Hildie said. "You don't owe me any explanations, Irish, but if you need a place to hide out for a few days, you know where to come." She turned to Dana. "Good luck, sister. From the little Gabe's told me, you're going to need it."

Dana reached over impulsively and gave her a hug. "Thanks, Hildie. For everything."

Dana followed Gabe as he ducked behind the bar, and she saw him open a cupboard door near the floor. "Ladies first," he announced. "Go on, there's plenty of room once you're in there."

"What is it, a secret passageway into the Quorum Building?" She wasn't especially claustrophobic, but she didn't relish the thought of crawling through a tunnel in the dark.

"It's a dumbwaiter, but it'll hold us. It was built for quick getaways in the bad old days before Repeal. Hildie's used it once or twice."

She shot a dubious glance at the other woman, who winked at her. "Close quarters if you have to share it with someone else, but I never minded."

What other choice did she have? Dana thought. She bent down and crept reluctantly into the dumbwaiter. There was more room than she'd expected, but when O'Shaunessy followed her and closed the door behind them, she realized that Hildie had been right. It was pitch-black inside the compartment, and although she had moved over as close to the wall as possible, she still could feel a solid masculine bulk pressed up against her.

"There's a button on your side. Press it." His voice came from about two inches from her left ear, and she started nervously. She felt around in the dark for the button.

"You got it." The dumbwaiter gave a jerk and then started moving slowly. "This takes us up to a closet in my office. It's slow, but safer than trying to use the stairs and running the risk of meeting Townsend's boys." He moved his arm out from between them and rested it on Dana's shoulders. "Sound travels in this shaft, so keep your voice down. When we get up there we'll grab what we need and come down the same way. We'll have to find somewhere to stay tonight."

"Why not Hildie's?" She was having trouble concentrating on O'Shaunessy's plan of action. Her other senses were compensating for her inability to see anything, and the rough weave of his jacket sleeve was a harsh caress against the nape of her neck. The faint scent of whiskey mingled in the enclosed space with the slightly salty tang of his skin, and where his leg pressed against hers she could feel the long hard muscles of his thigh. Dana found herself leaning into the curve of his arm and abruptly sat up straight, blushing furiously in the dark. She was acting like a kid in the Tunnel of Love, for heaven's sake!

"Too risky. They were expecting us to head back here, and after a while they'll start scouring the neighborhood. They know I've got friends in the area." Gabe's words were casual enough, but he leaned closer to Dana and tightened his hold on her. "We'll have to find a motel out of the city for a few days while we decide what to do."

She thought she detected a cat-at-the-cream tone in his voice that told her he wasn't altogether unhappy that circumstances were forcing them together. What exactly did he think they were going to do, stuck in a motel room? Her overactive imagination supplied an answer immediately and she hurriedly pushed the image away. She couldn't afford to let him distract her from the challenge she faced. She had to get back to her world. She had to have some time in his office to attempt a return.

With a muffled clang, the dumbwaiter shuddered to a halt, and he released his hold on her. Quietly he slid the door open, letting in a crack of light from the half-open closet door in front of them.

"I'm going to check out the office. If something goes wrong, push the button again and get back to Hildie. She'll help you."

He moved silently into the closet, and was silhouetted against the light as he cautiously pushed open its door and walked into the room. He was out of sight for a few seconds, and then he returned.

"Coast's clear," he whispered. "Get your stuff while I open the safe. We need some traveling money."

Dana went straight to the untidy heap of slats on the floor. The room looked like a brawl had taken place in it, she thought. There was the chair she'd knocked over, and the telephone was on the floor. She'd done that during their brief struggle this morning, when he'd been trying to take her to the police. She caught sight of a square manila corner showing at the edge of the slats.

The file! Her heart pounding, she opened it and peered inside. Everything still seemed to be there, she noted in relief, and lying on top of the papers and photos was the coroner's report on the poor woman who had died in her stead. She hugged the folder tightly to her chest, as emotions she had been trying to suppress all day surfaced without warning. In the last few hours, the life that she had lived in the future had seemed to be receding, becoming more and more unobtainable.

Being jolted through time five years ago had almost caused her to lose her grip on sanity. This time she had been able to handle the disorientation better, but she still had the feeling of being an observer in a strange land. She didn't belong here. Even the way she was beginning to feel about Gabe was all wrong. Although they might be drawn to each other, they belonged in two different times—times that never should have overlapped.

"I just can't be a part of this world again!" She hardly knew that she had spoken aloud. "Unless I accept the consequences of becoming Dana Torrence once more."

And those consequences could be fatal.

Just the fact that she had become involved with Gabe seemed too close a parallel to the life she had escaped from five years ago. If she didn't reverse the chain of events that she had inadvertently set in motion last night, she was in danger of following the same cycle that had almost destroyed her before, as Dana Torrence.

Holding the file, the one thing that validated her existence in the future, brought everything back into focus again. She and Sebastian had argued over its contents yesterday! They had stood in this room together while he had told her that she was about to be given her own movie to direct. That hadn't happened a lifetime from now, but less than twenty-four hours ago. She had to hold on to that. Twenty-four hours was a measure of time that could be spanned, and she was determined to cross that bridge again.

But how? She flicked a cautious glance at Gabe, already closing the safe. In a moment he would insist on leaving. He was right; the longer they stayed here, the more chance there was that they'd be discovered. She only had a few moments, if that. Could she tap into whatever psychic power had transported her before?

Her eyes were drawn again to the coroner's report. Its bureaucratic style of writing couldn't disguise the stark horror of the subject. Random lines caught her eye. "…body was unidentifiable…length of time before it was found…no known next of kin."

Would being stranded here mean that she would follow the dead woman's doomed path? A cold ribbon of fear threaded through her and the page trembled in her hand. Without surprise, she noticed that her fingers had left damp prints on the paper and she let the file fall from her hands. It slid across the wooden floor.

The chilling image of death and a lonely grave described in the document haunted her like a premonition of her own fate, and she felt as if she was reading her obituary. Was that why she had been returned to this time—to work out the cycle that her disappearance had interrupted before? Was it futile to try to escape whatever this life had in store for her? As she heard the hollow clang of Gabe securing the safe, her hopes for a miracle faded and she closed her eyes in defeat. What had she expected—that she could simply wish her way back to her time? She was trapped in this world, she thought despairingly. How long would she survive?

A ghostly fragrance of white roses seemed to drift into the room.

"Aren't you taking—what the hell!"

Gabe's startled exclamation tore across her consciousness, and Dana's eyes flew open. He had picked up the fallen file and was still holding it, but his shocked gaze went past her.

A *hole* had been ripped across the middle of the room. At first glance it looked as if the building had been split in two by an earthquake, but immediately Dana realized that no ordinary explanation could account for what she was seeing.

The oak floorboards that she was standing on just ceased to exist as they neared the split. No splintering or broken edges; at one point they were there. Then they weren't. The dirty mustard-colored walls were the same. Where Gabe stood by the safe, the walls seemed as solid as ever, the plaster smooth and uncracked. They simply *disappeared* at the boundary between his office and the void, to be replaced by what seemed to be a glassy, shimmering curtain of emptiness. It was as if the air itself had liquefied at that point, but there was a desolate, alien quality to it that made Dana take an instinctive step back.

And then she looked beyond the void. Her heart, already racing frantically, missed a beat.

The Hart production office, this same room but years in the future, was visible through the strange disturbance that divided the office. She could barely make out the pale cream-sponged walls and the sleek designer furniture, but there was no doubt that it was there. She could even see the vase of roses on the table, could smell their fragrance. It had worked! There was a way out of this nightmare! She moved eagerly to the void.

"Dana!" Gabe called out her name and started toward her.

She met his uncomprehending gaze with her own, and hesitated. Some part of her wanted to stay with him, she realized suddenly. They had parted once before; she knew that now, and the attraction between them had been so powerful that they had haunted each other's dreams since, but she had no choice. Ever since she had returned to this time she'd felt as if she was being swept into a dangerous whirlpool, a certain doom, and this was her one way out. How could she even think of staying? Feeling as if she was being torn in two, she turned her face away and moved swiftly to the boundary. Then she saw them.

Standing in the Hart office, white-faced and staring, were Sebastian and Edwina. Sebastian looked stunned as he stared across the swirling, unstable void, and his eyes met Dana's with a jolt of recognition. This was it! She steeled her emotions into action. This was her chance to return, perhaps her only chance—she couldn't lose this opportunity! She didn't allow herself to look back at Gabe. She stumbled forward and thrust her hand into the void, counting on her old friend to understand what he had to do.

They had always worked well as a team. Without hesitating, Sebastian moved forward but even as she watched him approach the hole, it began to diminish. He called her name and reached out his hand for her.

Immediately an intense cold seemed to penetrate her bones, and she could see by the pain in Seb's expression that he was experiencing it too. When their fingers touched an unpleasant buzzing sensation ran through her and she almost lost her grasp, but she held on desperately. She felt him start to pull her through the opening, Edwina now holding on to his other hand and helping. The numbing cold started to envelop her arm.

Suddenly the office door behind her crashed open. Out of the corner of her eye she saw Gabe wrench his gaze from her and go for his gun. He was too late. Three men burst in, their attention riveted on him, and one of them brought the barrel of his gun down across the detective's head. Gabe crumpled to the floor.

"Gabe!" She hardly knew that the cry of despair had come from herself, but as it did she released her tenuous grip on Sebastian's hand. She felt him clutch wildly for her, but in that instant she made her decision. Gabe was hurt, perhaps dead! She *couldn't* let him go again! Dana felt a dizzy falling sensation. Her ears were ringing as if all the winds in the world were howling through them, and as she looked one final time at Sebastian, it was like peering through the wrong end of a telescope. The last thing she saw was the agony on his face, and then the void between them closed as completely as if it had never existed.

"No tricks, little lady, or you'll get the same as your boyfriend here."

Dana whirled around to face Gabe's attackers. They couldn't have noticed anything out of the ordinary, and she realized that the incident with the time-hole must have taken only a second or two. They'd been occupied, judging from Gabe's prone body lying at the door. Her heart contracted in fear.

"What have you done to him?" One of the men stepped forward, but she brushed off his hand with contempt. "Go ahead and shoot. I'm an unarmed woman against three of you. That's probably your style." She bent over Gabe, and gently pushed the hair back from his forehead. It felt like rough silk in her fingers. An ugly welt was rising just below the hairline and the color in his face had faded to an unnatural gray.

They've killed him, she thought hopelessly. She'd come back into his life and led him to his death. If she hadn't tried to go through the time-hole they would have been safely away by now.

"You're still here." Gabe's voice was a weak rasp, and his eyes were clouded with pain, but all Dana could comprehend was that he was alive and talking. A wild joy filled her heart.

"Are you all right? No, don't try to sit up," she commanded unsteadily.

"Very touching, lady. What are you, Florence Nightingale?" The man who spoke seemed to be the leader of the group and Dana shot him a look of pure hatred. He was smaller than the other two, and wore a tight-fitting blue suit. A thin mustache outlined his upper lip. "Get him on his feet, boys, and down to the car. I'll take care of her."

Dana opened her mouth to protest, but before she could get a word out a thin arm snaked around her throat and a damp rag was pressed against her face. Frantically, she tried to struggle to a standing position, but even as she started to rise, her mind fogged over and her limbs went limp.

She just had time to identify the sickly sweet smell as chloroform before she passed out.

Chapter Four

She was going to be carsick, she thought groggily. Funny, she'd never suffered from it before. Maybe she was coming down with the flu or something. Weakly she pushed herself to a sitting position, hung her head between her knees and prayed for the nausea to pass.

"Boss, the dame looks like she's going to be sick. You wanna stop the car?"

"Open the damn window if you want, but I'm not stopping. We're almost at the casino." Dana felt too awful to react, but she recognized the voice as that of the man with the mustache. Another wave of nausea passed over her. She'd been chloroformed. That was why she felt so sick.

She heard a window being rolled down. Rough hands pulled her upright and propped her up so that her face was angled into the cool air.

"Don't get any cute ideas. Your boyfriend's right beside me and I'll blow his kneecap off if you try anything."

Even without the threat she would have been incapable of attempting an escape, Dana admitted to herself. She let her head loll against the door frame of the car for what seemed an eternity. Every few minutes her stomach would heave, and it took all her strength not to vomit. She was determined not to humiliate herself in that way in front of these goons.

Finally the nausea abated enough that she felt capable of opening her eyes. The swift California twilight was fading into night, and she realized that she had no idea how long she'd been unconscious. The car's headlights cut a swathe through the dusk-shadowed road ahead of them, occasionally picking out tiny reflections in the eyes of animals in the adjacent fields. The man with the mustache was driving like a maniac, but at least their speed created a bracing slipstream, erasing the effects of the chloroform.

Alert and revitalized, she reluctantly drew away from the window. Her movements were deliberately sluggish, as if she was still incapacitated, and she let her head slump against the seat. The man beside her tensed, but relaxed again as she pretended to close her eyes. Through her lashes Dana took in her traveling companions.

O'Shaunessy, obviously still unconscious, was jammed up against the other door, a length of stout-looking rope cutting into the flesh on his wrists. There was a dried trickle of blood on his temple and the skin around his right eye was mottled and discolored.

He hadn't had a chance back there in his office with Townsend's errand boys, Dana thought; not while he was still off balance from witnessing that unbelievable phenomenon with the time-hole, as she'd decided to call it. What else could it be? She'd not only seen Sebastian on the other side of that weird, shimmering barrier, but she'd also felt the grip of his hand as he'd tried to pull her through. It definitely had been some kind of bridge between this time and the future.

She'd known that, since she'd already had to accept the concept of traveling through time. But what had Gabe thought when he'd been confronted so suddenly with it?

She never should have involved him in all this. She'd known when she'd walked into his office that day five years ago and pleaded with him to change his surveillance report on her, that she was asking him to put his life on the line. She'd known the risk, and he hadn't. Perhaps he'd had his suspicions, perhaps he'd even guessed that the job Townsend had given him had nothing to do with morality clauses, but he'd had no idea of the true nature of the assignment. He'd just been trying to make a living. And now he was facing almost certain death.

That day five years ago!

It took a moment before she comprehended what she had just been thinking. She stiffened in shock. Her memory was returning!

"Hey, lady, no sudden moves." The man beside her had his hand on his gun, and the two in the front seat glanced around quickly.

"Sorry," Dana mumbled. "My stomach keeps seizing up."

Her heart was pounding so loudly that she thought it must be audible to her captors, but after a suspicious glare the man with the gun seemed satisfied with her explanation. He stared in boredom out the window again.

Carefully she clasped her hands together to stop them trembling. It had happened! She'd remembered going to Gabe's office five years ago; had remembered asking him to keep her whereabouts that day a secret from Townsend! She'd just recovered a huge chunk of her past, she thought shakily. A portion of her memory simply existed again, as if it had never been lost.

The memory of her previous meeting with O'Shaunessy must have returned in the moment that she had seen him attacked by the intruders in his office. In that split second, even as she clung to Sebastian's hand, the lifeline that would restore her to the world she had left, she had known that she couldn't run out on Gabe again. Seeing him fall, wounded, to the floor, had brought back the sense of loss she'd experienced before when she had walked away from his arms and into a hail of bullets.

The link between them had stretched through time. The spark that had been struck during that encounter had burned down the barriers between them; barriers of time and space that normally could never be overcome.

She hardly knew the man, Dana thought. They had shared a moment of attraction, one kiss. How had that generated such power that both of their lives had been changed? She looked over at him. Black hair fell carelessly across his brow; his lashes, dark and thick, contrasted sharply with the pallor of his face and his brilliant blue eyes were closed. From the moment she had first seen him five years ago, she remembered, she had found him more than attractive. Instinctively she had felt that they shared a common thread of destiny.

She frowned. Now she really was allowing herself to fall into the personality of the woman she had once been. Since the moment she had accepted that she had been Dana Torrence, she'd been terrified that she would play out the fate originally intended for the actress. But in assuming that, Dana realized, she was forgetting that the most important factor in this deadly equation had been changed—herself. She no longer thought or acted the way she would have five years ago.

Could she thwart fate by keeping this revelation in mind? A tiny glimmer of hope dawned. If she reacted to this situation like the woman she had become, strong and independent, could she change what was in store for her? Would the path of doom that Dana Torrence had been following alter its course, allowing her to return to her other life?

Her other life. The only way that she knew to get back to it was through the time-hole in the Quorum Building, but that was out of the question right now. Gabe's office had been staked out, and even if she managed to escape these thugs, that would be the first place they'd look for her. A plan began to form in her mind. If only she knew why she was such a threat to her enemies, then she could expose them, and they'd have to leave her alone! She'd be free to make another attempt at the time-hole. It was a long shot, but what other chance did she have?

The first step would be finding out who had wanted her dead five years ago, and why, but the single memory that she'd reclaimed wasn't much help. Earlier today, Gabe had said he'd followed her to a newspaper office, but she had no recollection of that.

Vague images of her previous life and scraps of trivial information fluttered through her mind. She could remember a dress she had once worn, for example. She could recall a tiny attic room, and it seemed to her that she had shared that room with another girl. But she couldn't put a name or a face to her roommate.

Her headache was returning. Now that she had made some progress, it was even more frustrating to accept the blankness that remained. It was almost a relief to be jolted out of her fruitless speculations when the car made an abrupt turn off the highway onto a graveled road.

"Rouse the shamus, Ed. Mr. Townsend won't want to waste time. He wants to ask these two some questions and they'd better be ready to talk." The man with the mustache glanced into the rearview mirror and Dana caught a glimpse of his eyes as he stared at her. They were about as full of expression as a couple of stones.

The man in the front passenger seat spoke for the first time. "We're taking them straight there? I thought you said we'd have some time alone with the dame. What the hell, she ain't Torrence. She doesn't know anything."

"Maybe later, Jackson. What's the matter, you ain't got lucky for a while?"

"Don't get wise with me, Frank. I knew you when you were just a lousy numbers runner, putting the chisel on every grocery store owner back in Chi-town. You don't impress me."

They braked so abruptly that she was thrown forward. The thin man turned to the one called Jackson and his voice was as cold as ice. "Get impressed, hood. I'm Mr. Townsend's right-hand man now, and you only got this job through me, for old times' sake. You better pray you're right about the dame. Torrence was your job, wasn't she?"

Her blood ran cold. This Jackson had been her attempted assassin! Even as the thought flashed through her mind, Frank reached across the other man and opened his door. "Go for a walk, wise guy. We'll meet you at the casino later."

Jackson hesitated, and in the next heartbeat Dana saw a gun pressed up against his temple. Frank spoke again. "It's your call, pal."

"Don't shoot, Frankie, I'm going!" Jackson fumbled with the door handle, getting out of the car so fast that he fell on the gravel outside. Without even waiting to see if he was clear of the tires, Frank floored the accelerator.

"You did right, boss. He was starting to get too smart."

"I don't have to worry about that with you, do I, Eddie? How's the shamus?"

"I'm all right, Frank. How's yourself?" Dana, still shaken, jumped when she heard Gabe speak. His voice was hoarse. "You just can't get good help these days, can you?"

To her surprise, the thin man laughed. "You never change, O'Shaunessy. That's what I like about you, always joking. Why didn't you ever come to work with us? We could have had some fun."

"Oh, I've managed to have fun on my own." Gabe lifted his bound hands and looked at them. By now they had started to swell. "I suppose there's no chance of loosening this rope, is there?"

"Nix on that, shamus. Eddie doesn't need another crack over the skull."

"Have a heart. My hands used to be one of my best features."

"Is that right? I always heard the ladies went for those beautiful blue eyes. What about it, sweetheart, was it his eyes?"

The car crested a hill as Frank threw the question over his shoulder at her. Before them, in what appeared to be the middle of nowhere, was a huge white building, blazing with lights. Dozens of cars filled the parking lot at the side of the casino, and she could hear the wail of a saxophone floating through the night. Her view was cut off as they turned from the main drive and headed towards the back of the building.

"Leave the dame out of it, Frank." Gabe sounded bored. "She's just someone I picked up for the afternoon. I told you I had my own way of having fun. Let her go."

"I'd like to oblige." Frank pulled up at a loading dock and opened his door. There was only one other car in the rear area, dark red and glittering with nickel plating in the harsh lights that illuminated the lot. "I really would. But Mr. Townsend said particularly that he wanted the dame." He pointed a gun at the detective. "Out."

Gabe shrugged and cast a veiled glance at her as they exited the car. She winced as Ed twisted her arm behind her back and marched her to the casino, their shadows huge and weirdly elongated in the glare of the lights. Behind her she could hear Gabe's dragging steps, and when they halted she saw that Frank stood back, covering them with his gun.

"Open the door, Ed. We're going through to the meat room."

In single file they walked through a cavernous loading bay, Dana on legs so shaky she felt she might fall. The only thing that kept her going was the thought of the gun pointed in her direction and her fear of doing anything that might startle the man holding it.

The room they entered was freezing cold, and lined with stainless steel tables. Along the ceiling ran a row of wicked-looking meat hooks, some supporting massive sides of beef. Dana stared at them, repulsed. This place, sterile and functional as it might seem, stank of death. She was suddenly convinced that she and Gabe weren't the first prisoners to be brought here, and just as suddenly, she realized that they weren't going to be allowed to leave. Frank had used names too carelessly. Eddie shoved Gabe into a chair and tied him to it with a length of packing cord.

The door opened. The man who entered the room was completely bald, and wearing a wide-shouldered suit that only served to emphasize his heavy build. His neck was so thick it looked as if the florid tie around his throat was about to strangle him, although Dana noticed that his feet, shod in gleaming two-tone shoes, were small and delicate. Despite his bulk he walked with an almost feminine grace.

But when he drew closer to her, his step faltered and rage flared briefly in the close-set eyes. At that moment, despite his dandyish clothing, he reminded her of nothing so much as a wild boar sighting prey. Then his glance passed over her to Frank and he gave his second-in-command a slight nod. An affable mask slipped over his features, so swiftly that Dana wondered if she had imagined his first reaction.

"Hello, all," he said pleasantly. As he spoke he idly tossed a silver key ring. "Frank, will you take my place on the floor for a while? This won't take long, but I hate to leave the suckers at the tables unattended. Oh, and tell the bar not to serve Mr. Flynn anything more. He's getting a little argumentative.''

Frank slipped quietly from the room and the bald man turned his attention back to Dana and Gabe. "I almost wish I'd put my money into orange groves, instead of investing in the hospitality business. But I must admit it's a lucrative little sideline. My position at Oval Studios doesn't really pay an adequate salary." The key ring left his hand, cut a silvery arc through the air, and returned again, to be enfolded in his palm.

This was the infamous Mr. Townsend, Dana thought. He had seemed to recognize her, but she was certain that if she'd ever met him face-to-face before, she would have remembered. There was a quality of mindless brutality about the man that made her skin crawl.

"Cut the small talk, Townsend. I told your boys that the girl doesn't know anything. Let her go before you start in with me." Gabe sounded as casual as if he was sitting in on a poker game, instead of bound to a chair. Eddie watched his every move.

"Please." The heavy man looked irritated. "I'm not a fool, Gabe. I know the girl's Dana Torrence and I know you think she is, too. You told Oakes that, this very afternoon. Yes, you were seen taking her into the station, and we thought it might be prudent to handle the investigation ourselves. The good lieutenant seemed to agree, after we persuaded him." He spread his pink hands in a helpless gesture. "The people I work for wouldn't thank me for letting her go without at least asking a few questions. After I get some answers, I'll have Eddie drive you back to the city. How's that for service?"

His air of bland good humor was too much for Dana. "You have no intention of letting us go!" Her hands were clenched so tightly that she could feel her nails digging into her palms.

O'Shaunessy shot a warning glance at her.

"Let's not be melodramatic, my dear. You actresses! Always so emotional." Townsend shook his head in disapproval at her. It took all of Dana's control not to rush at the man and tear the mocking smile from his rosebud lips, but she realized that Gabe, with his calm, unflurried facade, was right. If ever she needed to come up with a rational plan of action, this was the time.

She and Gabe had no weapons between them. He was even more defenseless than she was right now; at least they hadn't bothered to confine her. They probably didn't think of her as a threat.

And that was their mistake, she thought slowly. The one weapon she did have was their attitude toward her. If she played up to that image and increased their disregard for her, she just might be able to take them by surprise.

It was better than nothing. She pouted, and flounced over to a chair.

"My hair's a mess, I didn't have time to change my clothes and that stuff that they knocked me out with made me sick to my stomach. Wouldn't you get emotional?" She studied her nails with exaggerated dismay. "And on top of that I've broken a nail!" she wailed petulantly. She looked around the room as if she expected to be offered an emery board.

Gabe forgot himself far enough to let his mouth hang open in shock. Then he closed it with a snap. "Jeez, why didn't I dump you when I had the chance?" He turned to Townsend. "This hellcat's been a real pain since I picked her up. She's responsible for the claw marks on my face."

"What do you expect? Some crazy guy tells me I look like a girl he knows, he wants to take me down to the cops and hang a murder rap on me. Is it my fault this Torrence dame walked out on you?" Dana glared at him and continued with her improvised Bette Davis dialogue. "There's a million blondes in this town, mister. Why pick on me?"

The fat man had been watching their exchange with increasing suspicion. "You told the police that you'd lost your memory, that you might be Dana Torrence but you didn't know."

She tossed her head. "It was the first thing I could think of. But I'm not her."

Townsend gave her a hard stare. "But you do look like her."

"Sure I do." She looked up at her accuser, a flash of real anger darkening her eyes. "Drive over to Central Casting sometime and take a look through the photos. Ninety percent of the girls in Hollywood look like me, because that's what sells, and we're for sale. Fair, slim— all the same, like slices of white bread. No one wants rye or whole wheat in the movies."

Her voice was low and vehement. She felt a bitter pain that had nothing to do with her current problems, and with a start she realized that her words had subconsciously stemmed from her experiences as Dana Torrence. She suddenly felt closer to her previous persona than she had thought possible. What had she endured in that life? Living in this time and this place, where such a high premium was put on outward appearances, and little value was found in a woman's intelligence and abilities, must have been soul-destroying.

Townsend was staring at her intently and Dana wondered if she had alerted his suspicions. But the intensity she had revealed seemed to have merely puzzled him, as if a pet kitten had shown its claws for no reason. Then the frown creasing his forehead disappeared and he chuckled.

"I agree, the competition is stiff in this corner of the world, dear girl. But you really have no worries. You have a certain something that sets you apart." He twirled the key chain lazily by one finger and let his gaze linger on her. "I only wish we had time to explore this topic."

With a last appraising look at her, he turned his attention back to O'Shaunessy. "However, we're wasting time. I'm still not convinced that this charming little lady isn't Miss Torrence, Gabe. I know you shanghaied her and took her to your friend Oakes because you were convinced she was. What made you so sure?"

Gabe shrugged. "All right, I guess it's time to come clean. I saw her walking by my office last night. I'd had a few drinks, and I don't know—she just looked so much like the Torrence dame I went a little crazy. You know what it's been like for me in the past five years."

"But Dana Torrence was killed, you saw her body in the morgue. Why did you expect to see her alive and on the street?" Townsend let the key ring dangle carelessly from his fingers but as he waited for an answer his heavy body seemed congealed in expectation.

That was it, Dana realized. That was what he really wanted to know. He'd had his own doubts about the identification of the body from the start, and whether or not he actually thought she was the missing actress, he needed to know if Gabe had any information about it. She thought back to what Frank had said to Jackson as he kicked him out of the car on their way here. *Torrence was your job.* It all made sense. One of Townsend's hit men had lied to him.

"I told you, I was drunk. Maybe I thought I was seeing a ghost," Gabe said sarcastically.

Townsend's features took on an ugly mottled color and Dana saw Eddie tense, glancing at him like a Rottweiler awaiting a command. At the other man's nod he sent his fist crashing into Gabe's face with so much force that the chair teetered for a moment on two legs. The PI's head snapped back with the blow.

"Stop him!" Dana rushed to Townsend, appalled, but as she saw his face she realized that it was no use appealing to him. His lips were parted and his eyes were half closed. His hands hung slackly at his side, and with a silvery tinkle the key ring fell from his fingers onto the concrete floor.

"Again, Eddie. But keep him alive." His voice was thick and slurred.

Once more the hamlike fist made contact with Gabe's already battered face. His upper lip bled badly as his head sagged down onto his chest, and bright crimson drops spattered his white shirt. Without the rope securing him he would have fallen to the floor.

"We can keep this up all night, shamus." Townsend roused himself with an effort. "Or you can tell me what you know about a certain yacht trip back in '30."

"Don't know…" Gabe shook his head slowly. He sounded drunk. "Don't know about…yacht…" Laboriously he lifted his head and peered at Townsend through his rapidly swelling eyes. "What yacht?"

"Don't be a hero. Whether this is the dame or not, you knew all the time that wasn't Torrence they found in that ditch. I don't know how you did it, but you must have helped her hide out after the shooting."

He paced back and forth in front of Gabe, his words coming slowly, as if he was thinking out loud. "I was told she was picked up later, that the job was finished properly and the body dumped, but I think you found her somewhere to stay until she could get out of town. You're a smart operator. You wouldn't put your neck on the line for any broad, no matter what she looked like."

He bent down and pushed Gabe's head back roughly. "What did she tell you about the yacht trip? What angle are you two playing?" Their faces were only inches apart as he screamed his question.

Dana could see Gabe's eyes, pain-filled blue slits, lose focus as his head was forced backward. She looked desperately around for something she could use as a weapon. There was another chair nearby. Could she reach it without Eddie noticing?

"Boss." Frank entered the room and stood a few feet from Townsend. He didn't even look at Gabe's bloody face.

"What is it?" With a vicious movement, Townsend slammed Gabe's head back down. He turned to Frank in irritation.

"It's Mr. Flynn. He's tearing the place up. Me and the boys can handle him, naturally, but I didn't think you'd want us to rough up someone like him. Bad for business. He'll listen to you."

"Hell!" With the tips of his fingers Townsend carefully plucked an electric-blue handkerchief from his suit pocket. Delicately he wiped his hands clean of Gabe's blood. "These damned movie stars. I'd like to get that Flynn in a back alley one night, but you're right. I'll give him the kid-glove treatment."

"Should I stay with Eddie?"

"Don't bother. Eddie can handle the girl, and the shamus'll give him about as much trouble as one of those." He jerked his thumb at the sides of beef hanging nearby. "When we get back I want you to start in on the dame, whether she's Torrence or not. I don't have all night," he instructed Frank as they left. The door closed behind them.

The odds were never going to get any better, Dana thought frantically. Gabe couldn't take much more punishment, and she had no illusions that they would treat her any differently, or that they would let her and Gabe leave even if she could tell them anything. She had to act fast, before Townsend came back. On legs that felt like rubber she walked over to Eddie. Townsend's last words had given her a glimmer of an idea.

"How come you let them treat you like that?" she asked.

Eddie didn't take his eyes off Gabe. "Like what?"

"Ordering you around all the time, not giving you any respect. Compared to you, Frank looks like a cream puff, and Townsend's so out of shape I doubt he can even bend down to tie up those fancy shoes of his." She put her hand on her hip provocatively, and tipped her head to one side as she looked him up and down. "You're a pretty impressive guy with those fists. Ever fight professionally?"

It was a lucky guess. Eddie turned his massive head to look at her. His doughy features held the first flicker of expression she had seen on them.

"Hey, how'd you know that? Sure, I used fight pro back in New York." He gestured toward his nose. "That's how this got broken, in my last fight. Big son of a gun got me off guard, but I showed him. That's one boxer that'll never see the ring again. They put me away for a couple of years in the slammer for it."

He tossed off this anecdote with obvious pride. Hoping her true feelings didn't show, Dana moved closer. "In jail! You were just doing your job." She looked around the room with feigned interest. "Is this where they keep the meat for the casino? They must go through a lot of steaks." She walked over to a side of beef and made herself touch it. It felt cold and clammy. She gave it a tentative push and it swung heavily on the hook.

"Yeah. Nothing but prime, too. Sometimes Mr. Townsend tells the kitchen to fry up a few for me, if I'm working late." He pointed at the steel pulley system that ran along the ceiling. "See, the butcher just has to push them along that rail to a cutting table. They weigh too much for him to carry."

"Like this?" Dana heaved at the meat and pushed it along the rail a few feet. Once it started moving, its own momentum helped, and it ran smoothly.

"Of course, I've carried them plenty of times. But I'm pretty strong."

A shiver of revulsion ran through her. Was he actually trying to impress her? Could he stand there and flirt, in front of a man he had beaten nearly into unconsciousness? It was grotesque, but she fixed a simper on her face. "I'll just bet you are."

"If they make me work you over I'll go as easy as I can. Be a shame to mess up that pretty face," he added generously.

She was dealing with a maniac, someone totally out of touch with reality, Dana decided. In one sentence he'd complimented her and threatened her at the same time. It was time to make her move.

"Maybe we could get together some time when you're not working," she said. Her voice was husky and full of promise. "I could really go for a man like you." She widened her eyes and looked past him to Gabe. "Hey, I thought you were just supposed to rough him up. I think you went too far, Eddie. He looks real bad."

Alarm chased the fatuous expression from his face and he turned to his prisoner. "Mr. Townsend'll kill me if I screwed up."

Dana hoped desperately that Gabe had heard her and could play along. If he opened his eyes now, her plan wouldn't even get off the ground.

"It looks like he's stopped breathing!" The ex-boxer sounded frantic. He fumbled with Gabe's jacket, feeling for a heartbeat.

Keep it up, Gabe, Dana prayed. She started pushing the enormous side of beef along the well-oiled pulley. *Just distract him for a few more seconds.* She started to run with it as the gangster bent over to put his ear to Gabe's chest.

The mass of bone and half-frozen flesh was about ten feet from her goal; then seven; then just five feet away and moving like a wrecking ball.

"Eddie!" With her last ounce of effort she gave the carcass a mighty shove and screamed out his name.

With a fighter's reflexes he straightened up and spun around, his gun in his hand, just as five hundred pounds of meat came rushing at him with the blow of a battering ram. It struck the upper half of his body with enough impact to lift him off his feet and knock him sideways. Dana saw his head make contact with the floor, and heard the sickening noise his skull made as he fell. The side of beef, swinging wildly back and forth on its hook, came to a stop inches from where Gabe was trapped in the chair. Dana ran to him.

"Eddie's unconscious." She felt sick, remembering the way the big man's head had struck the floor. "Maybe— maybe dead. But we don't have much time."

He didn't respond and suddenly a terrible thought struck her.

Maybe Gabe's act for Big Eddie hadn't been an act at all.

Chapter Five

She expected Townsend to enter the room at any moment. "Gabe!" She shook him as hard as she dared. "Gabe, you've got to wake up!"

He opened one eye. "Get his gun," he whispered weakly.

Limp with relief, Dana looked around. It had flown out of Eddie's hand as he had fallen and she ran over to it, picking it up gingerly. It felt heavy and evil in her hand.

"I've got to find something to cut those ropes with." Her voice was tremulous and high-pitched. She wouldn't let herself look at the man on the floor. Had she killed him?

"Forget me, sweetheart, get out while you can. I'd only slow you down." Gabe drew a rasping breath and fresh blood spilled from his lip. She turned on him, her nerves stretched past the breaking point.

"Don't you ever say something so stupid to me again! We're partners, remember?" She ran up to him and started wrestling with the knots that held him. "I'm not losing you again, you hardheaded Irish fool," she said, barely thinking the words through before she said them.

"Temper of a redhead," Gabe mumbled. He was starting to fade away into unconsciousness. "Pants pocket... got a knife..." he managed.

With shaking hands she reached in his pocket. His thigh felt hard and well-muscled beneath her probing fingers, and she forced herself to ignore the faint flutter of desire that she felt. She found the jackknife and withdrew her hand hastily.

"You're sick, Dana, sick," she hissed under her breath, sawing frantically at the ropes. Townsend and his hired gun would be back any second, and her libido had chosen this totally inappropriate moment to make its presence known. And over a man who should probably be in the hospital from his injuries.

"Talking to yourself, darlin'?" Gabe turned his head painfully over his shoulder to watch as she struggled with the last rope. A gleam of blue showed between his swollen eyelids, and his mouth was still bleeding, but as the final rope fell to the floor he seemed to gather his strength. He tried to stand. Determinedly he pushed himself to an upright position, but then his face went ashen and a sheen of sweat beaded his forehead. He swayed back into the chair.

"I can't make it. You're going to have to hide out in the hills for the night, and you'd better start running. I just can't do it."

She stared at him. It was true. He was in no shape for a cross-country trek. From the way he was breathing it seemed possible that he had a broken rib, on top of the injuries to his face.

"Then I'm not going."

He opened his mouth to argue with her, but Dana put her fingers lightly on his lips. "My mind's made up, Gabe. I ran out on you once. This time I'm staying."

She stood up, looking for a cloth or a rag to clean the blood from his eyes. If they were both going to die, at least she could make sure they were left their dignity.

"Send help as soon as you make it to a phone, but get out of here!" Gabe looked angrier than she'd ever seen him. "Do you think I want to die knowing that you stayed because of me?"

And do you think I could live with myself if I left you now? she answered him silently. She turned from him, unable to bear the desperation she saw etched on his features.

Then she saw their ticket to freedom.

Lying in a silvery heap on the floor where Townsend had dropped them were his keys. Hardly able to believe her eyes, she pounced on them and held them out.

"They're Townsend's! That must have been his car parked out back. Come on, it's our only chance!"

He stared at them uncomprehendingly for a moment. Then a ghost of a grin lit his battered features. "You'll have to help me, but if I can't make it to the parking lot then I deserve to be shot."

With Dana supporting him, he managed to rise from the chair. Her discovery seemed to have given him a last reserve of strength and this time he was able to stay on his feet. "Give me the gun. If they come back, stay out of the line of fire and run like hell, and I mean it this time."

Thankfully she handed the heavy weapon over to him and together they limped to the door. Dana opened it. Behind her was the room where she had thought she would die, and a man who might be dead by her hand. She walked into the loading bay without looking back. Perhaps later she would feel regret at what she'd been forced to do, but right now all she could concentrate on was the fact that they still weren't safe. As soon as Townsend entered the room he and Frank would be after them. Gabe must have been thinking along the same lines, because he was moving as fast as he could.

Their worst fears were realized soon enough. As they got out into the cool night, she heard a shout from the building behind them and she turned to him in horror. "They're after us!"

"Get to the car and unlock it," he commanded. "I'll be there in a minute."

She hesitated, and then slipped out from under his arm and ran through the gravel to the red car. The stark lighting in the lot worked to her advantage as she tried one key after another in the car door, thanking her lucky stars when the third one fitted smoothly. Now to start the thing. She'd driven a manual shift before, but these old cars seemed to be even more complicated.

Dana reached down and pulled out the choke lever as she'd seen Gabe do earlier. At the same time she turned the ignition and with a powerful roar, the engine came to life. It was the sweetest sound she'd ever heard, but there was no time to savor her triumph. Two explosions split the air in rapid succession.

Gabe! Had he been shot? She felt the blood drain from her face as she saw him stumble towards the car, a momentary look of surprise on his face as he saw her at the wheel. He scrambled in awkwardly, collapsing against the seat.

"Are you all right?" The engine was so loud that she had to shout, but before he could answer her, Townsend and Frank burst out of the building and ran toward them, the fat man overtaking his wiry employee.

"Push the damn choke in!" Gabe gasped. "Are you sure you know how to drive?"

Dana gave him a cold glance. "I've survived the L.A. freeways. I think I can handle a parking lot." She stared grimly through the windshield as she depressed the clutch pedal.

"Hold on. This just might be the ride of your life," she said tersely.

"Dear God," he muttered, and braced himself against

the dashboard just in time. Gravel sprayed up as the tires engaged and they shot backward out of the parking space, and then Dana reversed direction, the gears grinding in protest. The car slewed sideways.

She was thrown against Gabe and heard him gasp in pain, but there was no time for apologies. She was too busy concentrating. She remembered how Townsend had watched Eddie use his lethal fists on Gabe's face, how he had disdainfully cleaned his fingers of Gabe's blood. A white-hot flame of pure rage sparked inside her. A little justice wouldn't be out of place, she thought. And she was tired of being the victim in Townsend's sadistic game plan.

Before she could change her mind, she turned the wheel and headed straight for him. The fat man's mouth dropped open in fear, and for a moment he stood his ground, as if he couldn't believe what was happening. His indecision turned to panic as he watched their approach, and then he turned and started running for the casino.

"Are you crazy? Let's get the hell out of here!"

Dana flicked an impatient glance at Gabe. "Don't worry, I know what I'm doing. He deserves a little scaring."

Like a cowboy cutting a steer out of the herd, she brought the car neatly in front of Townsend, blocking his escape route. With a desperate look on his face, he turned and headed back into the parking lot. The sweat poured off him as he struggled to evade his own vehicle, now bearing down on him. His dress shoes were no help as he slipped wildly on the gravel.

"Not so exciting when you're the victim, is it?" she murmured, turning the wheel as she caught up with him. She missed him by a couple of well-calculated inches.

It was little enough for what he'd put Gabe through, she thought, but she didn't want to give the man a stroke. She'd just wanted him to have a taste of his own medicine, and from the look of him, she'd accomplished that. It was time to leave before more of his employees heard the commotion. But she'd forgotten about his sidekick.

"Get down, boss!" Frank called out a warning to Townsend and grabbed a bulky object from the trunk of the other car. Dana caught the movement out of the corner of her eye and reacted immediately, slamming the accelerator down to the floor.

"Holy St. Christopher, just let me get out of this alive and I swear I'll never let her drive again," Gabe whispered hoarsely.

Ignoring him, she darted a look into the rearview mirror. Frank had taken up a position behind them, and even while she watched, a stitch-work of red and yellow flames zig-zagged through the night with murderous beauty.

"Gabe, watch out!" She ducked instinctively as the thud of bullets hit the bodywork of the car. Thinking quickly, she jammed the wheel hard to one side, and then the other. Weaving and clawing for traction on the treacherous gravel, they drove through the lot at top speed, but her evasive maneuvers weren't enough to dodge the deadly rain of bullets completely. The outside mirror on Gabe's side shattered as it was struck. There was a pinging noise as the fender was hit.

Please God, don't let them hit the gas tank, Dana prayed silently, resolutely shutting her mind to the images that thought conveyed. Her prayer was promptly answered, as with a jolt they left the parking lot and started climbing the access road. But it was too soon to breathe a sigh of relief.

A swift glance back showed her the tiny figures of Townsend and Frank climbing into the other car.

"They're coming after us." This was it, she thought hopelessly. They hadn't had enough of a head start to lose their pursuers. Sooner or later, Frank and his machine gun would start spraying bullets at them again, and eventually she and Gabe would be taken prisoner once more. Or killed. Their escape had just delayed the inevitable.

"Let them. They won't get far with two flat tires." Gabe looked at her, finally relaxing his death grip on the edge of the seat. "What did you think I was doing back there, picking up a road map?"

The iron control she had clamped over her emotions fell apart. "Those shots I heard were you?"

"I shot out their tires. I knew they'd try to follow us," he added. "Listen, why don't you pull over now and let me take the wheel? Or at least ease up on the speed, you're making me nervous."

If she had any sense at all, Dana thought furiously, she *would* pull over. Just long enough to dump this infuriating, ungrateful man into the nearest ditch.

"I'm making you nervous? I thought you'd been shot back there. You could have told me!" To her dismay, she felt the hot prickle of tears behind her eyelids and she blinked rapidly, hoping he hadn't noticed.

"When did I have the chance to tell you anything? You were too busy playing bullfighter with Townsend in the parking lot!"

Her tears disappeared like magic at his accusation. "I had complete control of this car at all times, O'Shaunessy. There was never any chance that I'd hit that creep, not that he deserved my consideration, and if you hadn't shut your eyes through the whole thing you would have known it."

"My eyes were closed because I was confessing my sins. It seemed an appropriate time."

"Please don't break off on my account, I'm sure you only got to chapter one," she snapped. "Reading *War and Peace* out loud would probably go faster."

"I'll save the good parts later for a bedtime story, but right now you'll just have to let your imagination go wild." Gabe glanced over at the speedometer and looked quickly away. "Will you *please* slow down? I'd like to find a place to hide out for the night, but it doesn't necessarily have to be the morgue."

Dana eased off the gas slightly, and tried to still her shaking hands. "I thought you'd been shot." She tried to keep the emotion out of her voice, and failed.

"Here." He handed her a handkerchief. "No, not shot. I think my nose might be broken and a couple of ribs feel cracked, though. Is that good enough?" His attempt at humor didn't have the desired effect.

"How can you joke about it?" She blew her nose and furtively dabbed at her eyes. Absently she handed the handkerchief back to him, missing his look of amusement as he took it. "Look at us—on the run, nowhere to hide. You should be in the hospital. On top of that, I probably killed a man."

"Eddie? He was breathing when we left. I had my eye on that bruiser." There was an unaccustomed gentleness in his voice. "The worst you'll get is assault with a side of beef."

This time it worked, and she managed a ghost of a laugh. "He was going to kill us, I know. But even so...murder. I don't know how I would have been able to live with that on my conscience."

"Self-defense isn't murder," Gabe said abruptly. He sat back, staring unseeingly out of the window at the dark. "But killing a man, no matter what the circumstances, is something you never get over. I'm glad it didn't come to that, for your sake."

Dana glanced over at him. His mouth was set in a grim line. The road was nearly empty, but every time they passed a car going the other way, its headlights swept his face, throwing his features into forbidding relief.

How much did she know about him? His past was almost as much a mystery as her own, and yet she'd tossed away what might have been her only chance to return to a safe, familiar world for his sake. Why? She'd told herself that she'd felt a sense of guilt over putting his life in jeopardy, but was it more than that?

She knew the answer to that question. She'd let go of Sebastian's hand for the same reason Gabe had endured five hard years of suspicion and the possibility of being charged with murder. It would have been simple for him to tell the police that he'd been following her on Townsend's instructions, but then he would have had to tell Townsend where she'd been that day. She'd begged him not to do that, and he'd kept his promise—not because they'd shared a moment of passion, but because for both of them, that moment had seemed like a continuation of something they'd experienced before.

Dana didn't know why she had pleaded with Gabe to keep her meeting with the reporter secret that day, but she clearly remembered how she had felt in his arms.

She had felt, for one brief second, as if she had come home to the only man she'd ever loved.

No! Her foot pressed down unconsciously on the gas and her hands tightened on the wheel before she forced herself to relax. No, Dana Torrence had been the one who'd attempted to turn an embrace with a stranger into *Romeo and Juliet*. But in her new life as Dana Smith, she was far more self-assured. She wasn't dependent on anyone.

"What happened back there at the office?" His voice came out of the dark beside her, interrupting her thoughts. "I got a pretty good crack on the head and I must have been hallucinating before Eddie put me out for good. I keep remembering the craziest things." Gabe laughed without conviction.

"Like what?" Her question was sharp with alarm, and

reluctantly she brought herself back to the problem at hand. She couldn't allow him to write off the time-hole as a hallucination. If he did, then they would be back at square one again, with him suspicious of her every action. "Like another dimension existing in the middle of the Quorum Building? Another reality?" She watched his face in the faint glow of the dashboard lights. He kept his eyes on the road ahead and didn't answer. "Don't try to write it off as a dream, Gabe. It really happened."

"I used to be a cop a long time ago—got shot in the line of duty." He seemed not to have heard her as he volunteered this rare glimpse of his past life. "The surgeon gave me a dose of morphine just before he dug the bullet out. Couldn't even feel that butcher digging around for the fragments. I was in a world of my own, as clear and real as anything I'd ever experienced. Just like today."

"I can assure you that I didn't inject you with anything," Dana retorted tartly. "What you saw was—"

"I know you didn't. I searched your pockets while you were sleeping last night, and you didn't have so much as an aspirin on you." He ignored the indignant glance she flashed at him. "But Frank must have given me something when I was unconscious—"

"Will you just listen to me for a moment?" It was her turn to interrupt. "You weren't hallucinating, it all really happened. That's what I wanted to tell you earlier." She took a deep breath and wondered how to explain the last twenty-four hours without sounding certifiable. "What you saw was your office, in the future. I traveled backward in time last night and today I was trying to reverse the process."

Well presented, Dana. Hit him over the head with it! She struggled to elaborate. "I know it's hard to believe, but I think that at the moment I was shot as Dana Torrence, I traveled in time to the 1990s. I've been living in that decade with no memory of my life here. Last night something pulled me back to this time.''

He laughed. "Too bad you didn't try that one on Townsend. It would have been worth it just to see his expression." Something about the tense set of her body alerted him and he sobered. "You're kidding, right?"

"I wish this was a joke, but it's not," she said tersely. "I'm telling you the truth."

"I don't get it. What's the point of spinning a yarn like this? When you were shot outside the Quorum there had to have been a second car that I missed while I was racing downstairs. Whoever was in it was too late to save you from being shot, but they managed to get you to a doctor in time. I won't judge you for whatever you had to do to survive, but tell me the truth." His eyes narrowed. "Don't take me for a fool, lady."

This wasn't going well, Dana thought. Even she had found the concept of time travel hard to accept at first, and it wouldn't be easy convincing him. But somehow she'd have to, if they wanted to survive Townsend and whoever he was working for.

"You were there." She forced herself to sound calm, but frustration mounted inside her. He was so hardheaded! Why was he denying the evidence of his own eyes? "What other explanation do you have for what you saw in your office?"

"I told you, Frank's dealt in dream-powder before. What's to stop him using it on me, to quiet me down?"

"I can stop this car right now and we can look over every square inch of your stubborn hide. I guarantee you won't find a puncture mark anywhere, because it didn't happen that way, O'Shaunessy!"

Gabe raised an eyebrow. "Maybe one of these days I'll strip for you, sweetheart, but not at the side of the road.

And you'll have to give me a better reason than that when I do.''

She took a deep breath and tried to hold on to her temper. Denial, she told herself; he was experiencing denial. Dr. Gottfried would classify this as a standard reaction to stress. She chose her next words with care.

"I know you saw the phenomenon. You have to accept that I'm telling you the truth, that there is such a thing as traveling between two times and that I've done it. I know how hard this is for you—"

"I've got a few bruises and maybe a broken bone or two, doll, but I'm not brain-damaged!" he interrupted impatiently. "You can go over your crazy story till the cows come home, but don't expect me to buy it. You ought to write for the pulp magazines.''

"You saw the time-hole with your own eyes! How can you close your mind to what happened back there at your office?" she demanded. "Is it so hard for you to trust me?''

"With your track record?''

"What's that supposed to mean? I admit I didn't tell you the truth as soon as I dropped in last night, O'Shaunessy, but I was busy being trussed like a Thanksgiving turkey! By you!" Dana glared at Gabe and saw him reach for his pocket. "And don't smoke in the car. It gives me a headache and in a few years they'll find out that it can kill you.''

He looked skeptical. "Smoking's bad for you? Where'd you hear that?''

"In the future!''

"Oh, right. The future. Did you happen to pick up any more useful information in the *future*, Miss Buck Rogers?" he ground out sarcastically. "Like who wins the World Series this year? The Kentucky Derby? I could use an inside line on something like that.''

"I must have been crazy to have stayed in this time with you," she exploded. "This could all have been a bad dream by now. But no, I was stupid enough to think you needed me."

"Need you? All you've done is give me grief from the first time we met, lady. It'll be a cold day in hell when I need that kind of help!"

"Fine. After tonight, you'll never have to see me again," Dana spat. "We'll pull off at the first motel and get some sleep. Tomorrow we go our separate ways. Agreed?"

"For Pete's sake, how long do you think you can survive on your own? After what you did to Townsend he'll be gunning for you worse than ever." Gabe looked at her with resignation. "You're my responsibility until I figure out what's behind all this."

She gripped the steering wheel as if it was his neck. "I'm your responsibility? You're here to look after me?"

"Yeah. I'm not enough of a heel to leave a woman alone in a situation like this. Don't worry, I'll stick around."

"Like I stuck around and took care of Eddie. Like I stuck around to cut you loose and get you out of that trap back there! Is that what you mean?" She realized that she was shouting but she didn't care.

He cleared his throat uncomfortably. "Okay, I admit you saved my hide. But the stakes are higher now, and Townsend won't get careless again. You need a man around."

Out of the corner of her eye Dana saw a dimly lit sign: Cabins for Rent. It wasn't Howard Johnson's, but she wasn't staying in this car another minute, she thought swiftly. She pulled the wheel hard over and shot off the highway into the motel lot, heading for the shadows beside the main unit.

"I need a man like a fish needs a bicycle, O'Shaunessy. Remember that line, you'll hear it again in about forty years." She turned to him and engaged the parking brake with a determined jerk. In the motel office a single light burned and she saw a figure look up. "I'll check us in."

Gabe reached for the door handle. "Like hell you will. Let me handle this."

"Take a look at your face in the mirror. You couldn't book a room in the Salvation Army right now," she retorted coldly.

She got out of the car and slammed the door, cutting off any further discussion. The man was a control freak, she thought. Typical of his generation, but a partnership with him just wouldn't be possible. And as for any deeper relationship…

"Stop right there, sister, and state your business."

The laconic command came from an unlikely figure standing in front of the motel office. Illuminated by the bare bulb above his head, he blocked her way; an old man in grimy coveralls and carpet slippers. Judging from the way his gray hair was sticking up at the back of his head, he'd obviously been awakened by the sound of them driving in. He looked like an eccentric grandfather, Dana thought.

Totally nonthreatening.

Except for the fact that he held a double-barreled shotgun aimed right at her.

"I seen you drive in with that fancy red automobile, lady. You can just head back to your friend at the casino and tell him that if he don't stop harassing me, I'll have the law on him. I've told him I'm not selling and that's my final word." He gestured impatiently and the barrel of the gun wavered. "Go on, get out of here!"

Maybe she should have phoned ahead for reservations, Dana thought light-headedly. She couldn't drag her eyes away from the shotgun, the twin barrels yawning hungrily at her just inches away. It looked like an antique, but she had no doubt it could still discharge a dangerous amount of buckshot.

"I'll give you to the count of five to get off my property," the old man threatened. "One. Two—"

"Wait a minute, you're making a mistake! Do I look like one of Townsend's women?" This was ridiculous. She hadn't time-traveled through decades to end up being gunned down by a short-sighted codger with a mouth full of chewing tobacco. "I'm on the run from him!"

He squinted at her doubtfully. "Come into the light where I can see you."

Obediently she took a couple of steps forward, acutely aware of the shotgun. Why hadn't Gabe appeared? Wasn't he wondering what was taking so long? Technically, their partnership wasn't supposed to end till tomorrow morning.

Perhaps she hadn't made that clear.

"If you're not working for that gangster, what are you doing here?" the motel owner demanded. He looked her up and down, apparently unimpressed with what he saw, and shifted the wad of tobacco from one cheek to the other. "I got to admit, you look like something the cat dragged in, not like the fancy pieces he picks up."

The compliments were certainly flying today, Dana thought. First Oakes, now this character. "Townsend kidnapped me. He thinks I'm someone else, someone he put a contract out on years ago." She saw no reason not to tell him the truth. "He got one of his thugs to work over the man I was with, and he was going to start on me, but we escaped in his car."

"Took his car, did you? That's an Auburn Speedster you swiped, brand new!" The old man grinned slowly and lowered the gun. "Townsend drove around in that thing like he was President Roosevelt himself. Almost ran over my dog last week."

She had an idea. "You can have the car in trade for a room tonight. My friend's in no shape to travel any further and that Auburn, or whatever you call it, is too conspicuous anyway. We have to ditch it."

The old man turned his head to one side and spat thoughtfully in the dirt. "Sounds good," he allowed cautiously. "My son works in a garage. He could have that beauty repainted and with new plates before the sun comes up. I figure that gangster owes me something for all the grief he's caused me, anyway. You got yourself a deal, lady." He extended a work-roughened hand. "Name's Trotter. How bad hurt is your friend?"

"Nothing fatal." Gabe limped out of the shadows toward them, his jacket pocket bulging suspiciously. "But I appreciate the offer of a room."

My hero, Dana thought ungratefully. She might have known he'd been covering her the whole time, since he didn't seem to think she could cross the street without his help. "*Two* rooms," she told Trotter, as he held open the screen door to his office. A moth flew in with them and the old man swatted at it as he propped his gun behind the counter. An overweight mongrel tapped his tail against the floor lazily, and Dana guessed it had been sheer luck, not agility, that had saved the dog from a fatal encounter with Townsend's driving.

"Good watchdog," Gabe complimented the old man. The mongrel rolled heavily onto its side and grinned up at them.

Dana glanced at him sharply, but Gabe's expression was bland. Trotter bent down with a grunt and ruffled the dog's ears affectionately. "Can't be too careful these days, and that Townsend fella's been trying to scare away my customers lately," he said, stepping over the dog. "Wants to buy my land cheap, tear down the cabins and build what he calls a multiunit motel here, with room service and everything.'' He snorted. "Hell, he must be nuts, pardon my French. I barely get enough business as it is. But I'll be darned if I knuckle under to a punk like him.''

He reached behind him and retrieved a brass key from the pegboard on the wall. "However, tonight's a different story. Got a convention of Fuller Brush men in town, and there's only one unit left, so that's all I can give you.'' He winked at Dana. "Don't worry, I'll write you down in the ledger as Mr. and Mrs. Smith. They stay here often.''

Gabe looked at her. "That okay with you, Mrs. Smith? After all, you stayed at my place last night.''

"That was different. I was tied up last night, I couldn't have left if I'd tried,'' Dana snapped, irritated at his assumed consideration.

Trotter suddenly became very busy with his ledger and she felt her face burn.

"The man doesn't want to know all the intimate details, sweetheart.'' Gabe signed the guest book with a scrawl and picked up the key. "Car's out back, Mr. Trotter. Tank's nearly full. Does that rate a bottle of whiskey along with the room?'' He glanced disapprovingly at Dana. "Don't worry, I won't let her get her hands on it.''

"I guess I could oblige. You got any transportation out of here tomorrow?'' The motel owner reached under the counter and came up with something wrapped in a brown paper bag. "Keep it out of sight. I don't want the traveling salesmen in here trying to buy my liquor.''

"I'll come over after we get settled in, and phone to have my own car driven out from the city.'' Gabe turned to go. "Ready, Mrs. Smith?''

This situation was rapidly getting out of hand, Dana thought, as they made their way along an overgrown path to the end cabin. An intimate evening alone with Gabe, who was no doubt going to make short work of his precious whiskey, was not on her agenda. The last thing she needed was to fend off a drunken Lothario tonight if she intended to leave early in the morning. It was amazing that he showed so little effect from his injuries. The man must have the constitution of an ox.

Even as the thought crossed her mind, he stumbled, and swore quietly. "Take the key and unlock the door, will you? Thank God I didn't drop the bottle."

She took the key from him in the dark and felt her way the last few feet to the cabin, her lips pressed together in exasperation. "Is drinking that important to you? Have you ever considered that you might have a problem with it?"

With a creak, the door swung open and Dana groped unsuccessfully for a light switch. She banged her hip on a piece of furniture and felt her patience rapidly eroding. Gabe stood dimly silhouetted in the doorway, making no effort to help.

"You could at least try to find a light around here before I break my neck!" she fumed. Her fingers came in contact with a lamp.

"I admit I have problems, but drinking's not one of them." He sounded immeasurably weary. "But it could be, after a few more days with you."

She turned. He was still propped up against the doorjamb, and as she took in his face—gray under his tan, with half-closed eyes—she realized that he was about to pass out. She sped to his side.

"Just take this." He shoved the paper bag at her and attempted to take a step toward the bed, a lumpy iron affair covered with a dingy chenille spread.

"Forget that!" Dana tossed the bottle onto the bed and ducked under one of his arms. "Come on, you can make it."

Two dragging steps across the tiny room, and Gabe collapsed on the bed, almost taking her with him. He lay there for a minute, his eyes closed against the light.

"I'm going to get Mr. Trotter to call a doctor for you."

"No doctors! The fewer strangers who know we're here, the better. Just open that bottle of whiskey for me."

She shook her head. "Sorry. I know that you're probably dying for a drink right now, but—"

"Dammit, woman, I need the alcohol to clean the cuts on my face! If my lip needs stitches you'll have to get hold of a needle and thread from somewhere and sterilize them. Believe me, cocktails for two is the last thing on my mind right now!"

"Stitch you up? I can't even hem a skirt!" Dana backed away from the bed in consternation. "Gabe, I'm really not qualified. And what if there's something else wrong with you, like a broken rib? Let me get a doctor."

"Those jerks were playing for keeps, sweetheart, and they know what kind of shape I'm in. Townsend probably has someone checking the hospitals right now, and you can bet that he's keeping tabs on the local quacks, too. It's too dangerous. Is there a towel in that bathroom that doesn't look like Typhoid Mary used it?" He tried to raise himself on the bed, but slumped back and closed his eyes.

It didn't help that he was probably right, Dana thought a moment later, coming back from the bathroom with the only towel there. His attitude still drove her up the wall. He was so stubborn, so—so *male!* 1930s male, she amended.

"This was all I could find—" She halted as she saw him. Still fully dressed, and with one leg off the bed, he'd fallen asleep in the few seconds she'd been out of the room. She could see the steady rise and fall of his breathing. Quietly she put the towel on the dresser and looked down at him.

Even in sleep, his face showed traces of the pain that

had been inflicted on him for her sake. There was a crease between his brows and faint lines bracketed his mouth with stress. His shirt was dappled with drying dots of blood, and his right cheekbone showed promise of sporting a well-developed bruise in the next few hours.

"Why didn't you tell them what they wanted to know?" she asked softly. "You could have turned me over to them at the office and they probably would have let you go. But you didn't."

She'd thought that going back to her own time would be running out on him, but now she realized he'd been right. She'd brought him nothing but trouble. If he didn't know where she'd gone, then Townsend would leave him alone. If she stayed, Gabe's stubborn code of ethics would put him in danger again.

A woman could look her whole life and not find a man like Gabriel O'Shaunessy, Dana reflected. Despite his faults, despite the way he drove her to exasperation with his old-fashioned attitude, he'd stood by her from the start. That kind of loyalty could almost make a woman fall for a man.

And that kind of loyalty could get him killed.

Chapter Six

Gabe awakened by degrees, feeling as if he'd gone a full ten rounds in the ring with Joe Louis. He was alone in the room, but through the closed bathroom door he heard the sound of the running shower. Disjointed memories swam through his sleep-fogged brain; a side of beef rushing through the air; a fat man running from a shiny car; a fist crashing into his face.

Dana telling him she'd traveled from the future.

"Hell." It all came back. He had to get the truth out of her. He had to talk to her, make her see how important it was that she stop playing games with him. He had to know why Townsend was after her. Gabe sat up in the bed.

Fire shot through his chest and he gasped.

Damn! He'd forgotten about his ribs. Gingerly he pushed the covers off his torso. The bandages that criss-crossed his chest were neatly taped and secured, but they certainly didn't have a professional look. Was that a label on one of them? He twisted his head painfully and tried to read the upside-down writing.

"Property of Shady Elms Motel" was stamped in indigo ink across the bandage. He looked again at the bathroom door, this time with a dawning respect. She must have been up all night looking after him when he'd passed out. The remains of the sacrificed sheet were tidily folded on a chair in the corner of the room, and beside it was the half-empty bottle of whiskey. He wrinkled his nose. He smelled like a distillery. Heaven knew how she'd had the strength to have done all that, after everything else she'd been through yesterday. But recalling the way she'd laid out Big Eddie, he was beginning to think nothing was beyond her.

Except for the crazy story she'd tried to tell him about traveling from the future.

He remembered the sinking feeling he'd had when she'd started to lie to him again. For a while there, he had been thinking he'd misjudged her these past five years, but that time-travel yarn had snapped him back to his senses. Sure, she'd saved his life, but who knew why? Maybe he just happened to fit in with her plans right now. But he couldn't figure out why she'd played nurse with him. She could have lifted his wallet and hitched a ride out of here as soon as he'd passed out. Instead, she'd stuck around.

He eased himself carefully off the bed, resolutely ignoring the stray thought of Dana standing under a stream of warm water, only a few feet away. It wasn't easy to keep her image out of his mind, dammit. Even at her most aggravating, the lady still managed to stir his senses. Who would guess that she hid a world of lies and deceit behind that innocent face?

Time travel! Did she think he was crazy?

He made his way stiffly across the room. By the rickety wooden dresser, he noticed that the linoleum floor was marked with splatters of dried blood. He put on his pants and reached for his shirt, grimacing when he saw that it was too damp to wear. She'd washed that too. He sat down, suddenly exhausted, his mind searching for answers.

The whole thing didn't add up. Why had she gone to so much trouble if she was just using him again?

For years he'd cursed himself for being fool enough to fall for her once. His reputation, already tarnished after being forced to resign from the police, had hit a new and permanent low when he'd been pulled in for questioning on the Torrence murder. The old-timers like Harry Oakes and Jake had stood by him, if only out of respect for his father's memory. They'd both served with Paddy O'Shaunessy before he'd been killed, but they were a powerless minority. Everyone else figured Gabe had lost it over some dame, snapped in a moment of passion and murdered her, and arranged to have her body dumped in the ditch where it was finally found.

They'd taken him to the morgue to view the body. He figured that they hoped he'd crack when confronted with it, but he'd seen death before. It saddened him that a young girl, snuffed out in the prime of her life, lay there on the cold steel autopsy table, but he knew she'd never been the woman he'd held. That woman, vital, mysterious and somehow linked to him, might have disappeared, but deep down he'd always known that she was still alive.

When Townsend had given him the job of following her, he hadn't thought twice about taking it. Surveillance jobs were boring, but this one paid well. He'd parked outside the house where she lived and waited for her to come out that first day, wishing that he'd brought a newspaper or something to keep the boredom at bay. And then he'd seen her. Townsend had shown him a picture of her, but all Gabe could think of was that it hadn't done her justice.

She'd stood on the porch of the boardinghouse where she lived, fumbling with the catch on her purse, the breeze teasing the hem of the flowered silk dress she was wearing and the mid-morning sun turning her hair to molten silver. With a little frown, she'd twisted around to check that the seams of her stockings were straight, and then she'd set off down the sidewalk toward the bus stop. He'd sat there, just staring at her receding figure until she was nearly out of sight, and then he'd hastily started his car and driven after her.

He hadn't been able to get her out of his mind since then. Watching her had been both heaven and hell for him—several times he'd considered telling Townsend that the deal was off; that he was giving up the job. Breaking all the rules of good surveillance, he'd sat at a nearby table in a restaurant while she laughed at someone else's jokes; sauntered casually by on the darkened street while she bid her escort good-night on the porch. Once, knowing that he was behaving like an amateur, he'd even brushed by her in a store and apologized, just to watch her smile abstractedly at him. That smile had fueled his fantasies for days.

And then she'd shown up at the Quorum Building and for one brief second his fantasies had become reality.

He'd never told anyone what had really happened at his office that day. He'd protected her the only way he could, by keeping his mouth shut, and that had bought him a mess of trouble. Now she was back, without even a thank-you, trying to sell him another tall tale. But this time she'd gone too far. She'd seized on his hallucination from whatever drug Townsend's boys had injected him with, and tried to persuade him that it had really happened.

Suddenly another explanation for her behavior occurred to Gabe. He sat very still. Perhaps she really did believe what she'd told him. Perhaps she was…unbalanced.

"Let's face it, boyo, the word you're looking for is crazy," he muttered to himself.

It made sense. She'd been on the lam for five years, and these were rough times for a woman alone and on the wrong side of the law. Maybe she'd gone over the edge. Now she'd created a fantasy that she could live with—the fantasy that she'd traveled in time and had been living a wonderful life in the future.

Moving quietly, he got up and went to his jacket for

cigarettes. Preoccupied with his thoughts, he fumbled in the pocket. It wasn't until his fingers felt an unfamiliar object tucked into the lining that he remembered the file he'd grabbed from the floor in his office.

Dana had thought the file would clear her with him, and Gabe hoped it had been worth a cracked rib and aching head. Lighting a cigarette, he made his way back to the rickety chair and turned impatiently to the file in his hand, wondering if the contents might provide a clue to her illness. He flipped aside several newsclippings without looking at them, and then he felt the breath go out of him as effectively as if Big Eddie had just KO'd him again.

It was a photo of himself, the one the papers had run when the cops had picked him up five years ago. Why would she be carrying that around? He turned it over, and read what was written there.

Gabriel O'Shaunessy, held and questioned, but never charged in D.T.'s murder. Possibly last person to see her before murder. Could be murderer? Check further.

The handwriting was unfamiliar and masculine. He frowned. Whoever had written it seemed confident that he could unearth the name of the murderer by a little research, but that didn't make sense. The so-called Torrence killing was still an open file with the police. What was going on here?

With renewed interest he examined the scraps of newspaper more carefully. They all had to do with the unsolved murder, but they treated it more as a Hollywood curiosity item than as hard news, and that puzzled him until he noticed the date of the clipping he held in his hand.

June 3, 1954.

A chill ran through him that had nothing to do with the temperature in the room. Almost twenty years from now! Could it be possible that she'd been telling the—

No. It was too damn impossible.

She must have had these scraps printed up. It wouldn't have been hard, Gabe thought slowly; anyone who'd worked in a newspaper office had been amused by lurid headlines created by bored typesetters. That had to be what these were. He took a deep drag on his cigarette. For a moment there he'd been the one who was losing his marbles. He'd almost started to believe that crazy story she'd told him! Sure, that was it—she'd had them printed up for her.

He placed the clipping back in the file and picked up another one, marveling at the attention to detail that had gone into its creation. The newsprint was brittle and yellowed, as if it really was decades old. Somebody had gone to a lot of trouble to feed the lady's fantasy. With a small start, Gabe noticed that the clipping he held bore tomorrow's date, and again he felt an eerie sense of foreboding, but this time he couldn't dismiss it. *Yesterday at 11:05 a.m. our time the small Pacific island of Tamarua was completely destroyed by an unexpected volcanic eruption...*

He impatiently turned the clipping over. There on the other side was what interested him, another column on Dana Torrence. The story was much like the others, except that the writer, quoting unnamed police sources, speculated that Dana Torrence, far from being killed, had actually been seen alive and was wanted by the police for questioning. The implication was that the police had somehow let her slip through their fingers, and Gabe could imagine Harry's fury when he read the piece.

He stopped reading suddenly. Hell, here he was imagining Oakes's reaction to something that he'd never see, a newspaper article that would never really exist, except in the deluded mind of an unfortunate woman. In frustration, he dropped the file to the floor, resolving to get rid of it before they left. If it was affecting him so strongly, it certainly couldn't be healthy for her to keep brooding over this stuff as if it was real.

He glanced over at the bathroom door. The lady might be crazy, but at least she'd be clean after all this time. What the hell was taking her so long? And why hadn't he heard even the slightest sound from her over the drumming of the shower? These walls were paper-thin…

Two heartbeats later he was on his feet and knocking at the bathroom door.

"Dana!" He paused and knocked again, louder. "Dana, come on out of there!"

He wrenched open the bathroom door and clouds of steam billowed into his face, obscuring his vision for a moment. When they cleared he found himself staring at an empty room, while behind him the shower still roared. He reached over, twisting off the taps with more force than the action called for.

It had to be because of her obsession with this time-travel thing. He'd shown her that he didn't believe in it, and she'd left, unable to deal with his skepticism. She'd been so unwilling to have him follow her that she'd rigged up this trick with the shower. Now she was out there somewhere, alone and vulnerable, on the run from the men who were trying to kill her.

He had to find her, fast.

When he strode into the motel office a few minutes later, Mr. Trotter was fiddling with the knobs of an ancient radio. He looked up from his task. "Message for you." He handed over a scrap of folded paper, shaking his head. "You're a fool to let that one get away. She had class." The radio emitted a squeal of static, and hastily he turned back to it.

Gabe grabbed the note, ignoring the old man. It was written in smudged pencil on the back of a receipt for the motel. There wasn't much to read.

Dear Gabe

You told me yesterday that there were some things you never forget. I'll never forget the way you stood by me from the start, but I can't involve you any further in this. It's time I faced my past all by myself. That's the only way I'll be able to return to the future, whether you believe it or not.

He crumpled the paper in his hand and slumped against the motel counter. She'd never make it alone. She'd need all her wits about her to escape from Townsend, but obviously this delusion about the future was as strong as ever.

"Got it," Trotter said as he continued wheeling the radio dial. He straightened up in triumph as the serious tones of a man reading the news came clearly through the radio's speaker. "'Fibber McGee and Molly' comes on in a few minutes. Me and Sam here never miss it." He prodded the sleeping dog with his foot.

"Did you see her leave? Do you know which way she went?" Gabe felt like grabbing the motel owner and shaking the answers out of him, but he knew his anger was really directed at himself. He'd been the one who'd told Dana that she'd built her hopes on a fantasy. He'd been the insensitive jerk who'd tried to make her face reality, when it should have been obvious that she was incapable of it. He tried to curb his impatience as the old man scratched his head.

"Seems to me she caught a ride with one of the salesmen. Most of them left an hour ago. Now, who did she leave with?" He pulled a flat tin of chewing tobacco from his vest pocket and inserted a hefty plug into his cheek. "That was just after she called about your car."

"My car?"

"That's right, she asked me to tell you. Said it was all arranged with Hildie, if I got the name correct, and someone would be here right away with it.'' Trotter snapped his arthritic fingers. ''Pete Dawson! She heard him mention he was heading downtown. She asked him if she could hitch a ride.''

That certainly narrowed it down, Gabe thought. To about twenty square miles of densely populated streets. He could wear out a lot of shoe leather following a lead like that. But why? What was she looking for there? A split second later he was cursing himself for his stupidity. Of course, she was heading for her former rooming house on Las Palmas! After all the time he'd spent watching the place five years ago, he'd have no trouble finding it as soon as his damned car got here.

He was deep in thought when he half heard the barely audible voice of the radio newscaster stumble over a word that sounded strangely familiar. A second later he sat up, unable to believe what he was hearing.

''Turn it up!''

Trotter looked at him. ''It's just the news. 'Fibber McGee' doesn't come on till—''

Gabe reached over the counter and twisted the volume knob himself. He felt as if he was turning to stone as the man's voice droned on.

''This just in on the teletype. The tiny Pacific island of Tamarua has reportedly been wiped out of existence by a terrible volcanic eruption fifteen minutes ago. We have no further details as yet, but we will monitor the tragedy as more information becomes available. And also in the news, gubernatorial hopeful James Mattson arrived in town today—''

Gabe didn't have the power to reach over and turn the sound down. He felt paralyzed. No, worse than that, he thought numbly. He felt as if the bottom had just dropped out of the world, and he was in free fall.

With a hand that shook, he reached into his jacket and

pulled out the slim file of clippings. The one he wanted was on the top.

It was unbelievable.

But there it was, in black and white.

Yesterday at 11:05 a.m. our time the small Pacific island of Tamarua was completely destroyed by an unexpected volcanic eruption...

He'd read those same words half an hour ago. *Before* this tragedy on the other side of the Pacific Ocean had taken place.

More than anything, he wanted to deny what he'd just learned, and restore his world to its previous foundations. But he couldn't lie to himself, or to Dana, any longer. Ever since he'd seen that impossible vision of his office suspended between two times yesterday, he'd tried to block it from his mind, even to the point of getting angry with her for trying to force him to accept it. He owed the lady a big apology, and he hoped desperately that he'd get the opportunity to tell her.

But if his car didn't show up soon, Gabe thought desperately, he might as well route that hope through St. Jude, the patron saint of lost causes.

DANA STARED UP at the shuttered dormer windows of the old Victorian house. As surely as if the memory had never left her, she *knew* that she had lived in one of those attic rooms. She'd known since this morning, when she'd awakened from an uneasy sleep, still fully clothed and huddled on the edge of the motel's uncomfortable, badly sprung bed. Taking up the rest of the mattress was a man, one tanned arm flung possessively across her shoulders; and all she could think of for the moment was that men weren't allowed in the rooms. That was Ma Harris's one hard-and-fast rule. Break that, and you'd find yourself out on the sidewalk in front of the rooming house...

...the rooming house at 96 Las Palmas, where she'd lived five years ago! The address had suddenly existed in her mind, along with a clutch of other memories.

When she'd realized what had happened, the first faint glimmerings of a plan had begun to form in her mind. She'd already decided not to involve Gabe further in the dangerous mystery that seemed to surround her past, but apart from putting as many miles between her and Townsend's casino as possible, she hadn't had a clue where to go. But remembering where she'd lived had given her flight a purpose: she would visit her old home to see if familiar surroundings jogged another fragment of memory loose. Enough fragments and she might begin to understand why people were trying to kill her.

She squared her shoulders, looking up at the house. She felt uncharacteristically at a loss. None of her belongings from five years ago would still be here, although it would be nice if she could find a diary with a day-to-day reconstruction of her previous life. She smiled wryly at the forlorn thought. Failing that unlikely miracle, perhaps Ma Harris could provide some clue to who her friends had been during the last few weeks of her life as Dana Torrence.

Or who her enemies had been, she thought somberly. If she was lucky, even a name might be enough to provide her with a starting point in this life-and-death treasure hunt.

"Here goes nothing," she murmured to herself as she started up the front walk, avoiding the broken paving stones and the worst of the weeds. Flakes of white paint hung from the once-gracious house and the old-fashioned porch was a minefield of dangerously loose boards. There didn't seem to be a doorbell, so she knocked firmly.

She felt a lurking feeling of unease as she waited for a response, but she dismissed it with impatience. For heaven's sake, this place, dilapidated as it was, had been her home at one time. It wouldn't win any *House Beautiful* awards, but the rent had been right for a struggling actress. Her fears were ridiculous.

Still, if it wasn't for the fact that she had resolved to face this thing alone from now on, she would have given anything to have Gabe beside her. Those broad shoulders and that wicked grin would dispel this sudden attack of nerves in a minute. Never mind that they couldn't exchange two sentences without arguing; at least when she was with him she felt alive. Right now she felt as if she'd wandered onto a Hitchcock set. She wouldn't be surprised if Norman Bates answered the door.

"Whatever you're sellin', I'm not interested!"

It wasn't Norman Bates, it was a woman. She had bright hennaed hair that was piled on top of her head in an untidy knot, and a crooked line of red lipstick bled into the wrinkles around her lips. She started to slam the door, a long ash falling from the cigarette in her claw-like hands to the front of the soiled negligee she wore.

"Mrs. Harris? Ma Harris?" Dana wedged a foot into the rapidly closing doorway.

"What's it to you?"

"Do you remember me? I used to live here years ago. I—" She felt a superstitious reluctance to continue, but she forced herself to go on. "I'm Dana Torrence."

Just saying the name felt like a violation, as if she had sounded out the last forbidden line in an unholy incantation and could now only wait for whatever danger she had called up to manifest itself. But instead, the older woman peered at her again. Her painted mouth stretched into a slow smile that fell short of her eyes.

"Dana Torrence! Is it really you, dear? They told me you'd been killed!" She hastily stepped aside and motioned to her to come in. "We had the police here, tromping all over my house with their dirty boots for days. Most of my young ladies moved out—they were always being questioned, their rooms were searched. Not an atmosphere conducive to the artistic temperament.''

Her tone had become lofty, her pronunciation affected. Dana remembered that her former landlady had once been an actress herself, in the early days of film. She still had the stagy mannerisms of a silent screen star, but nothing else remained of the imperious beauty she claimed to have been. Myrna had heard rumours that Ma Harris—Evangeline Harris as she had been known in her heyday—had been a regular customer of the Count, a shadowy figure well known for dealing in cocaine on the movie lots.

Myrna!

Dana felt the now-familiar tingle down her spine. Another memory regained, and an important one! Myrna had been her roommate five years ago; her confidante and mentor. She had shown Dana Torrence the ropes when she'd arrived in Hollywood, had gone out on casting calls with her. Together they had transformed Dana from a starstruck farmer's daughter to a platinum-blond would-be starlet. If anyone held the key to the mystery in her past, Myrna did.

''What fun we had in those days, didn't we?'' Ma Harris led the way down a dismal hall, stumbling once when the high heel of one of her grubby feathered mules caught on the cracked linoleum. She drifted regally into the kitchen, her chiffon wrapper billowing dangerously close to the open flame on the gas range where a kettle was coming to a boil. The room, with its old-fashioned cupboards and painted wainscoting, showed the same evidence of disrepair as the rest of the house. A potted plant, stunted and dying, sat in the middle of the table.

''You young girls, so hopeful, so lovely. It wasn't that long ago that I myself had come to this marvelous city of dreams, so I felt almost like an older sister to you all. But

I mustn't be jealous. I had my day in the sun." She reached for a tin caddy on the windowsill. "Tea? I won't take no for an answer, I'm just dying to hear what really happened when you disappeared that day."

Dana had no desire to indulge in a cosy tête-à-tête with Ma Harris. The longer she spent in the woman's company, the more she recalled just how much she had disliked her. The landlady had never had a friendly relationship with any of her boarders, despite her rose-colored version of the past. Promptly at eight-o'-clock every Monday morning she had knocked on their doors, demanding her week's rent in advance, and any girl who didn't have the cash ready to hand over was given an hour to pack and be out. The only one who had ever been able to sweet-talk her had been Myrna. But still, Dana thought, she was here to learn about her past. She sipped reluctantly at the over-sugared tea and gave Ma Harris the version of her disappearance that she'd given the police.

"So I've been working as a waitress in San Francisco, and until I arrived here two days ago I had no idea of my past identity," she concluded.

"My dear, how thrilling and romantic! It sounds just like a movie! You're absolutely sure you remember nothing?" The woman's gaze sharpened.

Dana tried to force down a mouthful of tea. "My memory seems to be returning in bits and pieces, but so slowly. I was hoping to talk to Myrna if she still lived here."

"Myrna! That tramp moved out a week after you disappeared. Owed me rent, too!" Ma Harris glanced at Dana's cup. "Finish your tea, dear. It's Lapsang Souchong, a weakness of mine."

She took a polite sip. It tasted awful. "Have you seen her since?"

"I went to see her, to collect my money. I'll tell you, our little Myrna was doing pretty well for herself; an apartment on Cahuenga near Yucca Street, fully furnished. There were dress boxes thrown around the living room— obviously she'd just come back from a shopping spree— and the room reeked of the awful perfume she always wore. *Nuits d'Arabie*, that heavy expensive scent. But she had the nerve to tell me she couldn't pay me!'' The landlady took a deep drag on her cigarette and blew out an angry stream of smoke. ''The next time I went there, about a month later, she was gone. She'd moved.''

''You never found out where?'' Dana's spirits sank with the news.

''Never. She did a midnight flit out of that place too, owing money. But a girl like Myrna always lands on her feet. She probably ended up with a rich studio boyfriend who hid her away in a love nest. A real platinum prospector, that one!''

Platinum prospector? Dana was momentarily diverted, and then she mentally translated. A gold digger. It sounded as if Myrna hadn't grieved too long over Dana's supposed death.

''Another dead end,'' Dana said disappointedly. ''I was hoping she could fill in some of the gaps.''

''You two certainly were close, dear, but I wouldn't say you were friends,'' Ma Harris commented. ''I think she only had time for you because you were attractive to the men. She used you to get an in at Oval Studios.''

Dana looked at her. Was this just another catty remark, or was there some truth in it? The older woman guessed at her suspicion and her heavily mascaraed eyes flashed defensively.

''It's true! You were just too naive to see what she was doing. The first night you stayed here, fresh off the bus, she came down and talked to me about you. Said she was going to give you some polish, help you buy the right kind of clothes, and then you two were going to be a team. She introduced you to a casting director at Oval and you both ended up getting parts in various pictures. Neither one of you was much of an actress, even for a poverty-row studio like Oval. Still, a pretty young thing like you, you didn't need talent.'' Ma Harris ground her cigarette out in a chipped saucer. ''Acting talent, I mean.''

''You're saying I took the casting-couch route,'' Dana said flatly. *Well, you wanted to know,* she told herself silently. Although she had accepted the possibility that her past had been less than spotless, it was still a shock to find out for sure. She felt suddenly weary and depressed, and then another thought occurred to her. Had Gabe known what she had been involved in back then? How much had he been told about her, when he'd been hired to follow her?

''Why not? You'd have been a fool not to.'' The older woman tossed her red hair coquettishly and rose from her seat. ''Even in my day, that kind of thing existed.''

Dana felt headachy, and the tea had left an unpleasant aftertaste in her mouth, although she had taken only two small sips. As Ma Harris turned to put her cup in the sink, Dana swiftly tipped the contents of her own into the plant. The landlady turned back to face her.

''I'm sorry I couldn't give you any more information about Myrna, but I still have a trunk full of your belongings upstairs. Did you want to look through them?'' Her voice was sympathetic and concerned, but her manner seemed nervous and distracted.

Dana barely noticed. This could be what she was looking for, she thought excitedly. Papers, letters, photographs—surely she would find something that would provide a clue to her involvement with Townsend and the employers he had so mysteriously referred to.

''Of course!'' She followed Ma Harris up two flights of

stairs, wishing that her head would clear a little. "I never imagined that you'd keep my things."

"Well, dear, to tell you the truth, I did sell a few of your dresses to cover the rent for that last week. After all, when they took that private investigator in for questioning, we all assumed you were dead. But everything else was just packed away and stored in your old room; I couldn't persuade anyone else to rent it after that, anyway."

She paused on the landing and opened the only door. "I'll leave you alone. You'll want to sort through it all, and besides, it's time for my—my medication. I'll close the door so you can have some privacy."

Dana stepped into the room, a frown creasing her forehead. All this concern for her feelings wasn't typical of the woman she remembered. Perhaps time had mellowed her, but the Ma Harris she'd known had never done anything out of the goodness of her heart. Still, what could the woman do to her? In a few minutes she'd be out of here and away from this empty echoing house that had once been her home, and with luck she'd have something more concrete than Ma Harris's rumors and innuendoes to take with her.

The only furniture in the room was an old iron bed. Beside it, shoved into a corner, was a battered tin trunk. A little nervously, she unlatched the lid and opened it wide.

She wasn't prepared for the emotions that flooded through her. With a cry, she picked up the object lying on top of the folded clothes, as a thousand painful memories whirled through her head and locked, one by one, into place.

"You take good care of Daddy and Kenny, you hear? You're the woman of the family now, baby. Momma's got to rest for a little while, sugar, the pain's getting worse."

"You hold it like this, aim carefully, and squeeze the

trigger real slow-like, Daughter. And remember, we ain't got spare ammo to waste, so choose your shot if you want to set meat on the table tonight.''

"Step aside, young lady. Tom, I'm real sorry to have to do this, but the bank's taking over the place. You gotta leave tonight."

"Okies, go home! Keep movin' or we'll have the law on you!''

"You take your night things over to that tent, Daughter. You'll be sleeping there with Mrs. Brewster and her little girls. Tomorrow we got to be up bright and early to start work in the groves.''

"Dana, I can't stand it no longer, seein' Daddy so sick, and us all working so hard for nothing. I'm hitchin' a freight out of here, gonna make me some real money, and then we can all be a family again.''

"Daughter, I don't know how to tell you this, but Kenny...they found his body in the Chicago train yards. He'd been beaten to death. Railroad cops, looks like.''

"Dana, your daddy needs a doctor. Me and Mr. Brewster would help if we could, but the twins gettin' sick last month wiped out our last dime, honey. It don't look good.''

"Sorry, Daughter...so sorry...''

The whirlwind of memories, her childhood and bitter teenage years culminating with the death of her father and her departure for Hollywood, existed in her mind as completely as if they had never been lost. Dana caught her breath in a dry sob. So much pain! So much sadness! No wonder she had tried to forget, but forgetting had been no solution. She had always felt the void in her soul that only her family could fill.

She stared at the lumpy toy bear she clutched to her chest. Knitted by her mother from blue and white yarn, with a once-jaunty red ribbon around its neck, it had been part of her childhood. It had been the only toy, she remembered, that she'd been allowed to take when they'd been forced to leave their home. Blue Bear had traveled with her halfway across the country, to the promised land of California, and his homely little body had been the one tangible link with those happier days before her mother's early death, her brother's brutal killing, and her father's lost dreams and sad end in a place far from his home.

She tried to swallow the painful lump in her throat. It wasn't fair! She'd already endured these losses before, but it was all new and freshly agonizing to her this second time around. She felt completely alone in her grief.

There was one person in this world that she felt would understand. Gabe. He'd lost family too. He masked his sorrow under a hard-boiled manner, but she'd caught glimpses of the vulnerable man beneath. Is that what she had seen in him, all those years ago? Had she felt instinctively that he was the one man she could turn to?

Gently she laid the toy bear on the floor beside her. Maybe. But what did it matter now? Circumstances beyond their control had ensured that she and Gabe could never be close. She had created a life for herself in another decade, and that was where she belonged, if she could return. Besides, Gabe hadn't even believed her.

Resolutely she turned back to her search. Clothes took up most of the space in the trunk, but buried at the bottom was a small packet of photographs and letters, and she took those. Time enough to look through them later when she was out of here, Dana thought. Her headache had returned, and with it her sense of unease. She grabbed Blue Bear and went to the door, intending to leave quietly without another encounter with her former landlady.

It was locked.

In disbelief, she tried again, jiggling the doorknob. She'd been locked in by Ma Harris! But why? Even as the ominous question presented itself she heard muffled footsteps mounting the stairs and she looked wildly around the bare room, but there was nowhere to hide. The heavy footsteps were coming closer, and now she heard Ma Harris's whispered voice.

"I made sure she wouldn't be a problem. She'll be sleeping like a baby with that dosed tea I gave her, don't worry. And while we're on the subject, don't you have a package for me?"

A deeper whisper answered her. "There. Top grade. Expensive habit you have, old lady, but I guess you earned it."

"Expensive?" The woman's voice was unexpectedly harsh. "I sold my soul for this stuff long ago. Sold my career, too! Yes, you could say I earned it. I really didn't think she'd come back here, but you were right. Our little arrangement has benefited both of us."

Ma Harris had sold her out, had contacted the killers who were after her! And Myrna's rumor had proved to be true, the woman had done it for the drugs she craved. Dana recognized the other voice now. Jackson, the man who had botched her murder once, had taken a gamble to redeem himself with his bosses. It had paid off and he'd tracked her down. He would make sure of her death this time.

She heard a key in the lock, and felt the adrenaline of fear course through her. Was there no way out of this trap? Her eyes fell on the window. It was a dormer, set in a steeply pitched roof, and her chances of escape by that route were slim. Dana swung it open wide and looked out. Not just slim, but practically nonexistent. Three stories below was a small brick patio. She'd never survive a fall onto that, but it looked like survival was an option that had been taken away from her. The best she could hope for was to go down fighting, instead of standing here like a cornered animal. Her leg swung over the sill just before the door opened.

"She's gone!"

"There's nowhere she—the window!"

Out on the roof, Dana heard their excited voices, but she could spare no thought for what they were saying. She was too busy trying to save herself from a broken neck. One false move, she thought, lying flat on the almost perpendicular surface, and she'd go sliding off this roof like a skier off a jump. And with no snowbank to break her fall, she reflected grimly. She edged along the sharp, gritty shingles, hardly noticing that her hands had started to bleed.

"We meet again." Jackson was leaning out of the window, a smile of triumph on his face. "For the third and last time." He brought his gun up almost casually and fired.

As the explosion ripped the air, Dana almost let go her precarious hold on the shingles. So this was what it felt like to be shot, she thought bemusedly. Funny, it didn't hurt at all.

Because he missed, stupid!

She lay there, frozen for a split second, as her brain kicked back into gear. He'd missed! She still had a chance. Risking a glance at the dormer window jutting out of the line of the roof, Dana saw that Jackson hadn't counted on the awkward angle. To be sure of hitting her, he'd have to lean out a lot farther, and if she moved into the lee of the dormer itself she'd force him to come out on the roof after her.

She took a deep breath and just as he took aim again she scuttled rapidly into the corner of the projection, thankfully grasping the edge of a shingle to steady herself. It broke off in her hand and in horror she felt herself sliding down the roof towards the edge.

"Dana!"

It was Gabe's voice. She was conjuring it up from her subconscious as she fell to her death, Dana thought briefly.

Oh, Gabe, I wish we—

Her foot hit something and her downward descent was halted. She closed her eyes and a shudder passed through her. She was safe for the moment, but already she could hear Jackson clambering out onto the roof. Even if he was no rock climber, as long as he could reach around the side of the dormer he could get her without having to let go of the windowsill. But the shock of her near fall had robbed her muscles of strength. More overpowering than the fear of Jackson's bullet was the thought of plunging once more down the roof. She slanted her eyes downward and saw that her left foot was braced against a metal bracket, the lightning rod that it had been designed to hold having long since rusted away.

"You've given me more trouble than you're worth, Torrence."

Slowly Dana raised her head and looked into the angry eyes of her killer. A few feet away, he was standing on the roof, safely holding on to the windowsill with one hand. In the other was the gun.

"I could have sworn you were dead that day on the sidewalk, but when our tame cop reported that you'd disappeared I had to do some fast talking to my boss. Even then he didn't believe me till I killed—" Jackson broke off suddenly and swallowed. A nerve in his cheek twitched. "Aw, what the hell. Just wanted you to know this one'll be a pleasure for me."

This is the last second of my life, Dana thought.

Chapter Seven

Everything seemed to occur in slow motion. As if she was watching a movie frame by frame, she saw Jackson's arm come up from his side; his hate-darkened eyes narrowed as he aimed at her, and his index finger started to tighten on the trigger. The world around her filled with violent noise and some part of her mind noted a frightened flock of birds rise from a telephone line, their wings beating jerkily in the same frame-by-frame fashion. As if he, too, was trying to fly, she saw Jackson's arms lift into the air; his body start to overbalance; his mouth open in a sound-less scream.

And then the movie speeded up and she saw him pitch sideways onto the roof, grasping for a handhold that wasn't there, his gun cartwheeling crazily through the sky. As he left the roof he finally found his voice. The blood-chilling scream cut off abruptly with a sickening thud on the bricks far below. She averted her eyes.

"Dana!" It couldn't be Gabe, but it was. "Okay, sweet-heart, stay where you are. I'm coming out to get you."

"No! It's too dangerous!"

"I don't know what men are like in the time you've been living in," he said, stepping out of the window and easing his way, inch by inch, towards her, "but I'm just a plain old 1930s kind of guy. I couldn't leave a lady stranded on a roof." One last step and he was close enough to grasp her hand.

Dana felt the strength of his fingers enclosing hers, and suddenly her fear subsided, to be replaced with confusion. Had she heard right? Had he just admitted that she had traveled in time?

"Now just crawl back with me. Take it easy, darlin'."

He was a man who used endearments easily. They meant nothing, she told herself as they cautiously covered the last few feet to safety. Still gripping her hand, he pushed her through the window and followed her into the room.

Then he exploded.

"Get one thing straight. Don't you ever pull a fool stunt like you did today again, or I swear—God, Dana! I nearly went crazy when I saw you sliding down that roof!" Blue eyes blazed down into hers. "Of all the stupid moves, coming here by yourself!" He pulled her to him and abruptly brought his mouth down on hers.

His kiss was hard with frustration and fear, and his arms encircled her so tightly she could hardly breathe, but as Dana's lips slowly parted under his, she felt as if some secret, hidden part of her was about to be unlocked and set free. For a moment she welcomed the release. It would be so easy with this man; so easy to let go, to give herself to him with an abandon she had never allowed herself to experience with anyone else. Why was she fighting it?

Her hands slid under his jacket, along the smooth cotton of his shirt, and her fingers spread open against the taut muscles of his shoulders. She felt the supple pliancy of well-oiled leather and tensed, her body stiff with apprehension.

He was wearing a gun.

Their lives were still in danger.

This was crazy!

Far off in the distance, but getting louder by the minute, came the scream of a siren, its eerie up-and-down wail another grim reminder of the danger they were in.

"We've got to get out of here." Dana pulled away from him abruptly, her voice toneless and her face turned from his. What was the matter with her? All it took was a pair of dark blue eyes and a crooked grin and she was melting like an ice cube in July. Was she that sex-starved? How could she have forgotten, even for a minute, that she was running for her life in an alien time?

Gabe looked like he was about to slam his fist through the wall. "You're right. I was out of line, kissing you like that." He shrugged bemusedly. "But somehow I get the feeling that you would have called time out sooner or later anyway." He didn't wait for an answer, but shot a glance at the pile of letters on top of the trunk where she had thrown them. "Is that what you came for?" He bent over and grabbed them, accidentally picking up a chiffon blouse with the papers.

"I don't need that."

"Never mind, let's just get out of here. Those sirens are headed this way." He raised one eyebrow as Dana ran back into the room, scooped a battered teddy bear off the floor and rejoined him.

"Could the police charge you with Jackson's murder?" she asked, as they took the stairs two at a time. "Did you shoot him?"

"He fell. If the police check my gun they'll see that it hasn't been fired," Gabe said flatly. "The guy fell, and good riddance to him."

He glanced quickly at her, and sighed. "Sorry, you've got a right to know. I pushed him as I saw him bring his gun up to fire. It was all I had time for—all I could think of was that I had to ruin his shot. But I won't lose any sleep over it."

"You saved my life." She heard the reluctance in her own voice and felt ashamed. Just because she'd had to rely on the man once didn't mean that she was losing her independence, for heaven's sake. Did she have to be so prickly? With an effort she smiled. "Thanks."

"Yeah, well—" He looked at her wryly. "I had to do something to justify my big mouth last night. I never did get around to thanking you for getting me out of that casino." As they approached the kitchen they heard a voice, and Gabe halted.

"Is this the city desk? I want a reporter over here right away, I've got a story for you... Yes, that's right, a scoop or whatever you call it." The woman's voice was sharp. "And I expect to be paid for the information, too!"

"Ma Harris, the landlady," whispered Dana with distaste, as they edged past the entrance to the kitchen, unseen by the woman on the telephone. "The second time today she's sold me out."

His expression was tight but he said nothing until they had slipped noiselessly out of the house. "My car's around the corner. Don't run, just look natural."

Even as he spoke, the approaching sirens reached a crescendo and two squad cars came squealing up to a stop at the rooming house. Gabe paused on the sidewalk, fumbled in his pocket for his lighter, and bent his head over a cigarette. "Play it cool," he murmured. "Don't let them think we're in a hurry to get away."

They'd been noticed. As three policemen ran up the dilapidated steps, a fourth started walking briskly towards them. Dana had an inspiration.

"Hey, wait a minute, honey!" She tugged at Gabe's sleeve and looked back at the house, deliberately raising her voice. "Look, cops and everything. Let's go see what the excitement is." She giggled. "Maybe we'll get our pictures in the paper, huh?"

The policeman slowed his pace. Alerted by Dana's piercing whine, a woman stepped out onto her porch, pink curlers in her hair, and stared curiously at the house. An old man across the street laid his hedge clippers down and called to his neighbor. Both of them started to cross the street to see what was happening.

"Come on, folks, there's nothing to see. Keep moving." The cop cast a disgusted look at Dana, who was still edging forward. "It's none of your business, lady. Get out of here." As she stared avidly at the scene, he frowned at Gabe. "Better get your girlfriend out of here, fella, before I have you both charged with loitering."

"Let's go, honey. The man's got a job to do."

With seeming reluctance, Dana fell into step beside Gabe. "How'd I do?" she asked under her breath.

He opened the car door for her. "I'm glad to see women's wiles don't change in the future."

She sat back in her seat, openmouthed. As he slid into the driver's seat and started the car she turned to him. "Have you been trying to tell me something? When you were on the roof with me you said—"

"Take a look at this." Gabe reached over and flipped down the glove compartment. He transferred his attention back to his driving. "The clipping on top is dated today." A thought struck him and he gave a surprised laugh. "On one side is Ma Harris's scoop. But it's the other side that convinced me."

He was silent while she read of the volcano in the South Pacific. Her head was bent over the clipping, her face hidden by a sheaf of hair that had fallen forward. He experienced a sudden and uncharacteristic attack of nerves. Would she forgive him for not believing her before?

Sure, it had been a crazy story, but he hadn't been exactly tactful last night. He could have given her the benefit of the doubt long enough to take a look at the file—any-

thing would have been better than dismissing her story the
way he had and forcing her into setting out alone this
morning. He remembered the sight of Dana falling down
the roof, and winced.

"This was verified somehow?" She closed the file, still
not looking at him.

"The radio. This morning," Gabe said. Her distant tone
was a bad sign, and he didn't blame her. She'd come into
this time with the suspicion that he was a possible murderer, judging from that inscribed photo of himself that
he'd seen, and yet she'd laid aside those doubts and taken
him on faith. He'd let her down.

"I owe you an apology. I had a good one all ready, too,
but now—" He glanced at her. "Hell, Dana! I'm just sorry
for hurting you like that. Your story was so damned far
out in left field, but I should have at least listened to you."

"You actually admit you were wrong?" Dana darted a
sideways glance at his set profile and then relented. "It
wasn't all your fault. I shouldn't have sprung it on you
like that. I could hardly believe that I'd traveled in time
myself, until I looked out of your office window—the
whole city had changed."

He hadn't realized he'd been holding his breath. He let
it out slowly. She'd not only had to cope with the shock
of finding herself in another time, but with his hostility,
and yet it seemed as if she was willing to overlook that.
Did that mean they were partners again? He hoped so,
because he didn't intend to take no for an answer. There
was no way that she could cope with Townsend's hired
killers all by herself, and he wasn't going to stand by and
let her risk her life again.

He almost spoke his thoughts aloud, but then he stopped
himself. He was getting the idea that women in the future
had become tired of being treated like fragile objects. He'd
have to do some changing himself if he didn't want to

drive her away again. He revised what he had been about to say.

"Townsend has a lot of resources. There's only one of you, and it's got to be tough dealing with this time-travel stuff, on top of running for your life. We made a good team last night. How about it?"

Dana looked unseeingly ahead. "I shouldn't have dragged you into this five years ago. You didn't know what was involved. It was wrong then and it would be just as irresponsible of me now. Especially since I still can't remember everything."

He shook his head. "I knew that with Townsend as my client, it wasn't a job I could be proud of. I got myself into this by closing my eyes and pocketing my fee, letting myself get as dirty as the crooked cops that I'd tried to expose on the force." As he spoke, Gabe saw the alleyway in Chinatown, the smiling face of Jack McGann. He resolutely fixed his attention on the road in front of him. He'd said too much.

"So that's why you became a PI." She shook her head, her lips pressed together firmly. "All the more reason then, for you to stay out of this. You wouldn't even be able to count on the police if you needed them and the few friends you had on the force, like Lieutenant Oakes, are being intimidated. No, Gabe." Her hands were clasped tightly in her lap. "Just forget you ever knew me."

A parked car pulled out ahead of them. With a squeal of tires, Gabe yanked the wheel over swiftly and took the empty spot.

"Can't you see that I care what happens to you?" He hit the heel of his hand on the steering wheel in frustration. "I let you walk out of my arms once and I heard the shots that took you down, saw your blood on the pavement. I went though hell when my father was killed and it was happening all over again."

The intensity of emotion in his voice shocked her. He'd been carrying that burden of guilt around for five years. For her. Finally she found her voice.

"But how can you blame yourself for that? You can't protect everyone, Gabe."

"I'd proven that before I even met you." His right hand left the wheel and absently rubbed the scar on his left forearm.

"But you can't wrap people in cotton wool. Nobody wants to be treated like a child, incapable of handling their own life!"

"It's not that." He leaned back in his seat, his expression grim. Dana, watching him, felt an unexpected compulsion to reach out and smooth the lines of tension that bracketed his mouth, but she resisted. At any moment he might retreat into his closemouthed self. Over the last two days she'd begun to understand that he was a man who normally kept his feelings private. Right now he was about to open up to her, and although she'd vowed to keep her emotional distance from him, she suddenly wanted to be the one with whom he shared his feelings.

"I watched my father die. I cradled his head in my lap and watched the life run out of him in a garbage-filled alley and there wasn't a damn thing I could do for him." His voice was low, nearly inaudible, as if he was talking to himself, not her.

"He was a cop too, but I was a young rookie and he was six months from retirement. A beat cop all his life, and proud of it. We'd switched shifts that night so that I could attend a lecture on ballistics. Mr. Ambition, bucking for promotion, taking all the extra courses I could." Gabe squinted through the windshield as if he was trying to see more than the street ahead of them.

"Dad was with my partner, Jack McGann. 'Smilin' Jack,' he was called. An older guy, knew everyone by their first name, everybody liked him. I thought he was the greatest, and if I ever wondered where he got the money to go to Santa Anita so often and drop a bundle on the ponies, well, I kept my suspicions to myself. If a kid like me started asking questions about McGann, he'd find his career cut short in a hurry.''

He gave a short laugh. It had years of bitterness and self-recrimination behind it.

''Yeah, I played the game. But that night the markers were called, and my father ended up paying the price.''

On the sidewalk stood an old woman selling polished, perfect-looking apples, and a young mother with a baby stopped to buy one. The sky, even here over the city, was a flawless summer blue, but Dana knew that Gabe saw none of it. He was kneeling on a killing ground, holding a man he loved and watching him die.

''How did it happen?'' she prompted him gently.

He flicked a glance at her as if he'd forgotten she was there, his eyes as blue and empty as the sky. When he spoke, his voice was flat. ''Jack had been working some kind of scam with the mob. They were new to L.A. then, but I guess Chicago was getting too crowded with Capone's boys, and this group decided to branch out. Anyway, Jack had been tight with them from the start, only I was too dumb or too scared to see what was happening. But that night my dad noticed something. He must have confronted McGann with it, and Jack panicked.'' He shook his head.

''He would have gotten away with killing my father, too, passed it off as a random cop-killing and patted my back at the funeral, only I got out of the lecture early and went to meet them. I knew where they'd be about that time, but they weren't there. Then I heard shouting, an argument or something, in an alley that ran behind a Chinese grocery store. I thought they'd been attacked, and I headed for the alley at a run. When I turned the corner, there were only two men there, and they both wore blue— my father, lying on his back on the pavement, and Smilin' Jack, pulling a knife out of his chest. He'd used a knife instead of his service revolver so it would look like an ordinary murder. He turned and saw me. He knew his plan wouldn't work then, not with me as a witness, and he came at me with that knife so fast I nearly didn't pull my gun in time.''

Gabe looked briefly at his left arm. ''I shot him point-blank. He died on the way to hospital.''

He pulled a pack of cigarettes from his pocket, took one out, and lit it with a hand that shook slightly. Dana rolled her window down and watched the slight breeze blow the blue smoke away. Nothing she could say would sound adequate, nothing anyone could say would lessen the memory for the man beside her. He'd been through hell and back.

''I was charged in McGann's death. Later the charges were dropped when his fingerprints and no one else's were found on the knife. But the department didn't want a scandal and they hushed the whole thing up. I was persuaded to resign. At least, that's what they called it. Really I was booted out and my name was mud from that time on.''

''They must have been thrilled when it looked like they could nail my supposed murder on you,'' she said. ''And they just might have. Crooked cops wouldn't let a little thing like a missing victim stop them. Why not bend the facts a little and say that you must have had enough time to hide my body, intending all the time to go back later and dump it where the other one was finally found?''

Gabe laughed mirthlessly. ''I think that's the way the scene was originally written, but luckily they couldn't go through with it that way. There was a secretary working late in the office across the street. She saw you step out of the Quorum and the shots coming from the car, but she was too scared to come forward at the time. After wrestling with her conscience, she finally got her nerve up and cleared me. They gave her the third degree trying to shake her story, but they couldn't.''

"How convenient that I was gunned down right outside your office.'' Somewhere at the back of her mind a theory was forming. It all seemed so implausible, but if she was right...

"A setup, with me as the fall guy?'' His expression grew very still. "And the police were there within minutes, as if they'd been waiting. But that would mean that someone with a lot of political clout was working with Townsend. And that from the day he hired me he intended to have you killed!''

"Two birds with one stone. Dana Torrence, who posed a threat of some kind, and Gabriel O'Shaunessy, who tried to blow the whistle on corruption once and who could be dangerous again.'' Dana paused.

There was a way to help Gabe work through his crippling guilt for the death of his father and the attack on her, but it would mean relinquishing some of her cherished independence. Could she handle that? Instinctively she wanted to retreat from the challenge, but her own reluctance decided her.

"We've got some powerful enemies, Gabe.''

"We? You still want to work with me on this?''

"As equal partners, yes.'' She held his gaze with her own. "There's a lot of digging ahead of us.''

His eyes darkened. "I know. We have to figure out why Townsend's after you, then we have to find out if he's working for someone else.'' He reached for her hand. "But first I want to get a few things straight.''

Dana waited for him to continue. All at once it seemed

vitally important that he continue to work with her, and she was disconcerted by her own apprehension.

"I've been doing a lot of thinking this morning, and it's obvious you belong in the 1990s, even if you did originally come from this time, Dana. You're used to looking after yourself, carving out a career. That just isn't the way it is yet, and we've got to get you back to your real world." His fingers tightened unconsciously over hers. "The truth is, I just don't know how to act around you. I guess I must seem primitive to you, but I'm used to women I can take care of and you just don't need that, do you?"

His words were a reflection of her own thoughts, but hearing him say them hurt. He was trying to distance himself from her, she thought, trying to warn her that this situation was only temporary. She attempted a laugh and drew her hand away from his. "Come on, just because I took charge for a while last night? You were unconscious, badly hurt!"

"You were great last night, taking out Eddie and then getting us out of there. But I shouldn't have let you shoulder all the responsibility. What if something had gone wrong?"

"Your problem is that you've worked alone for so long you don't know how to operate with someone else. Plus you have the typical male attitude of your time," she retorted. "You just can't handle the fact that a woman can think for herself, can you?" Even as she spoke she realized that she was overreacting, but the usual tight control she exercised over her emotions seemed to vanish in any confrontation with Gabriel O'Shaunessy.

"Knock it off, sweetheart. You're a bright lady. No one's trying to take that away from you. I'm just saying that you seem to be trying to prove how little you need me. That's not a partnership."

Was she really hearing this? Dana thought incredulously. The idea was ridiculous! She'd worked with men before, with no problem. In fact, the last few years with Sebastian had been a perfect working relationship. *Only because you kept him at arm's length. Only because you made it plain to him that was all it would ever be—a working friendship.*

It wasn't true! Or was it? Had she been running away from intimacy for so long that it had become part of her personality?

Gabe had been honest with her. It was only fair that she try to explain herself to him, however hard she found it. Her throat tightened. With anyone else, she would have let the moment pass, placing another brick in the wall of privacy surrounding her inner feelings, but for the first time in her life she wanted to tear down that wall. For the first time it seemed like a prison, rather than protection.

"When...when I opened that trunk in my old room I remembered my childhood..."

Gabe had been about to start the car and drive off, but he halted as she began to speak. A chill ran down his spine at the hopeless quality in Dana's voice, and he realized that she was reaching back into a past so painful that she hadn't been able to face it for years. Her words were slow and hesitant. He turned toward her in the car seat.

"My mother died when I was young. A hard life and no money for medical attention finally took their toll, I guess." Dana faltered. "After that, things just went from bad to worse, and when my father lost the farm to the bank, he set out for California with me and my brother Kenny, looking for work." She leaned her head against the cool glass of the car door and closed her eyes, reliving the heartache and confusion of the frightened child she had once been.

"We were treated like outcasts. Trash, they called us. Dad was one of the lucky few who found work out here, but the grove owner ran a company store and charged an exorbitant rent for the shack he let us live in. It was a condition of employment that you bought from his store and lived on his property, so every payday found us deeper in debt.'' She paused. Her hands were a tight ball in her lap.

''What happened?'' Gabe's face was somber. Dana found it impossible to go on, but then she felt his hands enclose hers, gently uncurling her fists and stroking away the tension.

''Kenny couldn't stand it. He was only sixteen when he hopped a freight train out of there, and just a few days away from his seventeenth birthday when they found him beaten to death in the Chicago train yards.''

''Railroad cops.'' Gabe sounded as if he'd just tasted something bitter.

''I was working as a waitress in a greasy spoon by then and we scraped together enough money to have Kenny's body sent back and buried near the old home place. But when my father fell ill a month later we were completely broke. He should have been in hospital, but that cost money we didn't have and when I finally got a doctor to go see him, it was too late.''

She turned to Gabe, her eyes blazing. ''He believed in the system, damn it! He worked hard all his life, never stepped out of line, never took a dime that he hadn't earned, and in the end he was a broken man. The system crushed him, just the way it crushed my mother and my brother! I swore that wasn't going to happen to me. I was going to make it any way I could, and I wasn't going to depend on anyone else to help me. I wasn't going to lose anyone else I cared about!''

Dana's hand went to her lips as if to retrieve the words she'd just spoken, but they echoed in the dusty silence of the parked vehicle.

"So you closed yourself off from everybody and came here." He deliberately kept his tone noncommittal. She was on the edge, and glib sympathy was the last thing she would want from him.

"Everyone left me." It was the whisper of a bereft child, not Dana's adult voice at all, and again Gabe felt that eerie chill. "Mom, Dad and Kenny. They all went away and left me alone." Dana's lashes squeezed shut and her hand tightened unconsciously in his. Her head was bent and a shaft of sunlight, dancing with dust motes, played incongruously on the rich sheen of her hair.

She was tough. She'd survived all that, plus the attempted murder five years ago and the time travel. She'd never bent under the weight of it all. And if she didn't, Gabe thought, she was in danger of breaking. Glaring at a passerby and wishing that he'd chosen a more private place to park, Gabe drew her closer to him. She felt like marble.

"You never let yourself grieve, did you? You've been so busy surviving that you haven't had time to cry." His hand touched lightly on her hair, feeling the spun-silk smoothness of it. "I did the same, only I used the bottle as my excuse. For two years after my father died, I drank to forget him. My mother had the priest come round to talk to me, and my sisters wore their knees raw praying for me, but I didn't care. When Ma and the girls moved to Boston, they begged me to come with them. But to tell you the truth, I was glad to see them go. I was determined to go to hell in my own way, and I didn't want them around while I did."

Through the thin material of her blouse he could feel Dana's shoulders, stiff and unyielding. Gabe continued, willing her to listen and hoping that his experience would touch some chord in her.

"And then one day I found myself kneeling in a gutter with your blood on my hands. I felt I'd brought you to

that just as surely as if I'd put the contract out on you, because I'd known from the start that Townsend was no good. But the drinking had made it easy to lie to myself."
He wondered if any of this was getting through to her, but even if it wasn't, Gabe realized, this was something that had to be said. He'd never before put into words what had happened to him that day, never acknowledged how close to the depths he'd sunk.

"I didn't stop drinking after that—hell, I'm a good Irish boy. But I stopped using whiskey to blot out the pain. I spent endless nights going over my father's death, and one night I started crying for him. I felt as if he was there with me, telling me to let it all out. After that I never felt his presence again, but I was ready to pick up the pieces of my life." He sighed. "I know it hurts, sweetheart. But you don't have to be strong all the time."

He waited a long moment for her reply, but it didn't come. She'd learned her lessons all too well. Never give in, never weaken. Or perhaps it was simply that she still didn't trust him enough to let her guard down. That last possibility was like a knife in his soul, although he couldn't imagine why. He'd said it himself—they had no future together. Why then did he want to take her in his arms, let her cry it all out, and convince her that he'd be there for her, whenever she decided she needed him?

Then he heard a strangled sound from the back of her throat, felt her arms wrap tightly around him, and saw her eyes, liquid green and spilling tears that had been held back for too many years. Gabe felt a sharp pain shaft through him, somewhere in the vicinity of his heart, and he suddenly knew that he would gladly take on all this woman's demons if it meant saving her from them.

He was in love, dammit.

Helluva time and place to find that out.

As her body shuddered with sobs, he cradled Dana's

head against his shoulder and tried to come to terms with this inconvenient revelation, but instead he found himself stroking the autumn glow of her hair and breathing in the sandalwood scent that clung to her skin, hoping that somehow his feelings for her would transfer themselves through his touch and comfort her. Not that he would ever put them into words. Sooner or later she'd have to return to her own time, and she wouldn't want anything holding her back. Like a broken-down PI from her past.

"I never cry," she mumbled against his jacket. "I always thought it was a sign of weakness."

"You're the strongest person I've ever met," he said quietly. "But don't shut me out. Let me help you."

Dana rested her head for a moment longer against his broad chest, breathing in the warm leather-and-tweed smell of him and feeling the steady beat of his heart. She felt curiously light and empty, as if she had finally let go of something that had been weighing her down for years. What was it? Certainly not the memories of her family: those she had finally regained. It was the child's sense of betrayal and abandonment that she had discarded, she thought. By facing her background as an adult, she had at last been able to react to it as an adult. With tears, and then with acceptance. And she owed that to Gabe.

She suddenly realized that she was clutching two sodden handfuls of his shirtfront, and drew awkwardly away from him. "I must look like a mess."

"You look gorgeous, runny nose and all," Gabe told her. He smiled, and she noticed a devastating dimple in his left cheek. "I've always been partial to green eyes with pink rims. Here." He handed her a handkerchief. "Get yourself mopped up and we'll grab a sandwich somewhere. Decide what we're going to do."

She blew her nose noisily. "Thanks for the shoulder to cry on." It was inadequate, but she knew that the slightest hint of emotion would be enough to start her crying again. As if to make up for lost time, she thought wryly. Gabe, with his casual teasing, seemed to realize that.

"I can't go anywhere looking like this. And you're not exactly *GQ* material, either." She blotted the last of the tearstains from her face and absently held his handkerchief out to him, missing the twitch of his lips as he gravely took it from her.

"*GQ*, whatever that is, be damned," he grinned. "I wasn't thinking of the Ritz, sweetheart—those fancy restaurants are just for tourists anyway. Let me show you a little place where us locals go for lunch."

Chapter Eight

"Woolworth's!"

Dana laughed in surprise as they entered. It was like being in a Norman Rockwell painting. If she hadn't been so hungry, she would have loved to wander around the nostalgic five-and-dime store, soaking up the atmosphere. The floors were wooden, creaking underfoot, and the display counters were curved oak and thick greenish glass. The cash registers were collector's items that gave out a cheerfully loud jangle whenever a sale was rung up.

But despite the prices, which to modern eyes were ridiculously low, few people seemed to be buying. Even children, tagging after shabbily dressed mothers, seemed to understand that the brightly colored tin trains and the stuffed animal toys were there only to be looked at, and as Gabe strode ahead of her to the lunch counter, Dana glimpsed the yearning in a little girl's face as she gazed longingly at a Shirley Temple doll; the doll's sausage curls were tied up with a jaunty satin bow, tiny Mary Janes were on its feet, and the frilly organza dress put the real child's patched overalls to shame.

"I'm beginning to remember why I wanted to forget this time," she said soberly to Gabe as they slid into an empty booth.

He followed her glance and his face hardened. "Yeah,

the kids. It gets to me, too. How much longer does this depression last, anyway?''

Dana picked up a menu. ''Until everybody starts gearing up for war again,'' she said flatly.

''Another war?'' He looked up, shocked. ''As bad as the Great War?''

''Worse.'' She snapped her menu shut. ''Look, Gabe. Things get worse before they get better, but even when they do improve, we end up with new problems, like pollution and international terrorists. I've had some crazy ideas since I got dropped into this time, like maybe trying to warn people about Hitler, or Pearl Harbor, but you've got to understand that everything I know, I learned secondhand during the five years that I lived in the future. I'm pretty hazy about dates and particulars.'' She wrinkled her brow. ''And besides, whenever I think about trying to change history a warning bell seems to go off in my brain, as if something is trying to tell me that it's impossible. I think that this time-travel phenomenon has rules that can't be broken.''

''Pollution. International terrorists.'' Gabe pronounced the ominous-sounding words. ''I don't even want to know about them. We've got enough trouble dealing with plain old American-style gangsters.''

''You folks ready to order?'' The waitress paused beside them, a pleated and starched maid's cap perched on her white-blond hair. Penciled eyebrows rose in interest as she took a second look at Gabe.

''Yeah, I'll have the twenty-five-cent lunch. With coffee.''

''That'd be the chicken sammich, right? With coleslaw and French fries.'' She whipped a stub of a pencil from behind her ear and scribbled on her order pad. Dana noticed that the girl's nails were bitten to the quick. Another small-town beauty who hadn't made it in the dream factory, she thought.

"And you, honey?" The waitress turned to her.

"The same, I guess."

"Comin' right up." The blonde sauntered behind the counter, her hips working overtime. She'd probably seen that walk doing justice to a silver mink stole and a bias-cut gown in a movie, but even under a waitress's uniform and apron, it did what it had been intended to do.

Gabe colored and jerked his attention back to the table, as he realized that Dana was watching him. "I thought I might ask her if I could get it toasted," he said weakly.

"Sure, she could probably heat it up for you," Dana agreed blandly. At that moment, he didn't look so much like a tough ex-cop, she thought, as a little kid caught with his fingers in the cookie jar. She had an instant glimpse of what he'd been like as a boy. A handful, she decided. But with enough Irish charm to talk his way out of anything.

He looked suspiciously at her, and then propped his chin in his hand, his elbow on the table. "Thing is, sometimes if you order something too hot, you can burn your mouth." His eyelashes fanned guilelessly across his cheekbones as he pretended an interest in the silverware.

"That's true. But ice cream's only a nickel. You could cool down with a scoop afterwards," Dana suggested innocently.

He shook his head. "Ice cream's too cold. Maybe if it was over a slice of cherry pie." He raised his gaze to her lips, and his stare was a mixture of the languid and the intense. "You know, when it starts to melt, sweet and warm…"

Her eyes were locked with his and her breath caught in her throat. There was nothing of the little boy about him now, she thought shakily. This game was for grown-ups. "That's the way you like it?" she managed weakly.

"Yeah. I love it like that." His voice was husky and held the faintest hint of a brogue. "When I can get it."

A surge of pure, unadulterated desire ran through her like a forbidden drug. He didn't even have to try, she thought incoherently. The man probably broke hearts just walking down the street.

"What's goin' on between you two just can't be legal. Not in a public place, anyway."

Dana looked up with a start and realized that their waitress was standing beside the table with their orders. She sat back hastily, her face flaming. "Sorry."

The woman set down the sandwiches and coffee. "I'm sorry too, honey. Sorry I didn't see him first." She ripped the top sheet off her pad and placed it under Gabe's cup. "Refills are free. In case you're interested."

Gabe lifted lazy blue eyes. "Thanks, sister, but I think this is all I can handle right now."

"Story of my life. Don't call us, we'll call you. Still," she adjusted her cap and shot Dana an envious look, "can't blame a girl for tryin', huh?" Her patented flounce was in evidence as she returned to the counter.

Dana reached for her coffee cup, hoping to reestablish an atmosphere of normalcy, but that was a mistake, she realized, as she slopped half of it in the saucer. She set the cup down with a loud clink.

"I think we should keep our relationship on a business-like footing," she finally said.

Gabe took a sip of coffee, wincing slightly at the hot liquid. "That's what I've been telling myself. But somehow it hasn't worked." He put his cup down. "I guess what you said earlier had some truth in it. I've never worked with a woman before and I keep seeing you as someone I'd like to—to—"

"Sleep with?" Dana finished for him.

"Among other things." He hesitated. "But we don't

have a chance, do we?'' Might as well lay his cards on the table. If there was any way she'd consider staying in this time, he wanted to know it now. But he knew her answer even before she spoke.

"If there's any way to return to the future, Gabe, I'll do it." She met his eyes. "I've created a career for myself there, a life with more opportunities than I'd ever have here. Perhaps if I was a man it would be different, but look how my life was going when I was Dana Torrence. I was a commodity. In the future I was working as an assistant director, and the night that I time-traveled back here I'd just been told that I was getting my own film to direct." There was a note of confidence in her voice that he didn't miss.

"What if you can't return?"

His question startled her and she blurted out the first words that came to mind. "But I have to get back!"

Gabe looked around him at the accustomed sights and sounds of his world. It was all alien to her. Although she'd regained some memory of her previous life, she'd completely discarded the familiarity she'd once had with this era. She probably saw it as old-fashioned and stifling.

And he couldn't blame her for wanting to return to that wider world she'd lost.

"Okay. I'll try to think of you as one of the boys. It'll be hard, but I'll give it a shot." One thing men of his generation were good at, he thought wryly, was hiding their feelings. But what the hell, at least his feeble joke had brought a half smile to those velvet lips.

Down boy, he cautioned himself. *The lady's out of bounds.*

"Maybe we can start by going through those papers and photos you found in your place on Las Palmas," he suggested, fishing them out of his pocket and handing them to her. "See if they jog a memory. It's a start." He picked up his sandwich again and began eating, although his appetite seemed to have disappeared.

Dana spread the meager collection on the table beside her plate, thankful to have something to concentrate on. And at least they were finally taking some steps, whether they were heading in the right direction or not, toward solving the mystery of her past. It was what she wanted, wasn't it? She resolutely shut her mind to the look she'd seen on Gabe's face when he'd asked her if their relationship had any chance. She'd told him the truth. There was no way she could stay in this time. Even if her life hadn't been in danger from Townsend, there was nothing for her here.

Except for the man sitting across the table from her, and attractive as he was, there was no guarantee that an affair between them would last. They were worlds apart in everything except their physical desire for one another. If she gave up her life in the future for that, she'd eventually regret it.

She realized that she'd been staring at a snapshot for several seconds without really seeing it, but all of a sudden the tiny, out-of-focus image seemed to jump out at her. She brought the picture closer, holding it carefully by one deckled edge.

"Find something?" Gabe had noticed her interest.

"I'm not sure," she answered slowly. The photo was a tightly cropped shot of three girls standing on a dock. Behind them the gleaming white bow of a boat was just visible. Dana recognized her own face under a spill of platinum hair, and the blond girl beside her, she knew instantly and without hesitation, was Myrna. She was laughing at the camera with her companions, but even this bad photo had captured the fiercely hungry look in Myrna's expression. She had reminded Dana of a young Joan Crawford, ready to sacrifice anything for her ambition.

"That's Myrna, my roommate at Ma Harris's," she told him.

He leaned over the table and studied the picture, squinting. "It's hard to make out. Did you get a line on her when you were talking to the old battle-ax this morning?"

She shook her head. "Apparently she moved a couple of times, but maybe we can track her down somehow. She roomed with me right up until I was shot, and roommates don't have many secrets from each other. I think she could help us a lot."

He tapped the picture with his finger. "The brunette. Who's she?"

Dana wrinkled her brow. "I'm not sure. She's really lovely, isn't she?" She closed her eyes, thinking. "Her face is familiar."

"She looks a little Oriental."

"Anna Ling!" She snapped her fingers. "I worked with her a few times, but I didn't know her as well as Myrna. You're right, I think she told me her mother was Chinese."

"So this Myrna's our best bet. I've got a friend who works at Central Casting, owes me a few favors," Gabe said. "Finish your sandwich and we'll drive over there and see if she's listed."

"I keep feeling that there's something else I should remember about those two." Dana took a couple of hasty bites of her food and a swallow of her nearly cold coffee. "But maybe Myrna can fill in any gaps."

Dana finished eating in silence, flipping through the other photographs. Most of the people in them were strangers to her, probably people she'd worked with, and she kept going back to the picture of Myrna, Anna and herself, again feeling that she was overlooking something. Even while she and Gabe were walking back to the car, she kept searching her memory. But after all these years of living with total amnesia, she'd learned that forcing herself to remember was futile. Let it go, she told herself while she waited for Gabe to unlock the car. If it was important, it would come back to her in time.

"We should have left the windows open. It'll be an oven in here," he commented, opening her door for her and then walking around to his own.

She got in and wrinkled her nose in distaste. The whole car smelled of a heavy, musky perfume, and it wasn't until she saw the blouse that Gabe had inadvertently retrieved from Ma Harris's house that she realized why. It gave off the cloying scent that had been Myrna's favorite, *Nuits d'Arabie*. Dana picked up the blouse with her fingertips, a slight frisson of repugnance running along her spine. What kind of person was her former roommate, that she would have worn Dana's clothes after she'd learned of her supposed death?

"Gabe, this is strange—" she started to say as he got into the car. But his expression stopped her.

"That perfume! Is it yours?" His face was pale under his tan, and as she handed the blouse to him he recoiled as if she was holding a rattlesnake.

"It's the blouse. I guess we couldn't smell it before when the windows were open, but it seems to have permeated the whole car. It reeks of Myrna's perfume." She was confused by his reaction. "What is it? Are you allergic to the smell?"

He took the limp piece of clothing from her gingerly, and then, as if overcome with revulsion, wadded it into a crumpled ball and threw it out of the window as far as he could. Dana could only stare as she saw it fall onto the street. A moment later a car ran over it, leaving dirty tire marks on the white fabric.

"Come on, let's get out of here." His face grim, he started the car and pulled out, almost causing an accident. Behind them an angry motorist sounded his horn.

"What's the matter?" Dana's voice rose in frustration. It was bad enough that her own mind was so clouded by amnesia that she felt as if she was trying to put together a jigsaw puzzle with most of the pieces missing. She didn't need him hiding things from her too.

"That scent—I've smelled it before. You say that's the perfume that Myrna used to wear?" He darted a look at her, his shoulders slumping at her nod of confirmation.

"What of it? Probably when we track her down through Central Casting we'll find out that she still wears it, but why should that mean anything?"

"It means that Myrna hasn't received any work through Central Casting for quite some time, that's what it means," he answered heavily. He turned to her. "Unless they needed someone to play a corpse."

"Play a—"

"She's dead," Gabe cut in harshly. "It was her body that they found in Orange County and inadvertently identified as Dana Torrence."

"How can you know that?" The blood drained from Dana's face, leaving a white, shocked mask. That vital, laughing girl in the photo with her, dead? All that ambition, so strong that it blazed through in a faded black and white snapshot, snuffed out?

"When they found the body, they called me into the morgue. I guess the cops still hoped they could shock me into confessing something." Gabe rubbed his face wearily. The skin under his eye was swollen from Big Eddie's fists and his whole body ached from the recent punishment it had endured, but his physical fatigue was nothing compared to the sudden sickness in his soul.

"She was just a girl I'd never seen before—the body was in pretty bad shape, but I was sure it wasn't you. Her purse was lying on an autopsy table nearby and as I left, some clumsy fool knocked it onto the floor, smashing her perfume bottle inside. Immediately the room was flooded with that awful scent. It was eerie. There she was, lying in that morgue drawer, long dead. And all around us that smell, the scent she'd used when she'd gone out on a date or dancing maybe, all dressed up to have a good time. For some reason it got to me."

"*Nuits d'Arabie,*" Dana said. "Arabian Nights. Ma Harris said that was the name of the perfume. That's what you smelled on the blouse?"

He nodded. "If I remember correctly, Sheherazade had to keep telling fairy tales to the king every night just to stay alive. I guess Myrna ran out of stories."

"Or maybe she had to die to keep the story going," she said slowly. It made a crazy kind of sense. "Something Jackson said on the roof—that his boss didn't believe I was dead until he'd killed someone else. What if Jackson killed Myrna when Townsend started doubting my death?"

Gabe's skepticism was apparent. "But the dead woman was carrying your ID and wearing your clothes, as if she was trying to pass herself off as you. How would Jackson have persuaded her to do all that, drive out with him to a deserted place, and then stand still while he put a bullet into her? Come on, Dana!"

"Jackson sounded as if he regretted having to kill Myrna," Dana insisted with stubborn conviction. "I think that he used her to keep tabs on me, and that there was more to their relationship than strictly business. She would have believed him if he'd asked her to pose as me after my disappearance, to give him an alibi or something. If they were lovers, she'd never suspect that he'd kill her." Her hand trembled as she found the photo of Myrna and stared at it. "Poor woman."

"If that's the way it happened, then she wasn't shedding

any tears over you. She betrayed you." Gabe's mouth was tight with anger.

"But she paid for it in the end," Dana said quietly. She started to put the photo with the others, glancing idly at the back of it. She stopped, bringing it closer. Words had been penciled on the back of the print, so faintly that she hadn't noticed them before. They were almost illegible.

"With M. and A. and the girl from Alabama."

It didn't make sense. She flipped the picture over again, and her own face stared back at her, along with Myrna's and Anna's. But there was no fourth person. Who was the mysterious girl from Alabama? Would she have been the one holding the camera?

"That's odd," she told Gabe. "Look at the writing on the back."

He paused for a stop sign and studied the photo, frowning. "That boat in the background. Wasn't Townsend asking me about a yacht?"

"That's right, when Eddie was working you over. But this picture doesn't really narrow it down much." Dana sighed in frustration.

"How about the inscription—the girl from Alabama? Did you ever work with someone with a Southern accent?"

"Not that I can recall. No Southern belles at all," she answered absently, retrieving the picture and looking at it again.

"Southern belles. What does that remind me—" Gabe broke off in mid-sentence. "The *'Bama Belle,*" he breathed. "It was in all the papers a few years ago—the yacht that belonged to William Atwell, the director. The one he disappeared from. That boat in the picture is the *'Bama Belle!*"

The *'Bama Belle.*

The name filled Dana with so powerful a mixture of fear

and despair that she felt as if a weight had been dropped on her chest, crushing the very breath out of her. Confused images and emotions swooped through her mind in a disorganized nightmare—

"Don't be a prude, Dana. Two days of sun and sea and a nice little present at the end of it. It's just a date. Little Myrna never steered you wrong before, did I?…"

"You're on file, Miss Torrence. We'll call you if anything suitable comes up…"

"Crackers and peanut butter again, Dana? I hope this doesn't mean you're going to have trouble making the rent this week…"

"I don't know, Myrna. The whole setup seems kind of funny to me, but if you're sure it's okay…"

"Great! I'll phone old sugar daddy Atwell and tell him you're coming. Then we'll look through your closet for some really cute outfits…"

"Mr. Atwell thinks Oriental girls are exotic, so he's invited me on these cruises before. That's right, Dana—it's kind of a date…

It's kind of a date…

"I was one of the girls on board the yacht the weekend that William Atwell was killed. Myrna was there, too." Dana let the photo drop into her lap with the others. Suddenly she grabbed the whole bundle and threw them into the back seat. When she turned around again her face was pale and still, as if it had been carved in ivory. "Anna was the third girl."

"The *'Bama Belle* scandal. Then you were on board as—" He didn't continue.

"As entertainment. Paid entertainment for him and his guests." She didn't elaborate. He could figure it out from there, she thought miserably. Too bad she'd been too innocent all those years ago to do the same, but back then Dana Torrence, beneath the outward Hollywood gloss she'd acquired, had still been a naive farmgirl. At least, Dana corrected herself bitterly, she'd boarded the yacht a naive farmgirl. Presumably her misconception about her role there hadn't lasted long. Not that she could remember specifics....

No wonder she had consigned her past life to the oblivion of amnesia. If only she had left it there, instead of raking up this sordid memory! She looked down at her hands, clenched together so tightly in her lap that her knuckles were white. It was impossible to believe that she'd actually been a part of something so tawdry, but the rest of her regained memories had proven true. She had to accept that this had happened, too.

Gabe drove in silence for a moment and then he spoke. "Anna's our only lead left. We might as well try Chinatown."

Wasn't he going to say anything about what she'd been hired for that weekend? Surely he understood what her role had been. Surely he had some reservations about working with her now, Dana thought, her self-reproach giving way to a spurt of anger. Men in this day and age had certain conceptions about how women should behave, and Gabe was most definitely a man of his time.

"One of these side streets should cut over to—yeah, there it is." He turned left, seemingly preoccupied with the driving, but she didn't miss the quick glance he flicked her way. "I've got a contact in Chinatown who should be able to help us. An old man, very wealthy, very respected in the community. I did him a favor once."

"How interesting." She bit off the words and the next moment she felt one of her hands being gently disentangled from its rigid grip. Gabe held it firmly in his, and slowly started to stroke his thumb along her palm. His touch was light, but strangely disturbing, and she found her self-control ebbing dangerously.

What was his game? Why didn't he just come out with what he was thinking, instead of avoiding the subject? Suddenly she thought she knew, and with that knowledge came an anguished humiliation. Of course, she thought, pulling her hand away abruptly and ignoring Gabe's startled look. The rules had changed. She was fair game now.

"Let me out of this car." Her fingers were already poised on the door handle.

"What's the matter?" He shot a glance at her, his eyes dark with concern.

Damn the man! Of all the hypocritical— Dana's lips set in a thin line, but she welcomed the rage that was building in her. At least it distracted her, if only for the moment, from her own self-condemnation.

"The partnership's dissolved, O'Shaunessy. Let me out." She turned away from him in frustration. They were moving too fast for her to jump out, but she almost felt like taking the chance. How could she have been so stupid as to fall for his velvet voice, his ready sympathy? Up until now he'd shown some respect for her, despite the fact that there was an almost electrical physical bond between them, but she had no illusions about his feelings toward her after what he'd just learned.

"What the hell's going on? What did I say?" Confused irritation sharpened his words but she'd had enough.

"Don't pretend with me, O'Shaunessy! What I did on that yacht *has* to make a difference in the way you see me. You live in the 1930s, for God's sake! Double-standard time, as far as men are concerned. I just don't want to wait around for the inevitable come-on!" She stared stonily ahead. "Let's leave it at that."

"Let's not," he ground out. He pulled over to the side of the road so sharply that her hands flew to the dashboard to brace herself. He turned off the engine. The planes of his face were chiseled as he turned to her, and a pulse beat hard at the side of his tanned throat.

"What makes you think I'll take an insult like that from you with a tip of my hat and a thank-you-ma'am? Because you're a woman? The only double standards around here are yours!"

"Don't deny that the current attitude—*your* attitude— toward someone like me is pretty judgmental—"

"Judgmental? Coming from you, that's almost funny." He was far from amused. "For the record, I don't judge you or any woman for doing what she has to, to survive. And neither should you."

"Me? I'm the one who sold herself, remember? I'm not condemning anyone."

"Sure you are. You just found out something about your past that you can't accept, can't forgive, but instead of facing it you're pushing your feelings about the whole thing onto me. It won't work, Dana. You can't lump me into your misconceived category of '1930s men,' and give me a complete set of knee-jerk reactions. You're doing exactly what you've accused me of."

Beneath the roughness of his tone, Dana heard an echo of the same hurt she had just been feeling. Her fingers slid from the door handle. There was an unpalatable kernel of truth in what he'd said. She'd turned on him to deflect her own guilt, attacking him when he'd tried to comfort her, like a wounded animal snapping at a helping hand.

And she'd judged herself harshly, too, or at least, the woman she'd once been. Circumstances beyond her control had made that woman what she was, had backed her into a corner of helplessness and fear. Dana Torrence had taken the only way out she knew.

"I wouldn't make the same decision today," she whispered, half to herself and half to the man sitting tensely beside her. "I'm not the same person anymore. I'm *not!*"

"You didn't have to tell me that. After forty-eight hours and a couple of life-and-death situations, I thought we were getting to know each other pretty well." He shrugged. "Obviously not." He sounded weary.

"I'm sorry." Her voice was pitched so low that Gabe, starting the car, almost didn't hear.

"What did you say?"

"I'm sorry." Tentatively she placed her hand on his. "Ever since I came back to this time, I've been so afraid that I wouldn't be able to return to the future. It seemed like all my experiences here were destructive, all my memories bad ones. I'd forgotten that there were people like you. Or maybe..." she caught her breath as enlightenment dawned "...maybe I'd just never met anyone like you."

Dana stopped, confused by her own feelings. Was she falling in love at last—and with a man who lived in another time, a time that she couldn't wait to escape from? It was impossible. Of course she cared for Gabe, and in another time, another place, she might even have allowed herself to give in to her emotions, weaken under the spell of those eyes, that mouth, his hands. But nothing was going to stop her from getting back to the world of the future, the world she'd made her own.

Nothing.

"I'd give ten bucks to know what's going on inside your head right now." He was watching her face. "But you're not about to tell me. So, apology accepted and let's start tracking down the mysterious Miss Anna Ling. Just don't jump to any more conclusions about me, will you?" He kept his tone light, but there was no mistaking the seriousness of his words. "I like to think there's a little mystery about me, too."

He turned the headlights on against the rapidly gathering dusk, and they drove in silence for a few blocks. He'd surprised her again, she thought. Another man would have felt justified in washing his hands of her, but Gabe seemed willing to give her a second chance. Heaven knew why— ever since they'd met she'd erected one fence after another between them, but he'd persisted with her. Only a man in love would take that kind of punishment.

But there was no way Gabriel O'Shaunessy was in love with her. She was everything he didn't want in a woman: independent, career-oriented and totally out of place in his world. Not to mention the fact that she was running for her life and she didn't even know why.

"We'll cut over to Los Angeles Street. There's a club there, the Dragon's Den. Mr. Chao is usually there around now."

They were heading toward the Union Station area, she realized, and for a moment she felt disoriented. Surely Chinatown was north of here. Then she remembered from her *Scarlet Street* research that the city's original Chinatown had been torn down to make way for the station. In her time, the Dragon's Den might well lie buried far below Union Station. He parked the car and they got out, Dana shivering as she looked around her.

Night had fallen, and the indigo shadows of the street were pierced with lights, from brazen neon stuttering on and off over the night clubs and bars to the hissing gas jets that wavered in front of piles of bok choy and sprouts in the Chinese vegetable stands, to the glowing strands of Oriental lanterns, like warm golden necklaces outside of the tiny restaurants. All gone, she thought, all bulldozed over in the future. Her knowledge of what was to come lent a surreal quality to the scene.

"Cold?" Gabe was already taking off his jacket and slipping it around her shoulders.

"Not really. Just a goose over my grave," she replied as they started walking.

"It couldn't be." He grinned, his teeth white against the

tan of his face. "Look. There they are, all safely penned up."

She followed his glance and saw an old woman sitting on an upturned box. All around her, in cagelike wooden crates, were glossy white geese, necks extended and bright orange beaks open as they squawked loudly against their captivity.

"This neighborhood still follows the old ways," Gabe commented.

Although the sidewalks were crowded, Dana realized that there was always a certain amount of space around them. As if to emphasize this, a group of older Chinese men, their hair tied in long thin plaits that hung down their backs, and dressed in traditional padded cotton jackets and felt shoes, parted and flowed around them, only resuming their conversation once she and Gabe were a few feet away.

He noticed her puzzlement. "They're very wary of strangers. Some of the older people still remember the night that Chinatown was looted and burned to the ground by white rioters, sixty years ago. Men, women and children were killed—just because of their race."

"Then how are we going to persuade anyone to help us find Anna Ling?" Dana asked. "With history like that behind them, no one's going to trust us when we start asking questions."

"Mr. Chao trusts me." Gabe didn't elaborate, but instead took her arm and led her up a shallow flight of wooden steps and stopped in front of a carved, red-lacquered door. "This is it."

Inside, the rooms were small and box-like, leading off a dimly lit hall. A blue haze of smoke hung in the air. Dana could hear the subdued murmur of voices from the rooms, but before they had taken two steps, they were stopped by a young Chinese man. He was dressed in an immaculately tailored suit that didn't completely hide the fact that he was wearing a gun.

"This place is not for tourists." His tone was courteous and final. He moved toward them as if to speed them on their way.

"One hand on me and you'll be looking for another job tomorrow, friend." Gabe smiled as he spoke, but there was steel beneath his casual manner. "I'm looking for Mr. Chao. Is he here?"

The other man paused. "Chao is a very common Chinese name. Like Smith, in English."

Gabe appeared to reflect on this. "The Mr. Chao I want to speak with may be familiar with a common Irish name. Tell him O'Shaunessy is here and needs to see him."

Black eyes held blue for a moment, and then the man nodded. "Wait here, please." He disappeared down the hall.

"What if he won't see you?" Dana whispered. Out of the corner of her eye she noticed two young men, obviously security, watching them.

"Mr. Chao is an honorable man, and to refuse to see me would be a dishonorable act, according to his code." Gabe appeared unconcerned. He leaned against the gold-papered wall and crossed his arms. "I did him a favor once."

"A favor? My grandson would not dismiss it so lightly. And neither do I." Behind them a figure drifted, wraith-like, out of the smoky atmosphere. He was very old, Dana saw, and his skin was stretched over the bones of his face like parchment over a skull. But his calm gaze, which lit first on Gabe and then herself, held the alertness of a man still in possession of all his faculties. He was wearing a heavily embroidered robe, and as she watched he made a small motion with one long-tipped finger. His security guards melted into the background hastily, and he tucked both hands back into his sleeves.

"Come this way, Mr. O'Shaunessy. And your friend, of course."

They followed him into one of the rooms and he shut the door behind them. He gestured graciously towards a couple of spindly, silk-upholstered chairs that appeared to be made of gilded bamboo, and Dana caught Gabe's dubious look before he carefully lowered himself into one.

"May I offer you tea? Refreshments?" Mr. Chao crossed the room and settled himself behind an ornate cedar-wood desk. He frowned. "Please excuse me for receiving you in such businesslike surroundings. I think of you as a friend, Mr. O'Shaunessy. However, I gained the impression that you preferred to keep your meeting with me private, and this room is totally secure. Was I wrong?"

"You were right, Mr. Chao." Gabe had unconsciously slipped into the formal cadence of the older man's speech. "And I regret that we have no time for tea. My business is not only private, but urgent."

"How may I assist you?" There was no hesitation in Mr. Chao's offer.

"I'm looking for a girl named Anna Ling. Her father was Chinese, and Anna looks Oriental. She was an actress in Hollywood for a time, but she may have come back to Chinatown to live, after being involved in the William Atwell scandal a few years ago."

"Is this Anna Ling in trouble?" the old man asked slowly.

"Not from us, but she may be in danger. I need to ask her some questions."

Mr. Chao turned his head slightly and Dana saw that he was studying a silk scroll hanging on the wall beside his desk. It was a brush-and-ink rendering of mountains and waterfalls. He turned his attention back to Gabe.

"It is hard for our younger generation to be content with the old ways. I try not to judge, but I cannot help grieving." He picked up the telephone and dialed a number, then spoke in rapid Cantonese for a few minutes. Replacing the receiver, he inclined his head towards them.

"Miss Ling is known, but not under that name. He will call me back shortly with an address." For the first time, he directed his attention to Dana, studying her intently.

"Forgive me." His eyes, under wrinkled lids, were open wide. "I am an old man, and sometimes forget my manners. But as an old man, I also have seen many mysteries, many wonders in my time. You are a traveler from a far place?"

There was more in his question than a courteous inquiry. *He knows,* thought Dana. *I don't know how, but he knows I've traveled in time.* She shot a startled look at Gabe.

"I have worried you. I'm sorry," Mr. Chao said. "It was only that I have always wondered if such a thing was possible. But my question was—indelicate."

The telephone rang and he picked it up. He listened in silence, wrote something on a piece of paper, and hung up. "This is the address where you will find the girl, Mr. O'Shaunessy." Gabe took the note from him. "It is as I feared; Miss Ling has strayed far from any path that will lead her to happiness. She works as a good-time girl from her apartment over this tea shop. Give this note to the proprietor and he will allow you to see her."

"I am grateful for your help." Gabe stood up, towering over the old man. He pressed his hands together and bowed formally.

"You saved my grandson from an ugly death once," Mr. Chao replied, bowing in return. "I can never repay you for that." He turned to Dana. "I should have liked to drink tea with you. I wish you good luck in your quest."

"Thank you." She felt an odd kinship with the old patriarch. He had time-traveled too, in a way; from a child-hood many years ago in a feudal country to respected old age in a strange and sometimes hostile new land. As she and Gabe made their way down the main hall, on impulse she looked over her shoulder. The old man stood in the doorway of his office, watching them leave.

"Mr. Chao!" He inclined his head politely as she called his name. "Mr. Chao—such a thing *is* possible."

Understanding flooded his wrinkled features. Her last glimpse of him was a frail hand raised in farewell and a grateful smile, as if she had given him a gift beyond price.

"Quite a character, isn't he?" Gabe said as the lac-quered doors swung shut behind them and they descended to the sidewalk. "He's a millionaire several times over, and not from his gambling clubs either. He started buying real estate forty years ago and he's made some pretty shrewd deals." He glanced at the paper in his hand. "The Two Cranes teahouse. It shouldn't be far. We'll walk."

"How did you save his grandson?"

He shrugged. "No big deal. A bunch of college boys came down to Chinatown for a night's excitement. After a few too many drinks, they thought it'd be fun to beat up on one of the inhabitants, and the victim happened to be Mr. Chao's grandson. Lucky for him I was making the rounds that night. Some of the older guys on the force wouldn't have interfered when they realized the victim was Chinese."

"But you did."

Gabe looked surprised. "Sure." He looked up at the sign above the restaurant they were just passing, oblivious to Dana's scrutiny.

He had an innate integrity, she thought. He wasn't per-fect—his Irish temper and his stubbornness saw to that.

But in the things that really mattered, Gabriel O'Shaunessy was true blue, and that was unfortunate.

It would be all too easy to fall in love with a man like him.

Chapter Nine

The Two Cranes teahouse proved hard to find.

"Could that be it?" Dana said at last, pointing across the street at a peeling sign with Chinese characters running vertically down its side. She saw Gabe's look of incomprehension. "No, above the sign—there's a picture of two birds flying. They might be cranes," she added dubiously. The picture was obviously painted by an amateur.

"Either that or the biggest damn pigeons I ever saw," he agreed. "Let's give it a shot."

The tea shop had seen better days. As they entered, two old men playing a variation of mah-jongg at a table looked up, but they let their glances stray past Gabe and Dana with the feigned disinterest that she had come to recognize as the older Chinese generation's form of courtesy. The only other customer in the place was slumped over his table, a small stone bottle at his elbow. His eyes barely flickered as they walked by.

"We don't serve meals." The speaker was a young man. He stood behind the zinc-topped serving counter, steam rising around him from a pair of copper tea kettles. Despite the green apron tied around his waist and the frayed cuffs of his white shirt, he projected a kind of hostile pride.

"Are you Joe Leung?" Gabe took his silence for confirmation. "We're looking for Anna Ling."

His words had a curiously deflating effect on the young Chinese man. His shoulders slumped as if the air had been let out of him, and he picked up a cloth and began polishing the already spotless counter. "That's nothing to do with me, mister. The lady just lives upstairs. She makes her own business arrangements." His face held no expression.

Dana heard the clicking mah-jongg tiles fall silent behind her, and out of the corner of her eye she saw that even the man with the bottle was watching them with bleary interest. Her face flamed.

"We just need to talk to her. Mr. Chao said—" She turned to Gabe in embarrassment. "Give him the note."

Silently the owner of the tea shop took the paper from Gabe's hand and read it. He handed it back to them. "I jumped the gun. Sorry." He gave them a lopsided smile. "It's just that sometimes men come in here and think I'm her—that I'm handling things for her. She's an old friend, nothing more."

She might even have believed him, thought Dana as he held aside a beaded curtain and gestured toward a set of stairs that led to the apartment above. But she'd seen the pain, quickly hidden, in his dark eyes when he'd thought that Gabe was one of Anna's clients. No, he wasn't her manager. But the slim, taut-featured young man with the tortured look was something more than just a friend to Anna.

"There's a back entrance too, but I took some tea up to her half an hour ago. She's alone right now." Joe shrugged. "You won't be interrupting anything." He let the curtain swing as he turned back to his counter. The beads made a lonely tapping sound as he disappeared.

There was only one door at the top of the stairs. Gabe

paused as he was about to knock, and sniffed the air. "Little lady's doing some cooking," he commented mildly.

Dana could smell it too; a sweetish miasma, much heavier than the scent given off by Mr. Chao's joss sticks. "Opium?" she asked incredulously.

"Why not?" His voice was suddenly bleak. "It's an escape for trapped people. What they don't realize is that it's just another prison after a while." He knocked at the door, the sound echoing in the empty landing.

There was no answer for a moment, and then they heard a hesitant shuffling noise approach the door.

"Joe, honey, I told you to leave me alone tonight. You're always worrying about me." The door opened a crack, enough for Dana to glimpse a blue-black tangle of hair obscuring a glazed almond-shaped eye. The eye focused on them, and widened.

"Who the hell are you?" Too late, Anna attempted to slam the door in their faces, but Gabe already had his foot in the opening.

"A friend, Anna. From five years ago." He put his shoulder against the door and pushed it open. "We just want to talk."

Dana followed him into the room in time to see Anna, dressed only in a lace-trimmed robe, run to a side table and pull open a drawer. She whirled around unsteadily, the soft light from a pink-shaded lamp gleaming on the nickel-plated gun in her hand, her slim, bare legs trembling.

"I have no friends from five years ago. They're all dead, just like you'll be—" Anna gasped as she saw Dana. Her exotically made-up eyes and the scarlet bloom of lipstick on her mouth were the only spots of color in her face as she stared at them.

"It's me, Anna. Dana Torrence." She kept her gaze on the other woman's face, but with every fiber of her being she was aware of the wavering pistol pointed in their direction. "I didn't die. But I'm still in danger, and so are you." She hoped that her voice sounded calm. Anna, drugged, frightened and armed with that tiny but lethal weapon, was as risky as a bottle of nitroglycerin in a juggling act. Dana held her breath.

"Joe Leung let us in. You trust him, don't you?" Gabe's voice was reassuring. "Put the gun down, Anna."

Flame-tipped fingers slowly relaxed their grip on the weapon. "Yeah, Joe's a good guy." Anna snapped the safety on and threw the gun onto the satin-covered divan behind her. "Too good for me."

She gave a brittle laugh and pulled the edges of her robe closer. On a low table in front of the divan was a jade ashtray containing a sticky lump of residue. Beside the ashtray was a matching table lighter and a half-empty pack of cigarettes. Anna lit one with a quick gesture and sat back on the divan, swinging her legs up onto the coffee-table. She let the smoke out in a nervous rush.

"Some party, that weekend. You been hiding out, too?"

How much should she tell her? Dana wondered. "I lost my memory after I was shot. Until today I didn't even remember you, and I still don't know what happened on board that yacht. We hoped you could help."

"Wish I could forget..." Anna closed her eyes and directed a stream of smoke toward the ceiling. A moment ago her voice had been sharp with worry. Now it was slurred.

"The drug's kicking in." Gabe pulled up a chair in front of Anna and brought his face close to hers. "Anna! You said all your friends from five years ago were dead. Who's dead?"

A small crystal clock on the table suddenly began to tinkle out the hours, making Dana jump. Anna brought the cigarette mechanically to her red lips, counting out loud along with the silvery chimes of the clock. "...five, six, seven, eight!'' she concluded dreamily. Her eyes opened, and without warning, tears spilled from her lower lashes and slid down her cheeks. "Eight. Just like that weekend." She lapsed into silence again.

"Eight o'clock. What happened at eight? Is that when Atwell was killed? His body was found later washed up near Santa Catalina, but I think he was shot, Anna. Did you see it happen?" Gabe looked at Dana in frustration. "She's in and out of reality here. Maybe we should come back later."

"William Atwell. Boyd Davis. Arthur Berlin. Myrna." The perfectly shaped nails gleamed like drops of blood, as Anna held her hands in front of them and ticked off the names on her fingers. "All dead. Dana Torrence—presumed dead. Anna Ling—'' She let her hands fall into her lap. "That girl died a long time ago," she whispered.

"But Arthur Berlin committed suicide," Gabe said, frowning. "That was the official verdict, anyhow."

"Oh, no." She sat up straighter, and for a moment looked entirely lucid. "That was the legend."

Beside her Dana heard Gabe make an exasperated sound, but she put a warning hand on his arm and leaned forward, intent. "What legend, Anna? What was the real story?"

"The legend was suicide. The real story was murder— all of them, murdered. And we're the only ones left."

Dana felt a deathly chill run down her spine at the unspoken implication. *We're the only ones left.* But for how long? And why? Despite Anna's ramblings, she hadn't given them any clue as to why everyone who'd been on the *'Bama Belle* that fateful weekend was doomed. They needed more information from her.

But the drug was overpowering her once more. She smiled at them as if she knew a secret, and shook her head, the heavy black curtain of hair swinging back and forth.

"There was a story my mother told me, from the old country," she said sleepily. "I thought it was just for children. She would warn me about the dragon that came down from the sky with his mate, but I used to tell her that the story didn't frighten me, that dragons couldn't fly down and kill people." She waved a hand toward the gold and scarlet draperies. "But now I have bars on my window, just in case."

The telephone started ringing in the other room. Unsteadily, she got to her feet and went to answer it. Dana watched her with despair.

"Dragons. Sure, we'll watch out for them," Gabe said in disgust. "Let's go, we're wasting time we haven't got."

Anna's voice rose from the other room. "But I don't see clients unless they've been recommended by one of my regulars." She paused, and then she spoke again, more agreeably. "That much? I—I guess I could make an exception. Sure, I'll be waiting." There was a click as she hung up the phone, and then they heard her running water in the bathroom.

"She's our only lead," Dana whispered swiftly. "Give her some time to come down from the opium. We can't give up until we find out what she knows."

"If her brain isn't completely gone. You can't trust anything she says, sweetheart. She probably doesn't even know herself, half the time." Gabe raked his hand through his hair.

"I have a visitor coming in a few minutes. You have to leave now."

Gone was the tear-stained, terrified woman of a few minutes ago. Anna's face was porcelain-perfect; fresh powder giving her skin a flawless matte finish, glossy lipstick newly applied to her mouth. She ran her little finger along the arch of each eyebrow, smoothing them into immaculate wings that accentuated the mystery of her tilted eyes. She noticed Dana's astonishment and gave a tiny smile.

"One to relax me, another to bring me down to earth. This is business, honey." She swayed, and steadied herself. "One hour. That's all he's paying for, and then it's back to dreamland for me."

Gabe was already at the door. His patience had been exhausted, Dana realized, but she still felt that Anna was their best hope, if only she would stop obscuring what she knew behind a fog of riddles.

"Can we talk to you later? We can wait downstairs until—" Was there any delicate way to put it? She took refuge in a veiled reference. "Until your friend leaves."

"He's no friend of mine. Not even a regular." The perfect face tightened and for a moment it was possible to see what Anna would look like when she was an old woman. "Although for the amount of money he mentioned, I'm willing to get acquainted. But you wouldn't understand." She reached down for the package of cigarettes, shook one out and lit it. "In the end, no amount was enough for you, was it? You just couldn't take that final step." She looked curiously at Dana's confused expression. "You really don't remember?"

From the back alleyway outside came the muffled thud of a car door being slammed. Anna hurriedly stubbed her cigarette out in the ashtray and took a quick look at herself in the mirror over the divan. She cinched the satin tie of her robe at her waist and took a deep breath. "All right. I'll come down to the tea shop as soon as I can and we'll talk. Don't worry—" she shot a sardonic glance at Gabe's skeptical look "—I can keep a clear head if I have to. But go now. The johns don't like being seen."

She hustled them out the door and darted a look down the hallway. Dana hadn't noticed the second flight of stairs at the other end of the hall before, but she guessed that they led to the private back entrance that the tea-shop owner had mentioned. Even as they stood there, they heard the sound of footsteps ascending.

"Go!" As Anna closed her apartment door she was framed for a second in the glow of the shaded lamps behind her, her slim figure outlined in the flimsy material of her robe, her hair an ink-black shadow falling over her shoulders. There was a fragile vulnerability about her silhouette, out of keeping with the self-sufficient image she'd tried to project.

Why did she feel so uneasy about leaving her? Dana wondered. She followed Gabe down the stairs and through the beaded curtain back into the tea room.

"Did you get what you wanted from her?" Joe, his face a polite mask, shook a handful of dried leaves and herbs into a hammered-iron teapot. With a linen cloth protecting his grip, he picked up a copper kettle. Steam obscured his features and a fragrant, flowery scent rose around him.

"She was a little the worse for wear," Gabe said bluntly. He glanced around the room and lowered his voice, although the two old mah-jongg players were now the only customers there. "That lady's going down a short and dangerous road."

The mask slipped momentarily, and pain flared in the black eyes. "I know."

"Can't you do anything to stop her?" Impulsively Dana put her hand on the man's wrist. "As an old friend, couldn't you try?" She felt the muscles tense beneath her touch before he shrugged her off.

"Anna won't listen to old friends. Not even old lovers." He stared blindly at the shabby room. "I've offered her everything—marriage, my business and my love." His voice broke on the last word. "Marriage is slavery, she says. My business will never make us rich. And my love...well, that she has whether she wants it or not."

He tossed the linen cloth on the counter and sat down beside Gabe, resting his elbows heavily on the table, his head bowed. "I don't know why I'm telling you this. But my family and friends don't understand why I feel the way I do about her. My father spits when he hears her name."

"Your family is old-fashioned Chinese?" Dana asked.

"They had a girl all picked out for me to marry. But she wasn't Anna." He looked up and attempted a smile. "I knew her before all this, you see. We grew up on the same block. Both of us wanted to leave the old ways behind, follow the American dream, make it in the big world beyond Chinatown. But even though things are better than they used to be, there's still a lot of prejudice against us. And Chinese people, like my parents, are against her because her father was American. He didn't even stick around long enough to know he had a daughter."

Attitudes would change, Dana knew. The next few decades would break down the destructive bias between people of different colors and beliefs. But it wouldn't be soon enough for Anna Ling and the man who loved her so hopelessly.

"I let her stay here. It rips me apart, knowing what happens up in that apartment, but at least she's not standing on a street corner somewhere." Joe rose wearily, moving like an old man. His lips twisted in a bitter grimace. "You know what's really funny? I named this place 'The Two Cranes' because in Chinese folklore cranes stand for fidelity and good luck. Painted the sign myself, thinking that someday we'd be like those birds, flying free but always together. Sad story, huh? Maybe they'll make a movie about it some day."

"Joe!"

They hadn't heard her coming down the stairs, but there she stood, still dressed in the satin robe. Anna took a step toward them, her movements curiously jerky and devoid of grace, clutching a handful of the beaded curtain to steady herself. Her eyes, enormous pools in the pallor of her face, were fixed on those of the man who had stood by her all her life.

"Joe. In my heart…" She seemed to be having trouble speaking, and all of a sudden Dana knew that it wasn't the drugs.

"In my heart I always flew by your side, too. Like the cranes."

Her last words came out in a whisper. Before anyone could move, Anna fell forward at their feet, brightly colored beads spilling and bouncing around her like precious jewels. Ruby red stained the back of her white satin robe, spreading out from the shaft of the knife still lodged there.

"Get down!"

Gabe was only a few feet away from Dana, but as he closed the gap between them he felt as if he was running the length of a football field. He reached her and let his momentum carry them both to the floor, shielding her body with his as the plate-glass window of the tea shop turned into deadly, flying shards. The coughing rattle of machine-gun fire came from the street outside. With the steam-fogged window gone, the movement that had caught his eye was now recognizable as two men with the snap-brims pulled low over their eyes and the death-dealing fifty-round cartridge drums of their Thompson submachine guns instantly identifiable.

"Leung! Stay down, man!"

Joe had risen from Anna's body. His face was contorted with grief, but as he realized what was happening, Dana saw the grief turn to rage. Ignoring Gabe's warning shout, he reached behind the counter.

"You haven't got a chance, Joe!" Gabe tried to stand, attempting to stop him, but the broken glass was a treacherous surface. Joe Leung, tea-shop owner, lover of Anna

Ling, and stubborn believer in dreams, stood in the middle of the shop surrounded by the wreckage of those dreams and raised the ancient pump-action shotgun to his shoulder.

Museum piece it may have been, but as it discharged with a roar Dana heard a cry of anger and pain from the street outside. Retaliation was swift and brutal. Again and again the counter was raked with murderous fire, the polished copper kettles slamming against the back wall, boiling water spraying from each bullet hole, glass jars of herbs exploding, the neat line of white china cups dancing madly on the shelf as they shattered.

And the slim Chinese man, caught full in the chest by a couple of rounds, spinning and falling to the floor beside the body of the woman he loved.

The firing stopped, a car door slammed and tires screamed in the night. For a moment all was silent and then, with a silvery tinkle, one last piece of glass fell from the window onto the sidewalk.

"Check on Joe, but be careful," Gabe whispered to Dana. "One of them might have stayed behind."

It was all he could do to keep from enfolding her in his arms and just holding her, feeling the beat of her heart and the warmth of her breath. It could have been her, dammit! It could have been her lying there, bloodied and torn like poor Leung. But there was no time for all that. He'd seen two men shooting, and the car had taken off at the same time as the door was being closed. That meant there had been a third man, a driver. He'd have heard two doors slamming, maybe more if whoever had knifed Anna hadn't been one of the shooters. He crept cautiously across the floor, noting with relief that the mah-jongg players, crouched under one of the tables, seemed to be all right.

Please God, don't let him get hurt! Dana prayed silently. She followed Gabe's retreating back with her eyes, her senses alert to any suspicious movement outside. He'd reacted so instantaneously to the gunfire that at first she hadn't realized what was happening. Her thoughts had been only of Anna, lying there like an exquisite broken doll. The next moment, Dana had found herself falling to the floor, Gabe's arms around her tightly, his chest a barrier between her and the glass and bullets. Despite the hell all around them, for those few seconds she'd felt no fear for herself, only a desperate panic that nothing should happen to him.

She saw him scanning the street from the cover of the doorway. What he saw seemed to reassure him, and he went outside, joining the throng of people who were gathered there. Voices, recovering from their shocked silence, filled the air with the staccato cadence of Cantonese. Dana felt a hesitant touch on her arm.

"Joe Leung dead, lady. You go. We take care of him." One of the old men, his padded jacket sparkling with bits of glass, looked gravely at her. His face was seamed with sorrow, but as she turned belatedly to look at the dead teashop owner, the old man firmly took her arm and shook his head.

"No look. Joe hit bad. You go now." His English was halting, but he needed no words to convey the mourning and compassion in his eyes. Joe Leung would be taken care of by friends. Dana stood up.

"He's dead?" Gabe paused in the doorway, his mouth bracketed by lines of strain.

She nodded. "They want us to leave."

He hesitated, taking in the situation, and then spoke a few faltering words to the men in their own language. Despite the circumstances, the old faces brightened at his attempt, and they answered him volubly. He spoke again, struggling with the unfamiliar and drawn-out vowels, but they seemed to understand him. One of the men nodded in agreement. Gabe bowed.

"Let's go." His look was grim as they left the destroyed tea shop and fought their way through the milling crowd outside. It was gathered around a body lying on the sidewalk, but Gabe took Dana's hand and kept moving.

"Joe Leung avenged his Anna," he commented briefly as they crossed the street.

"That was the man who killed her? Are you sure?" The image of the knife jutting out of Anna's back was one she'd never forget, and Dana's voice hardened. The man lying outside the Two Cranes had received an easier death than he'd deserved.

"He had a leather scabbard at his belt. Joe's aim was truer than he realized." Gabe jerked his head at an alleyway between the buildings. "We can cut through here to where the car's parked."

The alley was ominously shadowed, but Dana welcomed the darkness. They'd been too conspicuous on the well-lit street. A tight knot had formed in her throat, and she had to force herself to ask the question that had been in her mind for the last few minutes.

"We led the killers to them, didn't we?"

Gabe stopped in mid-stride. He gripped her shoulders and turned her to face him. "No. It was the other way around. They'd had Anna's place staked out for a couple of nights hoping you'd show up. The old men said that the third customer, the one who pretended to be drunk, was a stranger. As soon as we went upstairs he left and used the phone-box outside." He gave her a gentle shake. "For pity's sake, sweetheart, don't feel guilty for what happened back there. Blame whoever's behind all this."

He needed a shave, there was a thread of dried blood above his eyebrow where he'd been hit by a stray piece of glass, and his bottom lip was still swollen from the night before. His tie was loose and his shirt had lost a couple of buttons in the last half hour. That velvet voice was sand-papered with fatigue.

And none of it mattered, Dana thought, looking up at him. She wanted him. The violence of her reaction shook her, but she welcomed the sensation. They were alive. Death had come close to both of them tonight; close enough to feel the brush of its wings, but it had passed them by this time. The world ceased to exist as her universe narrowed to his mouth, his hands spreading wide on her back and the musky scent of his skin.

Gabe's eyes were still locked on hers. He didn't move, but Dana could feel the muscles in his arms tense and harden. It was her call, she realized. He was letting her make the rules.

She brought her hands up to his chest, pushing aside the ruined shirt and seeking the heat of his body. The tips of her fingernails raked lightly on his skin as if to brand him with tiny half-moons and she saw that devastating dark blue gaze lose focus for a moment and those thick black lashes flicker briefly as he fought for control. And lost.

When he closed the last remaining space between them, her lips met his with an unhurried inevitability. She thought she knew what to expect, but her body reacted as if this was a new and sinful delight it had never experienced.

A fuse ignited within her. Slow-burning but growing in intensity, it made its way along her thighs, her stomach, her breasts; leaving a trail of heat and building toward a flash-point deep in her being. It seemed as though steam must be rising from her skin. She let her hands follow the coarse arrow of hair that tapered off below Gabe's ribcage, and one last obstructive button tore loose from his shirt. His stomach was flat and smooth, and as her hands traced a teasing pattern she felt a shudder run through him. He deepened the kiss, his mouth no longer giving and receiving in unison with hers, but taking possession with his tongue.

Dana gasped and their lips parted, but Gabe continued. His mouth moved to her cheekbone, and then to her closed eyes, licking like a tiger cub after cream.

"I lose my mind when I touch you." His mouth was close to her ear and she couldn't miss the husky, desperate note in his voice. "In another minute we'll be over the edge."

"Yes," Dana breathed. It was an effort to speak when all she wanted to do was to give herself up to the exquisite torture he was inflicting upon her.

"But we've got to get out of here." Gabe tipped her head backward, his mouth on the suddenly weak column of her neck. "Make me stop," he murmured.

He was right. They had to leave. There were a million good reasons to end this, but none of them mattered right now, she thought incoherently. He pushed past the lace of her bra, his hands cupping the weight of her breasts, and pure sensation flooded her, overriding all logic and caution.

Then, as if from a great distance, she heard the sound of a voice and an unearthly shrieking coming along the alleyway behind them. Immediately Gabe tensed. For a moment he tightened his hold on her, then he carefully put her from him, looking swiftly over her shoulder into the shadows. She saw him grin reluctantly, his teeth very white in the half-light.

"Our friend the goose lady, taking them home for the night."

The old woman kept up a running argument with her charges as she trundled by with a rickety hand-cart of cages, but her eyes brightened knowingly as she passed them. The ghostly white birds were visible long after her stout figure had melted into the night but by then Gabe and Dana were no longer watching. They covered the last half block to the car in silence.

Once he was behind the wheel and driving, Gabe spoke. "We're crazy. That could have been anyone." He looked over at her in resignation.

Dana's head was bent, her fingers fumbling with the buttons of her blouse. Hadn't the scene at the tearoom been warning enough that their enemies played for keeps? They'd taken an insane chance in the alley, oblivious to the danger they were in.

"It was my fault," she said in agitation. "I wasn't thinking straight. I—" She struggled with a particularly stubborn button and felt it come loose in her hand. It seemed like the last straw, and she threw it angrily onto the floor. "I've never behaved like that before in my life! What got into me?"

"Don't sound so stricken." A corner of his mouth lifted briefly and his voice was unconcerned. "It was a common reaction. We were nearly killed back there and some part of you needed to reaffirm the fact that you were still alive. Glad I was handy."

He made it sound as if she would have turned to anyone in the situation, she thought. Perversely, she felt riled by the way he downplayed the incident. "What about you?" she retorted shortly. "You should be used to narrow escapes in your business, but you seemed just as enthusiastic about reaffirming the fact that *you* were still alive."

"That's different."

"A classically male defense," she accused him. "How is it different?"

He looked at her as if she was feeble-minded, and then shrugged. "I feel that way about you all the time, sweetheart. Given half a chance, I'd have you in my bed twenty-four hours a day. But that breaks the rules of our partnership, doesn't it?'' He slowed the car, pulled into a parking space at the curb and grinned wickedly at her disconcerted expression. His eyes were cobalt blue and as guileless as a child's. He nodded at a nearby bar. ''I could use a drink right about now. Also I need to make a phone call. Close your mouth, darlin', you look like a fish.''

The man was just too exasperating! Dana fumed as they entered the establishment. Why did he always leave her feeling like she'd just been checkmated by a grand master? She sat down at a table as he got change from a waitress and headed for the phone. An accomplished flirt, she thought, depressed—even the sophisticated Hildie hadn't been immune to his charm. Trying to unravel the mystery of the *'Bama Belle* would definitely be easier than figuring out Gabriel O'Shaunessy. With an effort, she wrenched her gaze from him. She had to stop obsessing about him, she told herself sternly. She had to concentrate on what they had learned from Anna Ling.

Dana sighed as she went over their conversation with Anna. It hadn't been much. The drug-induced ramblings of the woman had seemed disjointed and irrelevant at the time, but had there been some core of reality to the conversation that Dana and Gabe missed? Anna had seemed insistent that everyone on the yacht that weekend had been marked for murder. Right, Dana thought. Start with that.

William Atwell. He'd been a brilliant director, a trail-blazer in silent films. Her teachers at the film institute had referred to him as a genius whose work would always be remembered, but his messy private life had tarnished his image. Dana rubbed her temples wearily. It was hard to separate what she'd known of the man when she'd been living in this era as a struggling actress, from what she'd learned about him as Dana Smith, studying film history in the 1990s.

A notorious womanizer, in his position of power at Oval

Studios he'd had his pick of young starlets. His behavior had strained even the elastic tolerance of the Roaring Twenties but unless a vengeful father had stowed away on Atwell's yacht that weekend, who else on board would have had reason to kill him? She, Myrna and Anna had all known what had been expected of them. She closed her eyes. However unpalatable, it was true. They'd gone of their own free will. They'd had no reason to kill the man.

Boyd Davis. His face came to her suddenly, another memory to add to her meager store. He'd been boyishly good-looking, a rising young star in Westerns. If he'd lived, he might have been Oval Studios' answer to Gary Cooper. There was more. Dana let the memory return, no longer subconsciously repressing it, but still weighed down by a leaden sense of shame for her former self.

She'd been asked along that weekend to be Boyd's escort. He'd met her at the docks; had come up to her as she'd arrived with Myrna and Anna, and offered to take her overnight case into his cabin. Myrna had put on her little-girl act and asked him to take their picture before they boarded. Boyd had complied good-naturedly but it had been obvious that her femme-fatale charm left him cold. Even now, Dana could recall how flattered she'd been when the studio's current heartthrob had directed all his attention to her, and how she'd tried to persuade herself that she was on a regular date with him. But it hadn't worked. By then her suspicions about why she'd been invited on the cruise were becoming harder to ignore.

She'd felt scared and uncomfortable with him as he unpacked in his cabin. The memory stopped there and she frowned. What had happened then? Had it been so bad that she was still blocking it, even now? Had he abused her?

No. She remembered now.

He'd stood in front of her, that matinee-idol face contorted with anguish and the broad shoulders shaking. He couldn't go through with it, he'd told her brokenly. The studio was trying to build up an image of him as America's dream man; a playboy heartbreaker. It was totally false. He'd been married to his high-school sweetheart for years; they had a little girl and another child on the way, but under the terms of his movie contract his family had to stay in the background. Don Juans made better copy than happily married fathers, and if the truth ever came out, his whole career would come crashing down. He'd begged her not to tell.

Dana had started crying herself then, and when Boyd finally gathered that she hadn't fully realized what would be expected of her, he'd put his arm around her and outlined his plan. They would put on an act for the weekend, playing the part of lovers for the benefit of everyone else on board. It would be their secret.

The relief had been enormous, for both of them.

Dana saw Gabe heading back to the table and she blinked away the moisture in her eyes. How close she'd come to disaster that day on the *'Bama Belle!* She wouldn't have been the first gullible girl to have found herself in a situation that she couldn't control. But fate, in the form of a doomed young man who in the end couldn't bring himself to play marital games, had intervened. Somehow, Anna had guessed part of it. *You just couldn't take that final step,* she'd said. No, however it had happened, Dana hadn't taken that final step, had been saved from something that would have haunted her for the rest of her life.

But Gabe's opinion of her had never been in question. He'd accepted her for what she was now.

He sat down across from her. "Don't kill me, but I ordered sandwiches for us."

"I'm beginning to forget any other food exists." She

produced a weak smile for his benefit. "Who were you phoning?"

"Len Connor, at the *Times*. He's an old friend of mine." Gabe paused as a plate heaped high with thick ham-and-cheese sandwiches was placed in front of them, along with a tall glass of beer for him and a coffee for Dana.

"Coffee. What a surprise."

Gabe looked worried. "Well, I knew you'd drink it. I wasn't so sure about beer."

"As long as you don't expect me to sleep tonight," she replied lightly. She realized what she'd said and hastily took a sandwich to cover her embarrassment, but Gabe didn't let it pass.

"You tease." He shot her a look of mock reproval.

"Shut up and eat," Dana told him, blushing.

"And she talks with her mouth full. My mother warned me about the girls you find in bars." He placed another sandwich on her plate. "Keep your strength up. We've got a long night still ahead of us, starting with a visit to the newspaper morgue."

Dana swallowed a bite before she spoke. "What do you expect to find there?"

"I asked Len whether there was any question about the suicide verdict on Arthur Berlin. He said there'd been plenty of unofficial talk right after his body was found, but that within hours a lid had been clamped on the whole thing. And guess who was doing the clamping?"

"Oval Studios?" Dana guessed.

"You got it. The head of Oval security, Townsend himself, was at the elbow of the grieving widow at Berlin's funeral. Len said she looked stunning in black."

"Babe Francis." Dana nodded thoughtfully. "They're still arguing about it over fifty years from now—was it murder or was it suicide?" If Berlin had been married to anyone else but Francis, Dana mused, it would soon have been forgotten. But as the producer-husband of the original "Incendiary Blonde," his death had gone down as a classic unsolved Hollywood mystery. "He left a note, didn't he?"

"It could have been a forgery, Len says. Anyway, there's a chance that Anna was right and he was murdered. It happened two weeks after the yacht trip."

"Did you check on Boyd Davis?"

"A fatal accident while doing one of his own stunts. It happens, but it's one more link in the chain." Gabe took a swallow of beer and set the glass down. "But his accident occurred months after Atwell's death, and a few days before I was hired to tail you. That's why we're going to search the back copies of the papers."

Gabe leaned forward. "If Atwell's death was murder, then maybe Berlin knew it at the time, and he was killed when it looked like he couldn't keep his mouth shut. Then the killings started again later, with Davis's accident, the attack on you, and finally Myrna's death. Anna Ling bought herself some time by disappearing into Chinatown, but eventually she was tracked down. The fact that someone was watching the tea shop proves that."

"So what are we looking for?" Despite the warmth in the stuffy room, Dana felt chilled. Atwell, Berlin, Davis, Myrna and Anna. It was a roll call of death, with one name missing.

"Whatever it was that convinced the killers they hadn't covered their tracks well enough. Whatever made them think that Boyd Davis had found something out and had told you."

"Yes, they might think that," Dana said slowly. "Later, whenever he had to attend a publicity function, he tried to get me as his date."

"Did you two have something going?" Gabe's words

were casual enough, but he waited for her answer with watchful eyes.

"No. His big secret was that he was a happily married man—the kiss of death for a Hollywood heartthrob." Dana smiled sadly. "He told me that weekend on the yacht because I'd been hired to—to be his escort. I was just too dumb to understand the setup at first. But as it turned out, we became friends. He was a nice man."

Gabe was silent for a moment. Then he reached over and took her hand. "I'm glad you remembered the truth, for your sake. But it never made any difference to me."

"I know." She looked down at the tablecloth, unable to let him see how much his simple declaration of faith meant to her.

"So do you remember talking to him before his accident? Did you go anywhere with him, see anyone?" Gabe's manner was matter-of-fact, giving her a chance to pull herself together.

"Let me think. I seem to remember attending a charity dance at the Cocoanut Grove with him. And the next day—" Her eyes widened in shock. "Of course! That was the last time I saw him. He was killed the next day in that accident! But Gabe, it doesn't make sense. If everyone on board that yacht's been killed, then who are the killings supposed to protect? We're going on the assumption that Atwell was murdered and that this is all a cover-up for that. But there's no one left who could have been his murderer!"

"We're also going on the assumption that there were only six people on board, but what if we're wrong?" His expression grew thoughtful. "Anna said something about the number eight. I assumed she meant the time, but what if she meant there were eight people there that weekend? Another couple that you didn't know about?"

"We were all on deck until we got out of the harbor.

How could anyone have come on board without being seen?'' She was missing something, Dana thought in frustration, something that Anna had said. It was the key to everything, if only she could identify it.

"That damned dragon story... That's it!'' There was a note of excitement in Gabe's voice.

"A flying dragon?'' She lifted a skeptical eyebrow.

"A flying boat, damn it! Two other people joined the party that night, when the yacht was at sea. That has to be it. And one of them was the murderer.'' He slammed some bills down on the table. "Come on. The haystack just got smaller and the needle got a little bigger. We'll pull the society photos of that dance and see if you can recognize anyone there that might fit our theory.''

WITHIN FIFTEEN MINUTES they were at the offices of the *Times*, a hive of activity despite the hour. Gabe's friend, wiry, balding and with the same trace of brogue in his voice, gave Dana a speculative glance but didn't press for an introduction. They sat in the visitors' reception area while he made a quick telephone call. Then he rejoined them.

"Can't spare you much time, buddy. My editor would have my head if he knew I was conducting a personal tour around the morgue instead of rewriting my piece about James Mattson's political chances this year.'' Len stifled a yawn and looked at his watch as he led the way to the basement, where the back copies of the paper were filed. "We go to press in an hour, but the hell with it. There's just no way I can make Mattson interesting. The guy's a regular saint and a shoo-in for governor.''

"Everybody's got a secret.'' Gabe sounded mildly disbelieving.

"Not him. Well, a mistress on the side,'' Len admitted, "but big deal. She's hardly ever seen in public with him, and everybody already knows about her. Even his wife, I hear. All very upper-class and civilized, boyo, not like our old neighborhood." He laughed. "Remember when Ma Riley found Pat had been stepping out with that waitress?"

Gabe looked blank for a moment and then he grinned. "Right down the middle of the street brandishing a rolling pin, Pat sobering up fast a few feet ahead of her. We kids were laying bets on the race," he told her.

"And you won. Three of my best cat's-eye marbles, and my prize aggie." Len held open a fire door for them and closed it carefully behind him. "The luck of the devil even then, and I guess you've needed it these last few days." It was a thinly disguised question. Despite his earlier fatigue, his eyes were sharp with curiosity as he glanced from Gabe to Dana meaningfully.

"I've always gotten by on luck and the loyalty of old friends, Len. Don't know where I'd be without them," Gabe drawled, giving nothing away.

"Come on, give me a break." They'd arrived at the records office and Len kept his voice low. "You call me out of the blue, ask a few cryptic questions about Arthur Berlin's supposed suicide, and the next thing I know you show up here with Dana Torrence. A dame that's supposed to be dead. So I get on the phone and make a few discreet inquiries, and I hear that maybe she's not dead yet, but that's not from lack of trying on the part of Mr. Dave Townsend and his merry band. Seems the fat man's in Dutch with his mob bosses on account of her, seeing as how he's let her slip through his fingers—her and some wisecracking Irishman."

"Just how discreet were these inquiries, pal?" Gabe's voice was colder than Dana had ever heard it. Len seemed taken aback.

"I wasn't born yesterday, O'Shaunessy. I was careful." Nevertheless, a shade of doubt crossed his face, but then he rallied. "What the hell, Gabe! I covered the Torrence killing five years ago. I almost lost my job because I wouldn't crucify you in print like everyone else, and now you think I'm selling you out for a story?"

They glared at each other for a moment, and then Gabe slowly shook his head. "We go back a long way, Len. But you're sure no one overheard the conversation? Did it go through the main switchboard?"

"You don't think the girls on the switchboard—" He swallowed the rest of his sentence and looked suddenly anxious. "I'll go upstairs and warn Walt at the main desk to double-check any strangers who come in looking for me. Why don't you get started here? Ask the kid at the desk to pull the issues you need."

He left the room at a trot, leaving Gabe staring after him with a worried frown.

Chapter Ten

"Do you really think they might trace us here?" Dana asked in an undertone a few minutes later. At their request, the bored-looking youth manning the records desk had ambled over to the banks of steel filing cabinets and was apathetically pulling open drawers.

"Probably not. But if Townsend's getting orders from the mob, then we can't take any chances. They've got informants all over the place." Gabe drummed his fingers on the counter while the clerk slowly made his way back up the aisle with an armful of newspapers.

"You gotta look at them at the table over there. No cutting, no marking up the paper, and no taking them out of the room," he informed them. Adenoids gave his voice an annoying whine.

"Thanks, sonny. I'll recommend you for a job at Fort Knox," Gabe said, shooting the clerk an impatient scowl that had him scuttling back to his desk. He handed her half the pile. "These are for the whole month before I was hired to tail you, but we'll concentrate on the Saturday and Sunday editions for now. The charity ball was probably held on a Friday or a Saturday, and written up for the next day's paper."

"I don't really know what we're looking for," Dana

muttered, thinking hard and trying to jog her memory as she scanned a society page.

"Anything about Boyd Davis that night. Who was at your table, who he danced with—anything that might give us some idea about the people he saw there at the Grove. He was killed the next day, so if he passed on any information to you, and obviously someone thinks he did because they hired me to watch you soon after, then it had to be that night. Chances are that he learned something there that led to his death."

"Bingo." She shoved the rest of the papers aside to make room, and read the society headline aloud. "*Widows' and Orphans' Benefit Attended by Hollywood Elite*. There are photos, but they're pretty grainy." Dana scanned the article hopefully, but finally sighed in disappointment. "Boyd's mentioned, but just in a list of who was there."

"Take a look at this." Gabe pointed at one of the smaller photographs. "Behind Clara Bow and John Gilbert. Isn't that you and Boyd? Who's he shaking hands with?"

The picture was of poor quality, but there was no mistaking Boyd's chiseled profile. Unmistakable too, was the blond girl beside him in the clinging gown. Dana stared at herself, half hidden behind Clara Bow, the legendary "It" girl of the silent screen, and for the first time, her memories of the past were pleasant.

"It was so exciting. Everyone who was anyone in Hollywood was there that night," she breathed. "I actually spilled my drink on Greta Garbo during dinner."

"Now we know why she wants to be alone," Gabe interjected impatiently. "But do you remember anything useful? Take a closer look at the picture." He turned as Len came back into the room, and Gabe shot him a questioning glance.

"Walt said no one's been looking for me tonight. He'll

phone down here and let me know if anyone does show up. Find anything?"

"Yeah, Dana's going to start a scrapbook," Gabe said dryly. "Photos of her with Clara Bow, her with Garbo, her with Clark Gable—"

"Her with James Mattson," Len added, looking over her shoulder. "He'll be at the Academy Awards tomorrow night. Want a couple of press passes? You two starstruck kids can get your pictures taken with all the big names."

If they didn't get killed first. So that was James Mattson, Dana thought. The name hadn't meant much to her when Len had spoken of him earlier, but on the evidence of this picture, she recalled meeting the man. She leaned closer, concentrating this time on the blurred figure of Mattson shaking hands with Boyd. His other arm was around the waist of his escort, but her face was turned from the camera.

A wave of nausea swept over her, so powerful that she felt as if she was about to faint.

"Boyd, you're as white as a sheet! What's the matter?"

"I can't explain now, but we've got to leave. God, I can't believe it! James Mattson, of all people! And that weekend on Atwell's yacht—"

"Careful, he's looking this way."

"I'm sure he saw it in my face, Dana. Look, we've got to get out of here and talk."

"Call for you, Mr. Connor." The records clerk, a long-suffering look on his face, was holding out the receiver to Len. "We're not supposed to tie up this phone."

Len ignored the rebuke, while Dana mentally cursed the inopportune interruption that had broken her train of thought. Try as she might, she couldn't recall what had happened after Boyd's frightened outburst that night. But even without the memory, she thought, it was obvious that both of them had met James Mattson on the *'Bama Belle,* and that somehow that meeting had spelled disaster.

"Gabe!" Len was beside them, his expression strained. "That was Walt upstairs—he says that a couple of punks are in the building, gunning for you. He tried to stop them and they knocked him down."

"Someone in your office will have told them where we are by now." Gabe looked around. "Is there an exit from here?"

"Yeah, it leads out to the employee parking lot."

"That's a fire exit, Mr. Connor. It's against the rules to use it unless there's a fire." The weedy young clerk pursed his lips disapprovingly and then gasped as Gabe strode around the counter and grabbed him by the lapels.

"Listen to me, buddy, and listen good. Any minute now two gorillas are going to come here looking for us. You tell them we left a while ago and you don't know where we were going, got it?"

"What's it worth to you?" the clerk blustered in weak defiance.

Gabe swore and sent him staggering back into his chair. He dug into his pocket and threw a bill onto the counter, his eyes locking onto the youth's shifting gaze. "There's a ten-spot. You'd better earn it, laddie."

"Someone's coming down the stairs!" Dana turned anxiously toward the exit as the sound of heavy shoes grew louder.

"We'll take my car, boyo. Come on!" Len darted through the maze of steel cabinets, Dana close on his heels. With one last glower at the clerk, Gabe followed, and none too soon. As they slipped out the back exit an adenoidal voice rose excitedly behind them.

"They went that way!"

"Son of a bitch! I knew I shouldn't have trusted that little weasel," Gabe ground out forcefully, as they ran through the poorly lit parking lot. "Let's see what this jalopy of yours can do, Len!"

Len had the motor racing and the clutch engaged. Even before Gabe had swung the door closed the ancient vehicle was rocketing wildly into the street.

"Just like that time we took the Halloran twins to that roadhouse, and the place got raided," Len yelled over his shoulder. "Remember that, Gabe? Jeez, trying to make the county line before the cops caught up to us, those crazy girls laughing their fool heads off and telling you to go faster."

"The Halloran twins?" Dana repeated. "Who were they?"

"You mean to say this son of a gun hasn't filled you in on all the details of his misbegotten youth?" Len winked. "Good thing you ran into me. The Halloran twins were—what would you call them, Gabe? Dancers? Showgirls? They worked at the Diamond Club. When they came on stage with those cute little feathered costumes—"

"Cut it out, Len." Gabe sounded embarrassed. He glanced over at her and shrugged weakly. "Just a couple of girls we knew way back when."

"Hmmm." Dana pursed her lips. "And I suppose you'll back him up on that, will you Len?"

"Hell, no. I'm a reporter. I'll spill the beans on him anytime you care to pump me." He laughed and looked in the rearview mirror. "No one's following us. We must have given them the slip. Where to?"

"Beats me, this whole town's getting too hot." Gabe looked at Dana. "Any ideas, sweetheart?"

"It's going to be hard finding a room at this time of night. After all the running around we've done today, do you think they'd suspect that we'd circle back to Hildie's?"

"Maybe not. And she's got some bouncers there that

could eat Townsend's boys for breakfast,'' he agreed thoughtfully. ''Len, head over to the Quorum Building and drop us off in the alley behind the Pelican Club. Then I think you should lay low for a couple of days, just in case.''

''When are you going to tell me what this is all about?'' The reporter sounded aggrieved.

''As soon as we find out ourselves, we'll give you an exclusive. Right now we're almost as much in the dark as you are.'' Gabe rubbed his jawline wearily.

''Maybe we should take it easy for a day or two,'' Dana suggested. She saw his incredulous look and pressed his arm warningly. Her voice was deliberately casual. ''Did you mean it when you said you could get us passes for the Academy Awards tomorrow night, Len?''

''Sure.'' He sounded surprised, but reached into his pocket and handed her a couple of stiff cardboard tickets. ''Show them at the door and if anyone asks, say you're with the paper. But what if Townsend's there?''

''He won't try anything in such a public place,'' she said breezily. ''You said yourself that James Mattson's attending, not to mention every star in Hollywood. Even if Townsend's got the backing of the mob, he still has to use some discretion.''

''Mattson.'' Len slapped his forehead in despair. ''I forgot all about that rewrite.''

''If he's as clean as you say he is, what's the point?'' Dana sounded bored. ''If you could dig up some dirt on him, then you'd have a story. Like, he cheats at cards. Or he's controlled by the mob.''

''Maybe he killed Atwell, honey.'' Gabe laughed for Len's benefit, but his eyes were on her as he spoke.

''You two should work up a comedy routine,'' Len growled. ''Just don't spread those kind of rumors tomorrow night, or his attorneys'll slap a slander suit on you.''

He slowed the car. "I'd love to listen to your crazy theories, but this is where you wanted to be dropped off. Anytime you need a chauffeur, Gabe, just call." He turned into the alleyway and stopped behind the club entrance. "Call a cab, I mean."

"Spoken like a true friend." Gabe grinned as they got out, and then he leaned through the window and gripped Len's shoulder. "Take my advice, boyo, and stay out of sight for a while. Don't go back to your apartment tonight."

"You stay healthy yourself, buddy. And your mysterious girlfriend." Len touched the brim of his hat in a mocking salute and drove away. Dana saw his taillights glow red at the end of the alley and then disappear as he turned onto the main street. The night, soft and black, seemed to enfold her and Gabe.

"You learned something from that newspaper photo. Please don't tell me we're up against the wealth and political influence of James Mattson." Gabe didn't sound hopeful as they headed for the Pelican's back entrance.

"I think that encounter between Boyd and Mattson at the charity ball was the trigger for the killings that followed," she said hesitantly. "But I don't know why. From what I can recall it seems that Mattson was on the yacht the weekend that Atwell was killed, and that when Boyd saw Mattson at the benefit he learned something that probably cost him his life."

"And now Townsend, who's head of security for Oval Studios and, according to Len, takes orders from the mob, is gunning for you. Which means that Mattson is tied in with that element."

Gabe jimmied the basement door of the Pelican Club as he had before, and they stepped into the dank subterranean hallway that led to the club. Dana shivered from the sudden coolness.

"No wonder they won't let up," she thought out loud. "Mattson's squeaky-clean image would be blown out of the water if it was known that he had any connection to the mob. And the fact that he was on Atwell's yacht that weekend must have been covered up too."

"He would have left as secretly as he boarded. Probably radioed his pilot to pick him up before you got back to harbor, but he wouldn't have gone to all this trouble just to hide his presence on the yacht." Gabe pressed the buzzer and looked at her grimly. "Most politicians wait until they get into office to get away with murder. Maybe the next governor of this state already did…"

HILDIE SHOWED NO SURPRISE at their unexpected appearance on her doorstep. She took one look at Dana's pale face and the harsh lines around Gabe's mouth, and led them to a spare bedroom in her personal quarters. As soon as they were alone, exhaustion hit Dana like a club, and while Gabe was in the washroom cleaning the scratches he'd received from the flying glass earlier that evening, she barely managed to strip off her clothes and tumble into bed before falling into oblivion.

Somewhere in the background of her dream, she heard Hildie's husky voice purring out an old torch song and the heartbreaking lyrics seeped into her subconscious, something about a one-man woman and a man that had gotten away. The throaty voice breathed the last line, and the words faded away. A wave of sadness and regret washed over Dana.

In her dream she was standing on a sidewalk, about to cross the street, when suddenly a crushing pain sent her staggering backward and she was falling, falling through space. The world around her was growing dark and flickering out to nothingness, but just before everything disappeared a man ran from the building behind her, anguish etched on his features and apprehension shadowing the piercing blue of his eyes. Then he was gone, and all she could feel was a cold so intense that she knew she must be dying, and a feeling of loss so deep that she welcomed the void.

Gabe had been trying to fit six feet two inches of exhausted Irishman onto the five-foot length of brocaded couch in Hildie's guest room when he heard the thin scream from the bed across the room. Barefoot, wearing only his pants and a pair of leather suspenders, he was beside Dana in a flash, his gun snatched up from the chair beside him, his eyes adjusting to the darkness instantaneously.

But the terror she was experiencing hadn't been created by an intruder, he realized a second later. It was in her own mind. Her body was curled defensively in a welter of ivory satin sheets; her hair was a damp tumble on the pillows. He laid his gun aside, switched on the rose-shaded bedside lamp and gently shook her awake.

She came to with a start, her eyes wide and staring, filled with a devastating sense of loss. Her gaze focused on Gabe and the pounding of her heart slowed, but the dream still held her in thrall. She raised her fingers to his face as if to reassure herself of his presence, touching the hard planes of his cheekbones, the unshaven line of his jaw.

"You were gone," she whispered. In the muted half-light she saw him shake his head in denial.

"No. I'm here, sweetheart. For as long as you need me, I'm here."

With the miasma of her nightmare still hanging over her, Dana finally let herself face the truth. He was the one, she thought. Her desperate denial of her feelings had been a futile attempt to protect herself from a replay of the pain she had felt when she'd lost him the first time, but she'd told Gabe that people couldn't be wrapped in cotton wool, and that held true for emotions too. Fate and time might separate them again, and if that happened she would have to deal with the searing loss of the man she loved, but tonight they were together. With so few memories, surely there was no harm in creating one now.

She held his eyes with hers and slowly pushed the satin sheets aside, the silky fabric moving like cool liquid over her thighs. Like a man compelled, his gaze moved from her face. She watched as he took in the swell of her breasts, inadequately concealed with a scrap of bra, the smoothness of her stomach, and the triangle of shell-pink lace panties.

God, she was more beautiful than he'd imagined, Gabe thought—and he'd imagined her countless times. But the reality was exquisite torture. She lay there like a seductively wrapped present, and he knew that the tiny ribbons at her hips and in the hollow between her breasts would give way with just one gentle tug. But for the first time in his life, he hesitated. Making love with her would seal his fate forever. She already had his heart, but after she left him—and he knew she eventually would—perhaps he'd be able to pick up the pieces and rebuild his life. Maybe he'd even learn to forget her one day. But not if he made love to her now. Then she'd own his very soul.

He pulled her toward him.

His mouth covered hers hungrily. Dana felt the muscles of his arms tighten like bands of steel, holding her a willing captive as his tongue explored her. His lips were hard and the unshaven shadow on his face was a thousand rough pinpricks, but all she was conscious of was the sweet heat of his mouth. He closed his teeth gently on her lower lip and ran his tongue along its trapped softness. His hands were buried in the weight of her hair.

"If this is all I'm ever going to have of you, let's make it last," he said huskily, his lips against her skin. His voice was silk over sandpaper and his eyes had darkened to an unfathomable midnight blue. "Pretend this night is forever."

She felt her hair being lifted from the nape of her neck. Leaving a kiss at the corner of her mouth, Gabe's lips moved deliberately to her ear and the sensitive skin behind it. Dana caught her breath as his tongue traced the delicate area, and she turned her head, almost unable to bear the sensation. Gently he brought her back.

"No, darlin'. This is just the beginning." He trailed a slow hand down her spine, slipping his fingers past the fragile barrier of her panties and cupping the peachlike curves waiting there. His hand moved farther, and lifted her slightly as he turned her over onto her front. Dana's fingers curled into the feathery fullness of the satin pillow.

"You taste like candy, sweetheart." As he spoke, Gabe lowered himself and bit softly at the back of her thigh. He moved higher, and to her other leg. "So good." His teeth nipped gently again and his hair stroked silkily between her thighs. Dana's breath caught in a gasp. His tongue flicked at the lace trim on her panties and she arched backward, presenting herself to his teasing mouth.

"Sweet darlin', I'm not a saint. Don't push me." His voice ragged, he pressed lightly on her silk-clad derriere, urging her back down to the bed. Then she felt the warmth of his breath at her hip and through half-closed eyes she saw him pulling the ridiculous beribboned bow of her panties with his teeth, his gaze gleaming wickedly as he saw her watching him.

"We O'Shaunessys never do anything the easy way. Or the fast way," he promised her. A dimple flashed in his tanned cheek and he bent his head to her other hip, this time dragging away the shell-pink scrap, no longer fastened around her. The material slid smoothly between Dana's legs, leaving her completely exposed to his gaze.

"You're the most perfect thing I've ever seen," Gabe whispered hoarsely. "Your skin is like velvet. Let me see everything, Dana honey. I need to see all of you."

It was as if she was in a trance, she thought. Her limbs were weightless, as if she was floating in a warm sea, and dreamlike, she turned onto her back. She drew one leg up a little, her knee bent, and in the lamplight she lazily pulled at the bow between her breasts, parting the lacy cups of her bra.

"This is all of me, Gabe. Is it what you want?" she asked. She hardly could believe that it was her, Dana Smith, saying the words. She'd always kept some part of herself under tight control, but she had no desire to control herself with him now. And he felt the same way, Dana saw. His lips were parted as he looked down through his eyelashes at her, and a pulse was beating hard at the side of his throat.

"All that I ever wanted." He could barely speak. Dear God, Gabe thought, he could barely draw breath. He felt like a drowning man going down for the third time, and as he brought his lips to the petal softness of her nipple, he let the waves of sensation carry him almost to the point of no return. But then he forced himself from her.

"Baby, don't look at me like that," he pleaded. Didn't she know what those liquid green eyes did to him? And her full bottom lip, swollen from his kisses, did she have to bite it like that? How was a man supposed to stay sane looking at all that lushness?

A man couldn't, Gabe told himself. So give in.

He held her hips, his fingers hard on their softness, and bent his head to the shadowed, honey-sweet delta between her legs, stroking her with the tip of his tongue as if he was coaxing nectar from a bloom. And Dana, all inhibition completely gone, felt champagne running through her, as each nerve ending in her body turned to a tiny, golden exploding bubble. Again and again his tongue flicked against the sensitive flowerlike bud, nestled like a gardenia in pink velvet. Again and again she felt the miniature explosions, building toward an overpowering excitement. She reached down for him, her nails scoring the tan of his shoulders.

She wanted to feel every square inch of him, Dana thought incoherently. With a frustrated motion, she pushed aside the supple leather of his suspenders.

He looked at her, his hair a careless tangle across black brows, his eyes a smoky, glazed blue. He saw what she wanted and without haste, he moved from her and stood beside the bed, shrugging out of the leather straps, and letting them hang loosely at his side. He started to unbutton his pants. But Dana's fingers were already completing the task, and he let her take over.

This was something she wanted to do herself, she thought. And Gabe seemed to know intuitively that to her, the act of undressing him was erotic in itself. She pushed his clothing over his hips and down the length of his legs to the floor, only letting her eyes travel upward again when she saw him step toward her.

He was all male. Gabe's legs were long and athletic, and in the subdued light from the lamp his skin had a burnished glow. As he moved she saw the powerful shift of muscles under his hide, like some big cat's, and if she allowed herself to lean forward a couple of inches, Dana knew she would feel that silky pelt against her lips. Below that flat stomach, from the dark thatch between those legs, was the final proof, if any was needed, of his complete masculinity.

"This is all of me, honey. Is it what you want?" His words were a teasing echo and one corner of his mouth lifted in a wry smile.

"All that I ever wanted," she breathed. With delicate

fingers she touched him where she had never touched any man before, and a shudder ran through his frame as if she had left a trail of liquid fire there. He started to lower himself to the bed, but then, with a visible effort, he stopped himself.

"You're sure this is what you want, Dana? You're not going to regret this tomorrow?" His body seemed carved from stone as he waited for her answer.

"Come to bed, O'Shaunessy," she said softly.

She felt the warmth of his overheated skin as he molded himself to her, and as his fingers twined in her hair she knew that she couldn't wait any longer. And neither could he. Her breath caught in an involuntary gasp as she felt him enter her, but when he paused she shook her head.

"Don't stop."

Her plea was barely above a whisper, but he heard. Slowly he resumed his possession of her, giving himself equally to her in the process. The room around them was a shadowy blur of light and dark through Dana's half-closed eyes; the only true reality was her awareness of him moving deeper and deeper into her, until she felt as if he was completely filling her.

"Sweetheart." Gabe's voice was a husky rasp. He raised himself higher, the muscles in his arms corded and slick with sweat. Taking his time, he withdrew slightly from her, and then filled her again. "I've wanted this for so long. I've dreamed about this." He thrust again, and her hips arched to meet his, striving to receive all of him.

"Is it…is it as good as you dreamed?" she gasped. She locked her fingers behind his back, pulling him toward her, feeling the fire they were creating licking at her.

"Better," he breathed. "Better. Tighter. And sweeter." He ground out the words like a man confessing his sins, punctuating each one with a steadily stronger thrust, Dana meeting him in increasing tempo.

She couldn't take much more, she thought incoherently. This was too good. This was too intense. She heard a low moaning sound and realized that it was coming from her own throat, a primitive cry for release, a wordless urging for Gabe to take her just that one last step into ecstasy. She was so close, she felt as if she was standing on the edge of a cliff poised to dive into the blue of a sea far, far below.

She felt him hard inside her and suddenly she was there, over the top and spiraling through an explosion of sensations, one after the other. Hot moistness bloomed deep within her and Dana knew that he was falling with her, both of them out of control. Convulsively she pressed her nails into the smooth flesh of his back, while incredible spasms racked her trembling body.

Through a haze, Gabe felt the pressure from her nails and welcomed it. It was as if she was marking him as hers alone, and that was what he wanted. From now on, he thought dazedly, he'd be no good for anyone else. He tightened his grip around her.

Losing her was going to rip his soul in two.

Chapter Eleven

"We're with the *Times*."

Gabe flashed their press passes carelessly at the door of the hotel and they were waved through into the lobby. On Hollywood Boulevard, down the street from the exuberant chinoiserie of Grauman's Chinese Theatre, the Roosevelt Hotel wasn't unfamiliar to Dana. It still stood in the 1990s; and in fact its Colonial Spanish decor had been carefully restored. But to see it tonight, packed with a galaxy of stars from the glittering age of Hollywood, was almost enough to lighten her somber mood.

Mink coats trailed casually from powdered shoulders, diamonds nestled in creamy cleavage, and platinum blond hair shimmered under the lights. A thin man, impeccable in evening dress and laughing with his companions, suddenly broke into a flurry of tap steps, his gleaming shoes striking the floor in a staccato rhythm, and Dana realized with a start that she was watching a young Fred Astaire give an impromptu performance.

But all she could think about was last night.

She'd come out of a troubled sleep early this morning with the memory of the previous night bittersweet in her mind and Gabe's arms still around her. As he felt her stir he'd brushed a kiss against the back of her neck. They'd made love a second time, a slow and sensuous consummation building to a climax so overpowering that she'd been able to blot out her heartache long enough to fall asleep again, but her dreams, fragmented and symbolic, had mirrored her confusion.

It had been a mistake to let herself fall in love with him when both of them had known it couldn't last. She glanced at him and saw he was watching her. As their gazes met, a shadow suddenly passed across the brilliant blue of his eyes, but his teeth gleamed whitely in a smile. He took her arm, and the warmth of his touch sent a frisson down her spine.

If she'd ever hoped that sleeping with the man might take the edge off this constant desire for him, Dana thought, she couldn't have been more wrong. He stood there, looking devastating in the stark black and white of his borrowed evening wear, and she felt her heart turn over. She'd only ever seen him in an old jacket and rumpled tie before, and his appeal had been potent enough then. But the crisp white of his shirt against the tan of his skin made him look like a raffish millionaire just back from a cruise, and the severe formality of the black suit only accentuated his magnetism.

"Keep an eye out for Mattson." Gabe forced himself to stop staring at Dana like a lovesick schoolboy and pretended to scan the crowd. If there was an award for "Most Beautiful," Dana would go home with an Oscar tonight, he decided. Even in slacks she'd been a knockout, but Hildie had lent her a dress that could hold its own with any of the expensive gowns here.

A deep green that reflected the color of her eyes, it molded itself to the lush curves of her body like a satin waterfall, with thin jeweled straps at the shoulders. They looked like fragile drops of water and matched the diamond clip that swept a burnished chestnut wave of her hair to one side.

That hair, Gabe thought. Last night it had spilled onto the pillow, glowing under the soft light like a flame. He'd wrapped it around his fingers, marveling at its silky texture and imprinting its faint fragrance onto his skin. She was everything he wanted. But if they cracked this case open tonight, he'd have to stand by and give an Oscar-winning performance of his own while he watched her walk away.

"It doesn't look as if he's here yet." Dana bent her head over the satin purse Hildie had provided, and pretended to fiddle with the clasp. She spoke in a low, nervous whisper. "What do we do now?"

Gabe looked blank for a moment, as if his thoughts had been far away. Then he grinned at her reassuringly. "We'll do the starstruck fan thing, that's what." He put his arm around her shoulder. "Just wander around and keep our eyes open. He's bound to show up before they start the awards presentation, and when he does, we'll make some excuse to talk to him. Mattson's a politician, he has to be sociable." He steered her through the crush of people.

Dana apologized as she brushed against a dark-haired man standing alone. He was scanning the newcomers as she was, but he turned and smiled her apology away, a deep dimple creasing his cheek. Then he caught sight of a slim blonde on the other side of the room and hurried off, the well-known one-sided grin infused with genuine warmth.

She stared after him in awe. *Clark Gable!* Clark Gable had smiled at her. She'd cried through *Gone With the Wind* at least six times. Who was he meeting? She craned her neck to catch a glimpse of his companion, and then sighed up happily at Gabe's puzzled expression.

"Carole Lombard. Gable and Lombard." There was pleased satisfaction in her voice.

He looked across the room and shook his head. "You've

got it all wrong, honey, those two aren't an item. Look, they're with other people."

She smiled a small, secret smile. "Then the affair's just beginning. But it turns into the most passionate Hollywood romance of all time, and in the end they get married. And I was here to see it."

Gabe laughed as her eyes misted over. "Hedda Hopper would love to have you on the payroll. You're the gossip columnist's dream come true. Do they live happily ever after?"

She watched as Gable and Lombard left the room with their escorts, and pain flared briefly in her eyes as she saw the vital, laughing blond beauty toss a veiled glance at the impossibly handsome man they called the King of Hollywood. "No. She dies in a plane crash and he never really gets over losing her."

A cloud passed over Gabe's features and his blue gaze followed the doomed couple unseeingly. Then he looked down at Dana and tipped her chin up. His eyes were dark with emotion and his voice was low and urgent. "But they had it for a while, didn't they? They were in love, and no matter what lousy trick fate played on them in the end, nobody could take that away. Even if you walked over there right now and told them what their futures hold, they'd probably figure it's worth it."

He wasn't talking about Gable and Lombard anymore, she knew. He was telling her how he felt. She nodded, unable to speak past the lump in her throat. He stared at her intensely for a long moment, and then smiled as if to lighten her mood.

"Just so you know, darlin'. Now, let's get ourselves a drink at the bar and start acting like investigators."

Academy Awards night in the 1930s wasn't the overblown extravaganza that it would later become, Dana thought, as she waited at a table for Gabe to bring back their drinks. It was more a casual gathering of friends and co-workers, like a yearly celebration of a small-town industry. Except that instead of secretaries and salesmen, the people around her were instantly recognizable all over the world.

"This glass is dirty!" A harsh, throaty voice rose in anger above the hum of conversation. Dana glanced over at the diamond-festooned woman with the bright red lipstick who was complaining to her companions. They looked resigned at her outburst, and only mildly embarrassed as she started to polish the glass with a handkerchief.

Joan Crawford. Obviously her mania for antiseptic cleanliness was already part of her personality. She probably carried a bottle of disinfectant in her purse, Dana thought in amusement. She was still smiling when she caught sight of a tall, distinguished-looking man enter the reception room with a raven-haired beauty on his arm. Her expression froze as she recognized James Mattson and the same fear that she had experienced when she'd seen him in the newspaper photo flooded through her. But this time it was much more powerful.

She felt like an iron band was tightening around her chest, constricting her breathing, and fearfully she waited for the now-familiar flashback to fill in the gaps of her memory. Just then, a crowd of people gathered around Mattson and his escort, and he was hidden from Dana's view. She immediately felt herself start to breathe again.

"Don't tell me. I saw him too. Here, drink this." Gabe was beside her, pressing a glass of brandy into her hand. He watched her take a faltering sip, the worried look only leaving his face when he saw a faint flush of color reappear on her cheeks.

"The bastard must be feeling pretty confident about his standings in the polls, he's even brought his mistress out tonight. Did you remember anything?'' he asked in a whisper.

"Nothing. But when I saw him I was terrified, Gabe. Terrified!'' Her fingers tightened on the stem of the glass and she tried in vain to see past the crowd to where Mattson was standing. "I'm sure I must have seen him kill Atwell. Why else would I react to him this way?''

"I think you're right. But we have to find out for sure.'' A muscle twitched in his jaw. "Are you up to this, sweetheart? I'm starting to get a real bad feeling.''

She drained the rest of her brandy and grimaced. "I have to get close enough to him to trigger my memory. Let's do it.'' She stood up, straightened her shoulders defiantly, and headed for the group of people surrounding the politician with Gabe a protective step behind her.

As they drew closer, her senses seemed to sharpen. The rich smoke from a Cuban cigar wafted from Mattson's circle, and a faint hint of bay rum cologne hung in the air. A woman gave a tinkling, flirtatious laugh and moved past Dana, trailing a cloud of Shalimar perfume. Expensive scents, Dana thought, wrinkling her nose. The smell of power and privilege. She had to be crazy, thinking she could take on a man like Mattson and win.

Crazy like Joe Leung, standing up for everything he loved against impossible odds.

Dana pushed her way into the circle, her hands clenched damply around her satin purse.

"Don't get me started on the dam project! We'll be here all night!'' Mattson's voice was deep and well modulated. His accent was the product of upper-echelon private schools, but the rueful self-mockery in his words made him immediately likeable. A man of the people, she thought with a spurt of anger. She felt Gabe standing reassuringly behind her and the very fact of his presence helped calm her.

"But I'm just here as a fan of the silver screen, so let's give politics a night off. Why don't we escort these lovely ladies into the other room and take our seats?" No actor here had his audience more in the palm of his hand than the charmingly manipulative Mattson. Even his oblique mention of the mistress he usually kept discreetly hidden away raised no eyebrows. His velvety suggestion might have been a royal command, and as the chattering crowd around him began to break up, Dana saw her chance.

"Mr. Mattson." She felt as if her smile was painted on, but she forced a note of enthusiasm into her voice. "I've heard so much about you, I just wanted to shake your hand. I'm sure your political career will be—"

She faltered as Mattson turned the full voltage of his professional persona onto her. He had the politician's trick of making the person to whom he was talking feel as if he or she was the only one in the room, and even sensing how dangerous he was, she felt her antagonism waver as she looked him full in the face. His hair was lightly touched with silver at the temples, and his eyes were a steady, clear gray. The only feature that marred the image of trustworthy leadership was his mouth. There was a weak, disconsolate droop to the corners of his lips, but even as Dana noticed this he smiled warmly at her and extended his hand. She held out her own.

"I'm sure your political career will be all you deserve," she ended lamely. Their hands met.

Nothing happened.

Come on, dammit! You know something about this man, let yourself remember what it is!

His handshake was firm, as if she was a valued friend that he hadn't seen for a while, and with a start Dana realized that she not only hadn't received a flashback, but that she wasn't even experiencing the wave of revulsion that he had earlier caused in her. What was happening?

"All I deserve! My God, that sounds ominous," Mattson chuckled. He turned to an aide beside him. "Pete, we should put this pretty young lady on the payroll. She'd soon have the office staff toeing the line!" He shook his head in amusement and then sobered. "But seriously, many thanks for your good wishes. It's been a pleasure meeting you."

Her hand was freed and the powerful magnet of his gaze released her as he turned away. Numb and empty, Dana watched him as he headed for the other room where the presentations had begun.

"Well?" Gabe sounded puzzled. "Did you remember him killing Atwell?"

"No." The single word came out in a flat monotone, and she hurried blindly past him to the sanctuary of their table. The room was empty now except for a few waiters, and even they were clustered around the doorway to catch a glimpse of the awards proceedings. She sat down and covered her face with her hands.

"How could I have been so wrong? When I first saw him enter, I was so sure! I even told myself that he terrified me." She raised glistening eyes to Gabe. "But just now I stood there, actually holding his hand, and all I saw was a practiced politician, delivering smooth lines and platitudes. I even found myself admiring his technique!"

"Perhaps if you saw him again," Gabe suggested, a worried frown creasing his brow.

"I felt nothing, don't you understand? The man meant nothing to me and he had nothing to do with the murder. For heaven's sake, Gabe, I'm beginning to understand how these flashbacks work. If I'd seen him do something as horrific as kill a man, meeting him would bring it all back to me." Her shoulders slumped in despair. "I've led you on a wild-goose chase. Even now the real killer could be waiting for us somewhere."

"So we made a mistake. But we must be on the right track. Townsend's interest in us proves that." He touched her hair with a tender finger. "It's not the end of the world. We'll go back to Hildie's and try to figure out where we went wrong. Come on." He brushed his knuckles lightly against her chin. "Where's the fighting spirit that took out Big Eddie in one round?"

"Don't patronize me, Gabe!" She jerked her face away from his hand, frustration and fear causing her to lash out. "That just makes me wish I was back in the future, where women aren't constantly being patted on the head and treated like children."

"I'm not treating you like a child, sweetheart. But tonight's been pretty nerve-racking for you and I just want to take care of—"

She cut him off. "I don't need to be taken care of! I'm used to having a career, my own apartment, people I work with who respect me! When I go out with a man, I pay my half of the check, and if an affair doesn't work out, we shake hands and go our separate ways in a civilized, adult manner. Why can't it be like that with you?"

Gabe's eyes were very blue, his expression was very still, and Dana knew she had just thrown away the most valuable thing she possessed.

He pushed back his chair and rose to his feet. "Sure and I'm only a foolish Irish romantic, darlin'," he said, his brogue exaggerated. "What more can you expect from a man in this primitive time?"

"Gabe, I didn't mean it—"

"Oh, you meant every word. That's the real reason you don't want to stay in this time, isn't it, Dana? Not because your life in the future was so much fuller. But because it was empty. You didn't allow anyone to intrude on your emotions, not even your friends." He looked suddenly weary. "No wonder you're so frantic to get back to your other life. I'm the one man you couldn't push away."

Hot tears prickled behind her eyelids, but she blinked them back angrily. "That's not true. I never felt my life was empty."

"Neither did I, till I met you." His gaze held hers for a long moment, and then he shrugged. "Let's go."

She'd lost him. From the finality of his tone, Dana knew that nothing she could say would wipe out the words she'd hurt him with. His accusations rang in her ears, and to her horror she felt the tears spill over. She averted her face.

"I'll meet you in the lobby. I need—I need to fix my makeup." It took every ounce of pride she had to keep her voice steady, but she managed it. Pride was all she had left, she thought dismally. Head held high, she walked away from him and with every step she took she felt the crack in her heart break open wider.

The pink-and-gold powder room was softly lit, but even the most flattering light couldn't disguise the fact that she'd been crying. She had to get herself under control before she faced him again. Taking a seat at the long bank of mirrors, she opened her purse. He was completely wrong about her, she thought, powdering the worst of the tear stains with a trembling hand. She loved him, but it was impossible for her to stay here. She *had* to get back to the life she built for herself. It was safe. It was orderly. And no one there had the power to make her feel like this.

The door behind her swung open and a woman walked in, but Dana didn't look up. Gabe had said her life was empty; but at least her emotions weren't on a constant roller coaster the way they were now. She'd never felt this much pain before. If this was love, she just couldn't live with it.

But never before had she felt the ecstasy that she'd experienced with Gabe. And if that was love, could she live without it?

"Sorry."

With a start, she realized that the woman standing at the mirror beside her had spoken. A gold lipstick case rolled off the counter into her lap and she picked it up automatically, handing it back with a mechanical smile, her mind still on Gabe.

In the mirror, her eyes met those of the raven-haired beauty she had last seen entering the room with James Mattson, and Dana's world suddenly went dark with remembered terror.

The cool night air lifted the strands of Dana's hair and she sat back in the deck chair, her legs curled up under her. A few hours ago the yacht had been blazing with lights and the latest Cole Porter tunes had been blaring full volume from the gramophone, but now everyone had gone to bed. Everyone except for William Atwell and the mysterious James Mattson. They'd been closeted in Atwell's office since Mattson had arrived, and even his method of arrival had seemed furtive.

Dana had seen the floatplane land, earlier this evening. By that time they were well out to sea and everyone else was dressing for dinner, but after her conversation with Boyd, she'd gone up on deck to watch the sunset. Pontoons glistening, the plane had bobbed gently a few feet from the yacht, while Mattson and his beautiful companion were helped aboard. Atwell had hustled them below, and with a roar, the plane had lifted from the water and flown off. Since then, Mattson and the woman hadn't been seen.

Boyd had advised her to keep quiet about the new arrivals. "Atwell's got heavy connections with organized crime, Dana. This whole party was probably set up as a cover to meet with Mattson, and the mob doesn't like it when people find out their secrets. Keep your mouth shut, for your own sake.''

At least the little mystery had kept her from dwelling on her own problems, but finally she'd had to confront them. She huddled deeper into the deck chair. Although nothing had happened between her and Boyd, she still felt soiled and ashamed. Better to leave Hollywood and all her dreams behind than end up in a situation like this again.

Behind her, the teak decking creaked as someone walked over to the railing. She sank back, hoping she was out of sight. Right now, all she wanted was to be alone to think. A match flared, and in the sudden yellow light a man's face was illuminated for a brief second. Then the tiny flame died, leaving only the dim red light from the bow to pierce the soft night.

Who was he? He hadn't been on board earlier. She had a swift impression of well-defined features, a slim and supple build clad in dark sweater and pants. Before she could puzzle it out any further, heavy footsteps ascended the stairs to the deck and from her vantage point, she saw the slim man look about swiftly, obviously hoping for an escape route.

But there was none. William Atwell paused unsteadily at the top of the stairs and looked at the stranger.

"Who the hell are you? What are you doing on my boat?"

Atwell's speech was slurred; his attitude belligerent, and she realized that his meeting with Mattson must have been well fueled with alcohol. She wanted to leave, but she had no desire to catch Atwell's drunken eye. She peered around the corner of her chair and watched the director lurch up to the other man.

"Answer me! Who let you on board?"

Casually, the slim figure pitched his cigarette into the water far below, its red tip arcing through the dark. Then *he turned to face Atwell, bending close to him and speaking in a low murmur. It was an innocuous enough gesture, and that made the director's reaction all the more startling.*

Staggering back from the stranger, Atwell let out a harsh, shocked laugh and swore loudly, his choice of phrase raw and insulting. The other man let out an angry breath, and then, apparently dismissing his opponent as beneath contempt, tried to walk past him to the stairs. Atwell grabbed him by the arm.

"Don't walk away from me! Do you realize that I could destroy you? That's right, one telephone call and both of you would be finished. Broken!" He laughed again. "Yeah, that stopped you. Now, let's go below and reopen negotiations. I don't think my offer will be turned down this time."

"And of course you'd keep the secret. Somehow I just can't believe that." The stranger's voice was light and clear, and as steady as if he was discussing the weather.

Then, with her hands on her mouth to hold back a scream, she saw him reach smoothly into his trouser pocket, take out a gun, and shoot William Atwell point-blank in the chest.

Chapter Twelve

"Are you ill?"

Dana's eyes flew open. It took a moment to recall where she was—in the powder room at the Roosevelt Hotel with the exquisite oval face of Mattson's mistress bending over her. She struggled to regain some semblance of composure, but her mind was racing. For some reason this last flashback had been delayed, she thought, since her meeting with Mattson must have triggered it. That *had* to mean he'd been involved in the murder and she remembered that Atwell had thought there was some connection between the politician and the stranger on deck. What had happened after the shooting?

Despite persistent rumors of murder, the official story had eventually been that Atwell had fallen overboard, and in fact, what remained of his body had been found weeks later. How had the murderer managed to heave his heavy-set victim over the railings alone?

He hadn't. The rest of the scene came back to her, crystal clear. She'd been frozen into immobility in the deck chair, and had heard the sharp intake of the murderer's breath when a footfall sounded on the stairs. The next moment she'd heard James Mattson's shocked voice as he almost stumbled over the corpse. From then on, the conversation was conducted in low whispers, and the next thing she'd heard was a splash as Atwell's body met the water. Mattson and the other man had gone hurriedly below.

It was funny, Dana thought slowly. She'd expected to be excited over regaining this memory, this vital key to the mystery she'd been trying to solve. But her first reaction had been to rush and tell Gabe what she'd found out, and after their argument, she didn't feel she had the right to ask him for help anymore. Everything faded into insignificance compared to the desolation that swept over her as she tried to imagine a life without him—even the life in the future that she'd thought she wanted.

It was as if a sudden light had been switched on, chasing away all the shadows and doubts in her mind and showing her the path she wanted to take. She was so lost in her thoughts that it came as a shock to see that the woman was still standing beside her, puzzled concern on her delicate features.

"Oh—it's nothing. Just an attack of dizziness," Dana answered belatedly, feeling sudden pity for the unfortunate beauty. With her protector exposed as an accessory to murder, what would the future hold for her? The James Mattsons of this world always seemed to leave a string of innocent victims, she reflected somberly.

Even the thought of him had the power to affect her. The oppressive fear that she had felt earlier had returned and she stood up abruptly. She realized that her sudden departure would appear rude, but she needed to terminate this incongruous and uncomfortable conversation with Mattson's mistress. She had to get out of here. She had to find Gabe.

As she walked the few feet to the door, she felt the other woman's eyes following her. No wonder, Dana thought shakily, as she caught a glimpse of her own face in the mirror. She looked as if she'd seen a ghost, and her behavior had been erratic. She'd probably frightened the poor woman. Even as the door closed behind Dana, she saw the other woman still standing in the middle of the room, as motionless as a porcelain doll. Through some trick in the placement of the powder room mirrors, it seemed as if there were two of her reflected there; both beautiful, both enigmatic, both staring straight at Dana.

Dana shivered as her high heels echoed across the expanse of marble floor toward the lobby, where Gabe would be waiting. The muted sound of applause drifted from the room where the awards presentation was under way, but aside from that the hotel could have been empty. Everyone, from the manager to the lowliest bellhop, had obviously deserted his post to watch the proceedings. She hastened her stride, but the clinging dress and fragile heels made walking difficult.

"Miss Torrence!"

In the empty reception room the light, clear voice rang out from behind her. Her first reaction was one of impatience as she turned and saw that Mattson's mistress, obviously still worried about her, had followed her out of the powder room. Reluctantly Dana halted, irritated by the delay but not wanting to appear rude. After all, she thought in resignation, the woman was just being kind.

How did she know my name?

The question shrieked through her mind as suddenly as an alarm bell being set off. Dana felt the skin on the back of her hands tingle unpleasantly, her muscles tightened as if to ready themselves for flight, and her heart skipped a beat. How had Mattson's mistress known her name? Even the politician himself hadn't shown a flicker of recognition when they'd met. No, the last time she'd gone under the name of Torrence had been five years ago, when all this had started. The woman knew that she'd been one of the passengers on the *'Bama Belle.*

The only passenger, aside from the mob-tainted politi-cian, his mistress and the unknown murderer that he'd helped, who was still alive and a threat.

Dana raised her eyes to the fixed gaze of the approach-ing woman and, without surprise, saw her take a small but lethal-looking gun from her sequined scarlet evening bag. Dark hair floating softly around her shoulders, she let the purse drop to the floor and kicked it carelessly aside with the tip of a satin shoe as she walked steadily closer. The soft ivory hands with their brilliant red nails looked in-congruous against the blued metal of the weapon, but as her perfectly shaped lips curved into a parody of a smile, Dana realized that underneath all the feminine trappings was a determined killer.

"Gabe!"

Even as she screamed out his name, a wave of thun-derous applause rose from the adjoining room, drowning her out.

"No one can hear you, Miss Torrence. This isn't the movies, you know." Pale fingers tightened on the trigger of the gun. "The heroine doesn't get saved in the last scene."

"If this isn't the movies," Dana croaked, "then I'm not going to make your day."

A brief flicker of confusion passed across the other woman's face, and Dana took advantage of her momentary distraction. With a snap of her wrist she skimmed her own purse across the remaining distance between them.

The gun made a curiously flat popping sound as it went off, but Dana was already running toward her one chance of escape. Discreetly hidden behind a potted palm was an exit door and she veered frantically toward it, praying that it was unlocked. Her shaking hands twisted at the knob and she emitted a thankful gasp when she felt it open. She stumbled through the doorway, and stopped.

The small, secluded garden that she found herself in was completely surrounded by a high brick wall. She was trapped.

"How convenient." The brunette closed the door behind her, the red of her dress no longer a blazing scarlet. The garden was dimly lit with romantic little fairy globes, glowing in the branches of the Japanese plum trees, and the faint light seemed to drain all color from the woman's clothing. Dana took a step backward.

"You're a very intelligent woman—more intelligent than I gave you credit for. You know there's no way out of here, Miss Torrence. This is where it all ends."

Keep her talking, Dana thought. Gabe would be wondering where she was by now, and if she could just buy herself a little time she might still get out of this alive. She saw the gun glint in the woman's hand.

"How much do you know about the man you're in love with?" she asked, trying to keep the tremor from her voice. "Do you know how many people he's had killed to keep the secret of his involvement in William Atwell's murder?"

"*His* involvement in—" The dark eyes widened, and then the woman recovered. "Where were you that night on the yacht?"

"On deck. I saw the whole thing, including James Mattson helping the man who murdered Atwell throw the body overboard. Why did he do it? What hold did the murderer have over him?"

The pale face looked away, and her voice softened. "The person who murdered William Atwell did it to save James. They're very old friends." She was silent for a moment.

"You and Mattson left in his private plane before the yacht reached harbor, didn't you?" prompted Dana. As she spoke, she thought she heard a muffled noise from the other side of the wall and hope flared in her. Was it Gabe? Was he just a few feet away from her? She prayed that Mattson's mistress hadn't heard it too.

"Yes. All three of us left the same way we came, on the plane."

She was lying, Dana thought. Mattson and his mistress had arrived alone.

"Arthur Berlin owed James a favor, and he promised that the police would never know we'd even been on board. Aside from Atwell, he was the only one who knew about the secret meeting that weekend. But he was always a weak link in the chain. It was better that he died."

Something in the careless tone alerted Dana. "It wasn't Mattson who authorized those killings, was it?" she thought out loud. "It was you!"

The woman laughed lightly. "You've guessed my secret, Miss Torrence. Yes, I told James's business associates to tie up all the loose ends. He was naive enough to think that Berlin wouldn't talk, but I didn't want to take the chance of his name being linked with what the papers were calling the "Murder Yacht." That would have ruined his career, and I couldn't let that happen. James Mattson is going to be the president of this country some day." Her voice rang with pride and Dana recoiled.

"How was Boyd Davis a threat to that plan? Why did you have him killed?"

The woman's face changed in the uncertain light, the high cheekbones becoming more prominent and the mouth a grim line. Like a film run out of sequence, in her mind Dana again saw the murder of William Atwell, but she forced the horrific memory aside to concentrate on what she was hearing.

"Boyd was the greatest threat of all. He knew much more than you did, Miss Torrence." She laughed, but the sound had no humor in it. "What a nightmare it was at the Cocoanut Grove when I met the two of you—an old friend and a new enemy!''

"Boyd knew you? And that made him dangerous to you…" Dana's voice trailed off as she tried desperately to recall what Boyd had told her the night before he died. The memory stayed stubbornly out of reach.

From the hotel came the muted sound of applause and cheering, audible even in the secluded garden. Mattson's mistress cocked her head. "They must have announced the winner for Best Picture. Too bad you'll never know which one won.'' She raised the gun.

A movement from the top of the brick wall caught Dana's eye, but she resolutely kept her gaze on the woman facing her. "Oh, I know what won,'' she babbled frantically. "*It Happened One Night* with Claudette Colbert and Gable. Have you seen it? I love the scene at the end when—watch out, Gabe!''

Mattson's mistress had whirled with feline speed, sensing that something was wrong, just as Gabe jumped lightly from the top of the wall to the ground. He covered her with his own gun.

"I've never killed a woman and I don't want to start now, lady. Drop it.'' The woman seemed to sag in defeat, and she let the hand holding the gun drop to her side. Gabe's voice softened. "I don't know what Mattson told you, but we're not the bad guys here, he is. Give me the gun and we'll let you walk away. It's him we want, not you.''

"Don't trust her, Gabe! *She's* the one who arranged all the killings—''

Dana's warning came too late. Reaching over for the woman's gun, he let his guard drop for a fatal second, and that was all the brunette needed. The gun jumped in her hand, a flash of blue sparked in the dark garden, and Gabe was flung backward.

He fell to the ground.

"No! Dear God, no!" Half screaming, half sobbing a denial, Dana stumbled to his side and dropped to her knees. "Gabe! Gabe, say something!" As she reached for him his jacket fell open, revealing a dark stain spreading rapidly on his white shirt-front.

"Oh, no." Dana drew back, her words a horrified whisper. She took in the unnatural pallor of his skin, the awkward angle of his limbs. An unbearable pain lanced through her. "*No!* You can't leave me, you can't!"

It couldn't end this way. Not after all they'd been through, not after they'd found each other again. Time had proved to be no barrier to their love. How could death triumph now?

But even as she pleaded with him her heart felt like it was being torn in two. He was gone. She'd lost him. And he'd died without knowing the most important thing of all. Tears blinded her as she cradled his head on her lap.

"I wasn't going back, Gabe. If you can hear me, I want you to know that. I couldn't have, darling." Her voice was a broken whisper. "I couldn't have lived without you—I *can't* live without you!"

"I'm sorry." The woman behind her spoke.

Dana stroked a strand of Gabe's hair from his forehead. The woman's words barely penetrated her consciousness.

"You loved him, didn't you? You would have done anything, sacrificed everything, to keep him with you. Perhaps you can understand why I've done the things I did. Why I have to do this one last thing for the man I love." She gestured with the gun. "Get up. I want it to look like a lovers' quarrel. Get up, I said!"

Slowly Dana got to her feet, swaying slightly, her eyes still on Gabe. What did it matter? Her life had ended a few minutes ago. Perhaps she could try to make another run for it, but she didn't really have a chance and she was tired of running away. Besides, there was no one to run to anymore.

Mattson's mistress raised the gun and started to pull the trigger.

"No, Olivia! No more!"

The explosion was deafening in the enclosed space. The brunette staggered backward a step, her hand to her breast and her unfired gun falling to the grass. Slowly she turned her head and looked with stunned recognition at the man who stood in the doorway of the hotel.

"James." Her beautiful eyes were wide and perplexed, as if she was glimpsing some mystery that was beyond human comprehension. "But I did it for you..."

Her head slumped suddenly sideways on the swanlike neck and she pitched forward at his feet. The glorious raven hair slipped sideways from her head, revealing a close-cropped cut underneath. Suddenly, in her mind, Dana heard Boyd's voice.

Olivia Hunt! I lived in the same rooming house as him in New York, when he was Oliver Dushane, working the boys' bars as a female impersonator. They were crazy about him there, and then one day he just vanished. The rumor was he'd finally fallen in love with someone and left town. Don't you see, Dana? He was the man you saw murder William Atwell! And I'm sure he recognized me just now!

Boyd's last revelation finally came back to Dana as the final piece of the puzzle fell smoothly into place.

"So that was the big secret," she said slowly. "The American public might accept you having a mistress. But not a male lover. Atwell found out that night on the yacht, didn't he?"

Mattson nodded, his eyes fixed despairingly on the crumpled body at his feet, the heavy pistol by his side.

The silver at his temples was a dull gray in the dim light, and he suddenly looked much older.

"Yes. Olivia—I never called him Oliver—took a stupid chance by going up on deck like that. When Atwell realized who he was he called him some terrible things. Vile!" He shook his head. "Atwell was a front man for the mob, and they'd been trying to get their claws into me for some time. I'd told him there was no deal, but of course after the murder I had to knuckle under to those gangsters. Ironic, isn't it?"

"Yeah, it's ironic, pal. Tell that to the dead tea-shop owner and his girl down in Chinatown. Tell Boyd Davis and the rest of them that it was just irony that killed them."

Gabe, sweat matting the tangled hair on his brow, got unsteadily to his feet, bracing himself against the garden wall for support. His gun was leveled on Mattson. "Your friend said you didn't know anything about the killings, but I think you knew and closed your eyes to it all. That's not irony, that's taking the coward's way out."

Dana stood rooted on the spot, hardly daring to believe that Gabe was alive. Then the stunned lassitude fell away from her and she flew to him, laughing and crying at the same time.

"How—oh, you lay there so still, you were bleeding so badly—you'll never know what I went through when I saw you and thought—oh, Gabe, I thought I'd lost you forever!"

She knew she was making no sense, but he seemed to understand. His free arm went around her and they held each other tightly.

"Your chest!" She drew away in consternation. "You're still bleeding. It *is* bad, isn't it?"

"I'm all right, sweetheart. Just a flesh wound, that's why it bled so much. Remember telling me that I should stop smoking?" He grinned wickedly at her. "I'm trying, honey. But it saved my life tonight.'' He reached into the breast pocket of his bullet-torn jacket and pulled out a badly dented steel cigarette case. ''Must have just skidded off this and plowed through the top layer of skin. It was like getting a punch to the heart, and I lost consciousness for a few minutes.''

''You must be the private investigator,'' Mattson said suddenly. ''The one they accused of murder.'' Gabe's eyes narrowed and the politician averted his gaze. ''You were right. Olivia gave the orders, but I knew. She met with a man called Townsend, a mob flunky. He reported to her by telephone, and I listened in on the extension.

''She wanted Miss Torrence watched in case Boyd Davis had told her what he knew, and if it looked as if she was about to go to the authorities, Townsend was to kill her. But it was even easier than that. Miss Torrence went to the newspaper instead. Unluckily for her, the reporter she spilled the story to was on the mob's payroll. Townsend said that framing the Irish detective for the Torrence murder would make everyone happy, because you'd already stirred up a lot of trouble when your father was killed. I—I told myself there was nothing I could do to stop it.''

''But you stopped it tonight,'' Dana said. ''Why?''

''When we spoke earlier I didn't know who you were at first,'' he said heavily. ''Then when I joined Olivia in the presentation room, I remembered you from that night at the Grove, and I must have shown how upset I was. When she asked me what the matter was, I foolishly told her. A few minutes later, she excused herself and left her seat.'' A look of shame crossed the patrician features. ''I sat there, applauding in all the right places, smiling at people, and all the time I knew that she was going to kill you. The other times, I could pretend to myself it was out of my hands, but this time I knew I had a chance to stop it.''

He looked at them both, and then bent down to the still body and touched the full lips with a gentle finger. "It had to end, my love. Forgive me."

"We're turning you over to the police," Gabe said. "You know that, don't you?"

"Of course. But if I could just have a minute alone here?" His voice was ragged with pain. "Please. To say goodbye."

Gabe looked around the tiny walled garden. "Sure. We'll be just inside." He took Dana's arm and made for the door.

"But he's still got the gun!" she protested in a low voice.

He nodded curtly and hurried her up the path. "That's right. He's still got the gun."

"But—" She felt herself being hustled through the door into the bright lights of the hotel. The potted palm tree shielded them from the crowd of people that was starting to drift, laughing and talking, from the presentation room. Gabe glanced down at his shirtfront and hastily buttoned his jacket, obscuring the bloodstains on his shirt.

"We look like hell, but that can't be helped. Come on, Dana, let's get out of here before—" They were already several feet from the door and heading toward the lobby when the gunshot rang out, but Gabe didn't break stride. "Don't look back, darlin'. Straight through to the lobby, and then we're home free."

"But you knew! You knew what he intended to do and you didn't stop him!" Startled faces had turned toward the sound in the garden, and out of the corner of her eye Dana saw one of Mattson's aides heading for the door at a trot, his hand reaching inside his jacket. But her gaze was fixed on the grim face of the man beside her.

"I owed him for saving your life, sweetheart. This was my way of repaying him." Gabe stopped suddenly, and swung her close to him, ignoring the excited voices around them as people began to realize that something terrible had happened. His breath was warm against her hair and his arms held her tightly.

"Sure I knew he wanted to kill himself. Think what a circus his life would have been if he'd lived. The newspapers, the scandal, the humiliation! The great love of his life, a foul joke for every two-bit comedian. Maybe he deserved it, but I couldn't do it to him."

"He always referred to Olivia as a female. I think he saw him that way," Dana said slowly. "You did the right thing, Gabe." She lifted her face to his. "How did you know I was in the garden?"

"I came looking for you just in time to see Olivia going out there with a gun. But I didn't want to charge in there after him and scare him into shooting you. Don't forget, I still thought he was just some poor dame who didn't know the whole score. Boy, was I wrong." His eyes darkened at the memory.

"I underestimated him too," Dana said. "I kept thinking that it was Mattson who terrified me, but the fear only came when he was with Olivia. Boyd was the only one who knew how dangerous Olivia was. That night at the Cocoanut Grove he told me everything, and when he was killed the next day, I decided to talk to the press."

"The meeting you asked me to keep from Townsend." Gabe nodded thoughtfully. "Too bad you picked the wrong reporter."

"I thought I'd lost you on the way to the newspaper office, but when I came out I saw you'd managed to follow me. That's why I went to your office." She swallowed nervously. "But that's not the important thing right now. Gabe, about what I said earlier—"

"O'Shaunessy!" The dapper figure in the nipped-in suit strolled casually up to them and jerked his head over his shoulder at the crowd. "Little excitement in the moonlight, huh? Mattson's dead, I hear. Suicide-murder, with his very strange girlfriend lying out there beside him."

"'Lo, Frankie. Wish I could say I was glad to see you," Gabe replied. His grip on Dana tightened protectively.

"Why not? I always liked you, Gabe. And with Mattson dead, I got no business with you now." He shrugged. "The contract's off. I'll pass the word."

Gabe gave the other man a hard stare. Then Dana felt him relax. "Thanks, Frankie. And I'll give you this for free. Tonight was just the tip of the iceberg. Once they start digging into Mattson's death, Townsend's big-shot friends are going to cut their losses and run, so it could be a good idea to get a head start."

The gangster looked thoughtful. "I figured that might be the way it was, but it's good to know for sure. See you around sometime, Irish." He grinned, showing pointed teeth. "Maybe you and Slugger there'll invite me to your wedding." Hands in his pockets, he walked into the crowd, disappearing almost immediately.

"Slugger!" Dana glared indignantly after him.

"I get the feeling that side-of-beef story has ended Big Eddie's career," Gabe gave a faint smile, then shrugged. "Well, where to, Slugger? I guess we should head over to the Quorum Building. No reason not to, now." His voice cracked on the last few words.

"He's *not* coming to our wedding, Gabe, and that's final."

He wasn't listening. "About what I said earlier—I was way out of line. It sounds like you're going back to a great life, sweetheart. I wish you luck on that movie you're making."

"But you can invite Len. I want to know more about those Halloran twins—those showgirls you wouldn't let him tell me about," Dana added.

"You'll probably end up with an Oscar." His grin was a weak imitation of the real thing. "Best Picture for nineteen-ninety—what was that about the Halloran twins?" His head jerked up and he stared at her.

"I want to know all about them before we get married. A girl doesn't like to think her husband's keeping secrets from her."

"Married? Husband? What—" Gabe's eyes were blue fire. "So help me, Dana, give it to me straight. Are you staying with me?"

She sobered. "You're the one I want to be with, whatever year it is." Her voice was soft and suddenly uncertain. "Unless you've changed your mind."

"You've been the woman for me since I first met you." He looked down at her, his heart in his eyes. "That never changed. It never will."

Standing there in the middle of the lobby of the Roosevelt Hotel, surrounded by the cream of Hollywood, Gabe tipped her head back and brought his mouth down on hers. His kiss was sweet and full of promise. The faint sounds of an orchestra drifted into the lobby, and Dana dreamily recognized the song she'd heard last night, the one that Hildie's voice had invested with such heartache and loss.

"The Man That Got Away"—an old Gershwin and Arlen tune. How inappropriate now, she thought happily. As her fingers spread wide on the back of his neck, she felt the sweetness of their embrace change to something more urgent, less controllable. They both moved apart at the same time.

"Let's go home, Slugger," Gabe said shakily.

Home, Dana thought. It wasn't a time or a place. It was the man she loved. This man.

She looked at him and smiled. "You read my mind, Irish."

Epilogue

"Relax, Sebastian. The twins aren't due for another two weeks." Edwina Hart's well-bred English whisper held a hint of amused exasperation. "They're not going to pop out right in the middle of your acceptance speech."

Her husband looked terrified at the prospect, and smiled weakly. "It might not be such a bad idea. I'm sure the audience would appreciate any method of shortening the speeches." He gripped her hand nervously as the nominees for Best Picture were announced, but suddenly Sebastian Hart's mind was miles away from the Dorothy Chandler Pavilion.

Barbara Walters had interviewed him earlier that day for one of her famous pre-Oscar specials. With her usual perceptiveness, she'd gone straight to the subject of Dana.

"You've won before, for *War Story,* your Vietnam film. Your work is well received at Cannes, year after year. And *Scarlet Street* has been hailed by the critics as a truly masterful film. So why, when you've already achieved such success, is it so important to you to win the Oscar this year?" She'd leaned forward, her eyes full of sympathetic understanding. "Or are you really winning it for someone else?"

He'd talked, then, of Dana. Of her promising career, cut tragically short by her mysterious disappearance; of her talent; of the enormous contribution she'd made to *Scarlet Street*. He'd admitted to Barbara that if *Scarlet Street* won he would think of it as a tribute to Dana Smith, as much as to himself.

But he didn't mention that day in the Quorum Building, when he'd seen Dana one last time. He and Edwina had decided never to tell anyone about that.

"After all, Sebastian, what would we say?" Edwina had asked. "That she seemed to be in this room, but in another time? Who'd believe us?"

He'd never forget the eerie scene; the shimmering division between her time and his; the deathly cold as he thrust his hand through the barrier and clasped Dana's. He couldn't forget how her face had been etched with agony as she'd let go and turned back for the man she'd called Gabe. There had been something in her voice he'd never heard before when she'd screamed out that name. She'd been in love with the man.

Maybe that was why she'd never returned. He liked to think so, but he'd never know for sure.

"Ladies and gentlemen, we have a very special announcement." The master of ceremonies paused while a murmur of anticipation ran through the crowd. "The presenter of the award for Best Picture has blazed the trails that today's filmmakers follow and has been on the receiving end of this award six times. Her films are considered timeless classics. Through the generosity of her Silver Shadows Bursary, she has made possible the careers of many of you here tonight. It is my great pleasure to welcome one of the most enduring legends of the industry— D. T. O'Shaunessy."

D. T. O'Shaunessy! Sebastian found himself on his feet with the rest of the packed auditorium as she walked up to the podium, escorted by a handsome, white-haired man.

The applause went on and on, a frenzied tribute to an incredible career.

And an incredible person, he thought. The Silver Shadows Bursary had helped him realize his dreams at a time when he was considering giving up. What an honor it would be to meet her!

"I thought she seldom attended these functions now," Edwina said as the applause finally died down and they took their seats. "Don't she and her husband live on a farm in Ireland and raise horses or something?"

"Derby winners, love," Sebastian whispered back. "She must have some special reason for wanting to present this award." He fell silent as the still-glamorous figure at the podium was handed a small white envelope. Her soft, clear voice rang out as she pronounced the eagerly awaited words.

"And the winner is—"

There was a breathless hush in the huge room and the only sound was the ripping of paper as she slit open the envelope. Sebastian sat frozen, his hand clasped tensely around Edwina's. That voice!

"*Scarlet Street,* produced and directed by Sebastian Hart!"

"Darling!" Edwina's arms were around him. She was laughing and crying at the same time and he felt a suspicious moisture in his own eyes as he kissed her. "Get up there before they give it to someone else!"

He was grinning like a maniac, he realized as he made his way to the stage. But who cared? It didn't come much more fabulous than this; winning the Academy Award for Best Picture and having it handed to him by his own personal idol. He started across the stage to the woman waiting at the podium, and then he caught his breath.

She stood there, tears of joy streaming down her face, her green eyes glistening with pride. The tall white-haired man beside her grinned and handed her a handkerchief. Her chestnut hair was an elegant silver chignon now, and there were laugh lines in the once-smooth skin, but—

No! It couldn't be, Sebastian told himself. He was imagining things. He took another step forward as she came to meet him.

"Hello, Seb." Those green eyes, so familiar, smiled up at him in fond remembrance. "It's been a long time."

The three McCullar brothers once stood strong against the lawlessness on their ranches. Then the events of one fateful night shattered their bond and sent them far from home. But their hearts remained with the ranch—and the women—they left behind. And now all three are coming

HOME TO TEXAS

Gayle Wilson has written a romantic, emotional and suspenseful new trilogy and created characters who will touch your heart. Don't miss any of the cowboy McCullar brothers in:

#461 RANSOM MY HEART
April

#466 WHISPER MY LOVE
May

#469 REMEMBER MY TOUCH
June

These are three cowboys' stories you won't want to miss!

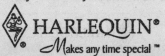

DEBBIE MACOMBER

invites you to the

HEART OF TEXAS

Join Debbie Macomber as she brings you the lives
and loves of the folks in the ranching community
of Promise, Texas.

If you loved Midnight Sons—don't miss
Heart of Texas! A brand-new six-book series
from Debbie Macomber.

Available in February 1998
at your favorite retail store.

Heart of Texas by Debbie Macomber

Lonesome Cowboy	February '98
Texas Two-Step	March '98
Caroline's Child	April '98
Dr. Texas	May '98
Nell's Cowboy	June '98
Lone Star Baby	July '98

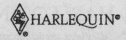

HARLEQUIN®

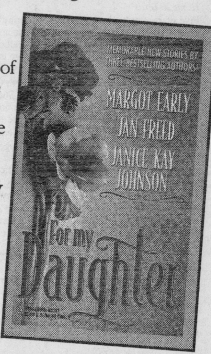

COMING NEXT MONTH

#469 REMEMBER MY TOUCH by Gayle Wilson
Home to Texas
Five years after her husband's murder, Jenny McCullen's life was
turned upside down by Matt Dawson, who aroused familiar passions.
Matt claimed to be a DEA agent on the trail of Mac's killer—but
Jenny's heart told her he was keeping more than his share of secrets.

#470 THE MISSING HOUR by Dawn Stewardson
P.I. Cole Radford worked alone—until Beth Gregory asked him to
solve a twenty-two-year-old murder case. She'd finally remembered
witnessing the murder, but insisted her memory was wrong. Now only
Cole stood between Beth and someone who wanted her dead....

#471 JODIE'S LITTLE SECRETS by Joanna Wayne
Single mom of twin baby boys, Jodie Gahagen saw her ordered life
destroyed when a stalker sent her running home. But once there, she
couldn't avoid Ray Kostner's probing questions. He knew Jodie was
hiding two secrets...but he never guessed he was their father.

#472 RUNAWAY HEART by Saranne Dawson
When C. Z. Morrison found by-the-book cop Zach Hollis as a fugitive,
she left behind her button-down ways and went on the run with him to
clear his name. With no safe haven except in each other's arms, would
their love overcome the odds?

AVAILABLE THIS MONTH:

Look us up on-line at: http://www.romance.net